# DESERT OF THE *Damned*

KATHY KULIG

# What the critics are saying...

ꕤ

**5 Blue Ribbons** "Kathy Kulig tells Lauren/Cimi and Deven/Kayab's tale with such passion and fervor that I was completely captivated by them—both past and present. From the wonders of the rainforest to the passionate relationship between Lauren and Deven this is a story that charms and leaves you with a sense of wonder…WILD JADE will take you on an adventure you won't soon forget—and will want to revisit." ~ *Romance Junkies Reviews*

**4 Lips** "*Seducing the Stones* is a fascinating story with a lot of emotion and adventure...Kathy Kulig has written a wonderful story that is both entertaining and captivating."

~ *Two Lips Reviews*

An Ellora's Cave Romantica Publication

www.ellorascave.com

Desert of the Damned

ISBN 9781419958656

Edited by Helen Woodall.
Photography and cover art by Les Byerley.

This book printed in the U.S.A. by Jasmine-Jade Enterprises, LLC.

Electronic book Publication December 2008
Trade paperback Publication February 2009

# DESERT OF THE DAMNED

ꝏ

# Dedication

ഗ

*For my enthusiastic and talented critique partners—Becky Bartlett, Kathleen Coddington and Karen Rose. And special thanks to Pattie Giordani, the grammar goddess, and Terri Prizzi, the brainstorming goddess.*


# Acknowledgements

ഗ

Authors do research even when creating paranormal worlds. I'm grateful to the following—Georgia G. Colasante MS. SM (NRM), Microbiology Manager. Janice Curran and Mitzi Flyte for their cat expertise. And my sister Carol Nicholas, past National Park Service employee and Hot Shot firefighter.


# Trademarks Acknowledgement

ഗ

The author acknowledges the trademarked status and trademark owners of the following wordmarks mentioned in this work of fiction:

Cinderella: Disney Enterprises, Inc.

Colt: New Colt Holding Corp.

Disney: Disney Enterprises, Inc.

Frankenstein: Universal City Studios, Inc.

Jeep: DaimlerChrysler Corporation

Magnum: Smith & Wesson Inc.

Ziploc: S. C. Johnson Home Storage, Inc.

# Chapter One

ꕥ

The smell of smoke drew Amy Weston out of a deep sleep. As her mind fought through her grogginess, she stared at the orange shadows flickering across her stucco walls. The waving colors nearly hypnotized her back to sleep then logic shook her fully awake.

Fire.

She bolted upright in bed.

From the window on the opposite wall she could see that the fire was outside. A chorus of toads and crickets sang their night song as the desert breeze stirred her sheer curtains. She rubbed sleep from her eyes and inhaled deeply.

Not dreaming.

Hopping out of bed, she rushed to the window and peered out. The glow of a campfire shone behind the saguaro cactus and the mesquite bushes about fifty yards from her house.

The silhouette of a man stood beside the fire. Dante Akando was summoning her.

The digital clock read twelve a.m. The hour. She groaned as if complaining but between her legs the throb of her pussy gave away her desire. Thanks to all the subtle teasing at work and impromptu meetings in Dante's office, where he'd described raw details of his sex games, her body hummed in anticipation.

He was good—very good—impossible to resist. And he was just what she needed right now—a man who had a taste for adventurous sex and was eager to explore the dark side of her passions. Like her, Dante didn't want any emotional ties.

She had been intrigued by his looks the day she was forced to transfer to the new division of Drake Diagnostic Labs and, since she didn't plan to stay long, having a brief affair with her boss didn't seem like a problem. The sexual chemistry had been immediate and bone deep. How could she say no? Someday she would find someone special and consider a more permanent arrangement but for the moment, she didn't need the hassles.

As much as her body ached for Dante, she should resist him. She had to get up for work early and she was exhausted. Did she dare ignore his campfire call and curl back in her comfortable bed? Her hand reached beneath her silk chemise and slid over her breasts. Her nipples were raw and erect, sensitive to the touch. She squeezed them and imagined Dante's hands on her then glided her hand down her flat belly, over the curly hair and patted her bud. In moments it was swollen and throbbing, aching for more. Oh, she wanted him all right. *Damn him. I'll never get back to sleep now.*

What was the use? The dancing lights on her bedroom walls grew brighter, signaling his impatience.

Tugging the thin chemise over her head, she tossed it on the floor, then yanked the Indian blanket from her bed. Why did he affect her this way? She walked back to the window but there was no sign of him—only the silhouettes of the saguaro cactus with its outstretched arms. Stepping into moccasins, she grabbed a flashlight, then strode out of her house.

The night air was cool and she pulled the red, black and orange blanket tightly around her. Dante had bought it for her at the flea market, not the trading post, so it probably was a Mexican blanket and not Indian but it was beautiful just the same and a thoughtful gift. Still, it was a puzzling gift considering Dante Akando said he was part Navajo. She would've thought he would only buy native crafts. As she followed the path off her property onto open land, the light of her flashlight and the campfire lit her way. The sky was dark, millions of brilliant stars glittered like shards of crystal.

Stepping around scrub pines and clumps of prickly pear cactus, she approached a large mesquite bush. On the other side of the spiny tree the campfire blazed.

Another Indian blanket lay beside the fire. Dante was nowhere around. But she knew he had to be close, watching her.

"Dante? I'm here." She pulled her blanket up to her chin. A breeze swirled around her and under, teasing her moist pussy. She felt a growing heat and moisture between her legs. Where was he? Every nerve simmered with anticipation. "Dante, come on. I'm here. We have to work tomorrow. I can't stay long."

She wasn't afraid of the desert night. He said the fire would keep her safe from the night creatures. Recalling his game of seduction, she dropped her covering and stretched out naked on the blanket, her body raw, exposed, vulnerable.

The flames crackled and sent sprays of sparks into the air. Peering into the dark shadows surrounding the campfire, Amy tried to spot her mysterious lover but saw no sign of him. She was supposed to wait.

As she closed her eyes, a shiver that was a slightly panicked feeling mixed with desire rippled through her body. Ignoring his instructions, she opened her eyes again and scanned the area. Still no Dante.

Only a cool breeze brushed over her skin, tightening her nipples to hard points. As she stared into the fire, her vision blurred. How long had she been there? She chuckled to herself. What if she fell asleep when Dante returned? How would he react? She suspected his ego wouldn't handle that well. Was this a test to see how long she'd wait? Well, she wouldn't wait for much longer. Damn, she forgot her watch. She had no idea how long she'd been out there.

Sighing heavily with impatience, she decided to go against his game and move. She stroked her breasts, drawing circles around her nipple with her fingertip. Maybe she could entice him. Her body sizzled with need, wanting his touch. He had promised to meet her. She wanted him on top of her now. She slid her hand across her breasts and squeezed each mound. Damn him, where was he?

The turpentine scent of the mesquite bushes and pungent earth drifted on the breeze. Her fingers pinched her nipples until they were sensitive and erect, then she slid her hand down across her stomach to her mound. She spread her folds, dipping one finger inside for a moment, then rubbed her bud until it swelled. She sucked in a breath.

"Mmmm. That looks nice," said a husky voice behind the massive saguaro cactus.

She jumped, removing her hand from her pussy and sat up. "Dante."

He gave a low, sultry laugh. The fever of wanting sex penetrated her very soul.

Dante stood over her, bare-chested and wearing buckskin pants. He was playing his role, she thought, claiming his part-Navajo heritage. In the firelight, she could see his dark brown, almost black eyes glinting with mischief and sensuality. As he moved to the campfire and tossed on a couple of dried branches, she admired his gleaming, straight black hair brushing over his broad shoulders.

The firelight did amazing things to enhance every muscle in his back and arms. She suspected he was taking his time, teasing her because he knew his power over her—his voice alone could awaken her lust. Every inch of her body ached for him. Their friendship had quickly moved into a physical, seductive phase. In past encounters he'd pleasured her beyond her imagination with only one complaint—he never completely fucked her.

"You moved," he said. "And your eyes are open."

"What?"

"You moved. You're supposed to wait with your arms over your head, your legs spread and your eyes closed. That's the game. Those were my instructions."

Tight-jawed, she sighed to herself and stared past him into the fire. He was good but was it worth it?

With the added wood, the bonfire blazed and the heat warmed her naked skin. She was mesmerized by the fingers of fire dancing above the logs. When she saw a small fur mound a few feet from the circle of stones she gasped, her hand cupping her mouth. "What's that?" She pointed.

Dante turned around. "Raccoon. A dead one."

"I didn't notice him when I first got here." She crossed her arms over her chest.

He smiled. "Not very observant, are you? Looks like he's been dead awhile."

She ignored his snide remark. "Poor thing. I wonder what happened." Was she stalling? Why was she suddenly feeling self-conscious around him? Or just frustrated?

He shrugged. Leaning over her, his round black stone pendant swung on a leather cord inches from her face. The stone was shaped like a spiral with white specks, reminding her of a galaxy.

"What kind of stone is that?" She reached up to touch it but he pressed her hand back down over her head. He held up the stone between two fingers, rubbing his thumb over the swirling pattern in the center.

"It's called a nebula stone."

"Is there a significance? Some stones are supposed to have certain New Age properties."

He made a face as if he was insulted by her comment. "Yes, it does have special properties. It's also called a cosmic window." He released the stone and began stroking her breasts. "It's used in meditation for grounding and also to help travel to inner domains." He pinched her nipple and she jerked.

"Where did you get it?"

He looked out into the desert night and said, "Mexico." Stroking her cheek with his finger, he lifted her chin and gave her a deep sensual kiss. His tongue was hot and demanding, his mouth hard and hungry. She moaned into the kiss as his hand slid down over her breasts and parted her legs. Her knees fell open as his fingers found her moist clit. "Forget about the pendant."

Taking her mouth again, he slipped a finger inside and plunged deep. She cried out. "Ah God…that feels amazing." She reached up to touch his rock-hard penis but he pulled away.

"Close your eyes and lie down. Arms over your head, legs spread. Keep your eyes closed." He pushed at her shoulder, a sly smile quirked at the side of his mouth.

She hesitated, her fingers dug into the blanket. This was just a game, not a relationship and she had agreed to this. She could stop it anytime. When she learned what he had in mind, harmless, safe-sex games, she had agreed. Only they hadn't had real sex yet. Not completely. But what they'd had so far was exciting and erotic. She lay back down and put her arms over her head, spread her legs and closed her eyes without saying a word.

"Good," he murmured. He knelt down beside her and thrust a wet finger deep inside her cunt.

Amy groaned and raised her hips. His finger was hot and he worked it until he hit her G-spot. Her body shuddered. "Dante." Finally tonight would be the night. He wouldn't tease her for another night. He would bury his cock inside her.

"You want it hard and fast or tortuously slow?" he groaned. She opened her eyes to look at his erection, bulging beneath his pants. She blinked her eyes. A swirling kaleidoscope of colors surrounded him. A reflection from the fire playing tricks on her tired eyes, she concluded as she gazed up at him. A look of disapproval passed over his face.

He withdrew his finger and stood up. Her body quivered, a trickle of moisture dripped down her pussy. Her cunt pulsed and ached. "Why did you stop?"

Unzipping his pants, he dropped them on the ground. His cock was hard, thick and resting against his belly. "You're supposed to keep your eyes closed," he said with a smile as he eased between her legs.

Yes. Oh yes. He wasn't going to tease her tonight. This time he would make love to her. She reached out to him and stroked his chest, keeping her eyes closed. The earthy, sage scent of him filled her nostrils. As he again pumped his fingers inside her, imitating the action of what would come, she groaned her impatience. "Oh, Dante, I want you deep inside me."

"Soon, soon..." The growl in his chest was wild sexual hunger, out of control. He leaned over her and captured her mouth with a kiss, his tongue flicking and dancing inside. Then he licked her neck, her earlobe and nipple. Amy arched against his mouth and cried out. He mumbled words against her skin that she couldn't make out but the rumbling vibrations sent ripples of desperate lust through every nerve.

"Do it, Dante. Take me." She gripped his hips and tried to pull him down onto her.

He chuckled as he plunged two fingers into her, ignoring her plea. His body hovered over her, kneeling between her legs, while he finger-fucked her. "Ride my hand. I can make you come a thousand different ways."

He'd so easily found her rhythm and she could come any moment but she resisted. Not this time. The other nights he had made her come, then left her before he came, before he made love to her. Why? She didn't understand. When she tried to ask him, he laughed it off by saying, "Didn't I please you?"

Tonight she wanted all of him. Never had a man made her feel this hot for sex. She didn't care about his elusive ways, his arrogance, or his manipulating sex games.

Using his thumb on her swollen clit nearly sent her over the edge. Her hips writhed, unable to fight the throbbing sensations building, her cunt clenching. She had to have him and it had to be tonight. The orgasms he'd given her the other nights had rocked through her body to the core. But tonight she would have his cock sunk deep to the hilt. "Dante, I can't wait. Fuck me, now." She pressed his shoulders down.

Dante chuckled. "Not yet."

"You're killing me."

"Hmmm."

"Please..."

"Not yet."

"I want your cock in me now. Or make me come now." Damn it, she couldn't wait a second longer. Her body craved him with more intensity than she ever felt. And she had to have him now.

Dante slid up her body and opened his mouth to kiss her but his lips were torturously close. She arched her back to kiss him. Finally he did and she pulled him down on top her. Now, he'd make love to her now.

"Spread your legs," he demanded. Then his laugh was almost mocking. He bent down to lick her.

"I'm wet enough." But it was too late. She couldn't hold back the climax that racked through her body. "Oh God, I'm coming." Gripping the blanket with her fists, she closed her eyes and let the wave after wave of sensation ripple over her.

"Yes," Dante breathed against her slit. Every part of her sex throbbed. "Yes..." She heard a low growl and at first thought it was from Dante. Then she realized the sound came from behind her. Something was moving toward them across the sand. Dante slowly lifted his head and his eyes widened in horror.

Leaning up on her elbows, Amy attempted to turn around but Dante pressed a hand to her chest. Amy glimpsed the shape of a mountain lion. She was about to cry out when Dante raised his hand again and everything went dark.

# Chapter Two

ꟃ

After a late dinner, park ranger Jake Montag sat in front of the blazing fire pit in his grandfather's backyard. Every muscle ached down to the bone from a long day of searching miles of hiking trails for more dead animals. Stretching his legs out, he crossed his boots and inhaled the smoke, detecting sage and mesquite. Jake stared past the fire across the scrub brush and cactus plain to the Rincon Mountains, admiring the shadowy silhouettes along the evening horizon.

"How many more today?" Bill Sike asked as he dragged a rusty lawn chair next to Jake. His gray braid swung down in front of his denim shirt. After handing Jake a mug of hot coffee, Bill sat in a chair and drank from his mug.

"Thanks." Jake stared at the coffee without drinking. "Nine. Three deer, two coyotes and four jackrabbits."

Bill hung his head and shook it. "It's happening again. Records say a little over fifty years ago was the last time the enemy came." Bill stood and walked to the edge of his scraggly patch of property behind his double-wide trailer and stared out across the open desert. The intensity of his gaze made Jake think his grandfather could see with night vision.

"No, don't start with your old folk tales again, Granddad."

Bill ignored him and, after a minute, strolled over to his small herb and vegetable garden, heavily protected by a chicken-wire fence. He tugged at the eagle feather, crystals and stones tied to the wire fence, apparently checking that the objects were secure. Jake's grandfather, a shaman, had infused the items with magic to ward off desert creatures from helping themselves to the garden's bounty. There might be other significance to the feather and stones but Jake, not being Navajo himself, had never grasped the spiritual side of Native Americans.

"We've called in consultants. A private testing lab, environmentalists, veterinarians, the Arizona Department of Health, we'll find the cause for the deaths. The problem is natural, we're sure. Water contaminates, parasite, bacterial infection, viral… If we have to we'll contact the CDC." The National Park Service usually didn't contact the Centers for Disease Control and Prevention unless they had reports of rabies. They hadn't yet confirmed any reason for the increased number of animal deaths in the park. "Don't worry, we'll find the cause."

"They wouldn't close the park? Would they?"

Jake considered the question. "No, fire or dangerous predators are the usual reasons for a temporary closing of a park. But if potential visitors hear about the animal deaths and the numbers of visitors decreases drastically, the park service might issue cutbacks and I could be out of a job."

Bill made a face. "You could always transfer to another park."

Jake leaned forward in his chair, elbows propped on his knees. "And would you move with me?"

Bill shook his head. "This is my home. I'll never leave."

"Didn't think so. I wouldn't want to leave you here alone."

"I'm not a helpless old man." Bill glared at him.

Jake had always admired his grandfather's stubborn independence and he wasn't about to tread on the old man's pride. "Never said you were. It would be hard for me to see you regularly, that's all."

The old man studied him for a long moment then nodded. "You don't think it's a predator?"

"The animals don't appear to have been mauled or bitten."

Bill shook his head. "Won't do you any good. The problem isn't natural. It's not of this Earth."

Cold pushed through Jake's veins. A hush settled around the backyard. Jake knew better than to argue with his grandfather. The man had been taking care of him since he was nine. Bill wasn't a blood relative but he was the closest to a parent he had. Jake sipped at the mug of coffee clutched between his hands. "Ugh, this is awful." He grimaced.

"It's a fresh pot." Bill laughed. "I like it strong."

Jake forced down another gulp of coffee, being polite. He didn't get to have dinner with his grandfather as often as he should. "Visitors are always warned to stay away from wild animals because of diseases like rabies. There's no reason to believe humans are in danger, so no plans to close the park, thank God."

"Trouble's going down in the desert and testing the water or animals isn't goin' to help it. Don't you see the pattern?"

Jake sighed and held his tongue. He didn't want to insult his grandfather and his superstitions. He'd be there all night unless he honored his grandfather's beliefs. "What do you think is happening?"

Bill stared at him for a long while before speaking. "Do you know the story of Coyote?"

His grandfather had told him and his brother Brad many Native American legends and myths over the years. "There are numerous stories about the Coyote Trickster. Is there one particular story you had in mind?"

Bill leaned forward in his chair, putting his coffee cup on the ground. "There is one story of Coyote and Badger." His grandfather took out a pouch of pipe tobacco from his shirt pocket, opened it and took out a pinch and flicked the brown leaves into the fire. "For cleansing and to carry our thoughts and prayers to the Great Spirit," Bill explained. "The offering of tobacco connects earth and sky, the physical and spiritual worlds." Bill inhaled deeply. "Smells of desert and mountains."

As the small cloud drifted past, Jake breathed in the sweet scent of tobacco and felt tension flow out of his body as if the puff of smoke had the power to draw all the negative energy out of him. Beads of sweat formed at his brow. He wiped at his forehead with the back of his hand and thought about moving his chair back away from the heat of the fire but he was too relaxed and didn't feel like getting up at the moment. "So what about Coyote and Badger? I hope it's not a long story because I should head home soon. I'm beat." As much as Jake adored his grandfather's Native American stories, he knew that some were very long. How many nights did he and his brother sit around this fire and listen to stories? Bill also told many stories before they went to bed. He couldn't recall the one about Coyote and Badger.

His grandfather narrowed his eyes. "Are you ready to listen to the teacher and be the apprentice?"

"Apprentice to what?" Jake gazed into the fire. His vision blurred. He doubted he'd make it though the whole story without falling asleep. Just like when he was a kid.

"Listen with your heart. Listen with your spirit. Because the enemy that has come to the desert won't stop with the animals. Humans will be next."

A jolt of fear shot through him. Not fear of this enemy but fear that his grandfather was beginning to show signs of senility. Bill was known to give predictions before but never this outrageous. He was going to have to come over more often and check on him. Jake took a gulp of coffee. "I'm listening."

Bill nodded in approval. "Coyote and Badger were in love with the same woman and they agreed to compete for her. Whoever had killed the most rabbits by the end of the day would win. Coyote tried to trick Badger by telling him he'd seen a rabbit go down a hole. When Badger went down the hole, Coyote blocked the hole with a rock and returned to the village with his kills first. But the people insisted on waiting for Badger who managed to dig himself out of the hole. Badger returned to the village and had the most kills. He won the woman. Coyote attempted to steal the woman away but he failed. Coyote then disappeared into the desert alone. This story is finished."

Jake smiled. "Interesting story. Thanks but I still don't understand how this applies to the deaths of the park animals or why I'm in danger."

Bill's eyes narrowed. "It's not a child's fable I'm telling you," he said sharply. "What's happening in the Sonoran Desert is much more serious. There's a mystical basis in its cause and only mystical weapons can fight it."

It was impossible to talk sense to an old Navajo man. Jake rubbed his forehead with his hand. "I didn't mean to insult you."

"No insult taken, son. I'm trying to tell you it's time to come to terms with your natural gifts. That will be your best–"

"No! I can't do that." Jake stood up and strode over to the fire.

"Your brother has embraced his abilities and is putting them to good use in the Special Forces. Why can't you?"

"I'm not Brad. My brother was always reckless and a show-off. It'll kill him one day."

"The other shamans are interested in learning of this Norwegian magic. They can help you and so can I."

"Tell them to talk to Brad." His brother was proud of the *Eigi Einhamr,* a rare Norwegian trait that was passed down through the male line. If Brad had been the one to find his father dead would his brother still embrace this burden?

"You're here, Brad's not."

"Brad can shift into other animals. I've never attempted that. And I don't care to try."

"Brad did not see his father shot by hunters. That ain't an easy thing for a nine-year-old."

Jake shook his head. A wave of nausea went through him. He gulped down most of the coffee and tossed the rest into the fire. "Shit, you make the worst coffee."

"Would you like a refill?" Bill asked like a smart-ass.

Jake made a face. "No, thanks. A second cup will probably kill me," he teased.

Jake tried to block out the memory of the night his father was killed but the images flashed through his mind. He was only nine but he remembered every detail. He had watched his father change into a wolf from his bedroom window. The wolf loped out into the desert, gone for hours. Jake fell asleep waiting for his return and the crack of a rifle shot jolted him awake. When he ran into the desert behind their house, he found his father, who had been in the process of removing the wolf skin. From the shoulders up, his father was in human form. The wolf skin draped down his back and the lower portion of the body was still in wolf form. He was dead, shot in the chest by a hunter.

"I knew my mother couldn't handle that her two sons had this gift, or curse. She deserted us," Jake said to his grandfather. "But I was stupid. I had to tell Alison about this gift. She couldn't handle it either and left me." He closed his eyes, remembering Alison's horrified expression when he demonstrated the transformation of *Eigi Einhamr*. She freaked and he panicked and tried to keep her from leaving. He ended up clawing her leg. She left for California and never returned. How could he ever be sure he wouldn't hurt anyone again?

When he opened his eyes, the stars appeared brighter and even seemed to vibrate. His gaze dropped to the saguaros behind Bill's house. A glowing aura surrounded the cacti. The trees also emitted a pale light. *What the hell…* Jake spun around, which was a mistake because the ground continued to spin when he stopped. "Bill, what the hell did you put in my coffee?"

Bill wasn't sitting in his chair and the fire had burned out. How long had he been staring up at the sky like a drunken or drugged fool? He searched the backyard for his grandfather. He couldn't find him anywhere. Panic gripped him. What was happening? Creatures darted across the desert, strange creatures, not earthly ones. They looked two-dimensional like the ancient paintings seen in the cliff dwellings. "Bill!"

"I'm here."

Bill sat in the lawn chair, smiling and the fire was again burning in the pit. Jake shook his head, trying to clear it. Another mistake. The movement only made him dizzier. He tried to look at his watch but his eyes wouldn't focus. "What was in the coffee? Peyote?"

"Only a little."

"Fuck."

"You must face Coyote," Bill said with the face of an owl.

Jake snickered. He was having a conversation with an owl. "Why do I need to see Coyote?" He couldn't stop chuckling.

"Because this Coyote is not of this world. This Coyote walks with an unknown tribe. He is dangerous and will soon harm more than the park animals." Bill's face changed from the owl back to normal and back to the owl again.

Jake stopped snickering. "You're serious, aren't you?"

Bill picked up a mountain lion skin from the lawn chair where Jake had been sitting earlier. "Deadly serious."

Jake took a step back.

"It's your heritage."

"My curse. Damn you." Jake kicked the lawn chair but didn't move as Bill approached with the mountain lion fur.

"You must adjust to the form to become a warrior and defeat Coyote."

Jake hung his head. Why couldn't he accept the *Eigi Einhamr* with ease like his brother Brad? Were animals and people in danger? Or was it just an old man's superstitions? In the past, his grandfather's predictions had been correct too many times. Resigned to his task, Jake asked, "How will I find this Coyote?"

Bill closed his eyes for a moment and sighed. "You will sense his power from a great distance. You may see his power as Northern Lights or a vortex of energy or you may hear the hum like live electric voltage. In your altered state you will know him."

"I don't know if I can do this." But the peyote broke down his inhibitions. Picking up the mountain lion fur, Jake slung it around his shoulders and imagined becoming one with the animal.

The vibration shattered through every muscle, every cell. A white flash of light shot slivers of pain to every joint. He dropped to the ground. His body changed, reformed to fit the animal skin. Four legs, four paws made contact with the hard-packed earth. He sniffed the air for prey. His human memory remained intact.

He must hunt Coyote.

"Not Coyote. Hunt for the rogue Coyote," the grandfather said, seeming to understand Jake's intentions.

In mountain lion form, Jake glanced over his shoulder at his grandfather and waited a moment until the message registered. *The rogue Coyote is the prey.* Jake loped across the yard, leapt over the fence and bounded off into the night.

*****

Jake, as the mountain lion, stalked the desert night like a brown ghost, racing around rocks, cacti and trees. With wide padded paws, he kicked up the soft sand and ventured toward a hum and vibration. Something he'd never sensed before. Adrenaline pumped through his veins, hardening his animal muscles, sharpening his senses. Nostrils flared, detecting a mixture of scents—the earth, the plants, a rabbit, the faint trail of a deer but not his quarry. Human memories and thoughts unraveled in his mind as the true quest of his hunt emerged.

He padded down a rocky slope, ignoring the temptation to hunt small prey. He must find Coyote and kill him.

Instinct directed him through the wilderness and open plains, like an invisible trail. If he veered off, the hum or vibration left his body, a change in direction accentuated the sensation. The energy drew him to his target. Several hundred yards ahead, below the next bluff, a pulsating glow highlighted the rim. Jake knew it was not a human structure emitting the light. Barren desert couldn't create that type of illumination.

As he reached the top of the bluff, the wind carried the scent of a man, his prey. He also detected a mixture of scents and vibrations in the air and since he dared not trust his unfamiliar form, he crept closer to inspect. He couldn't afford to make a mistake.

At the sound of voices, his ears twitched forward and he skulked around bushes until he detected movement, then froze. Next to a fire a man and woman were mating. The man was between the woman's legs and pleasuring her with his mouth and fingers. "Ride my hand. I can make you come a thousand different ways."

Firelight glinted on the woman's body as she writhed in pleasure, her hips rising to meet the man's touches. The man pushed her thighs farther apart. Even in his animal form Jake could admire the woman's body, the inward dip of her waist, the curve of her hips and full breasts. Part of him thought his presence there was wrong, observing them, intruding on their sexual encounter. And part couldn't deny his own desire heating up while watching her in throes of passion. Raising his snout to the breeze, he breathed in the tangy sent of sex. The animal side and human side were aroused.

She cupped her breasts while the man continued licking her. She tossed her head and blonde hair tumbled around the blanket. "Dante, I can't wait. Fuck me now." The woman pulled his shoulders down.

The man chuckled as he seemed to bring her to the edge of orgasm then stop. "Not yet," he said.

"You're killing me."

"Hmmm."

"Please..."

"Not yet," the man said.

Damn. Jake crouched, tail lashing the air.

The man slid up her body and Jake thought he was going to enter her but instead he hovered a few inches above her. At the height of desire this man was making her wait. Anguish and pleasure tightened the muscles of her face as she struggled to draw him down onto her. Her lover smiled and resisted. The man liked to tease, pure torture. The human side of Jake couldn't help but be turned-on by the scene. Why was he watching these two lovers? That man was his prey, wasn't he? Why was Jake waiting? He studied the man, then the woman. There was nothing unusual about them except for the light glowing around them. But was it possible he would see that with any couple making love? What if he had the wrong man? Could the woman be Coyote? He had to be sure. He hadn't been in animal form in so long, how could he trust his senses?

Then a golden light around the woman grew bright and concentrated around her head. The radiance flowed from her and entered the man between his lips. When the light faded the man smiled, as if pleased with his deed. Jake growled low in his throat. There was something unnatural in what he'd just witnessed.

She arched her back to kiss her lover. Was she aware of what had happened? Finally the man kissed her and she pulled him down on top of her. Would he mate with her now or kill her? Jake advanced closer, hiding behind a mesquite bush.

"I want your cock in me now. Or make me come now."

Head down, eyes locked on his prey, Jake moved out from behind the mesquite.

"Spread your legs," the man demanded. His laugh was almost mocking. He bent down to lick her more. She moved her hips away from him but his hands held her thighs steady so she wouldn't twist away.

"I'm wet enough." Her body jerked. "Oh God, I'm coming."

If the man made a move to harm her, Jake thought. Yes, he had to be the prey. He could see the light pulsing around the man now. Then the image of Coyote was superimposed over the man's face. Jake growled. He crept closer, in the open now but the man had not seen him yet.

The heat of the fire caressed his fur. Soon he'd taste blood… He hesitated, not moving, barely breathing. Blood? The human side questioned how he could suggest such a thing but he knew the creature had to die if this was the beast his grandfather had warned him about. He remembered the peyote. Peyote could cause hallucinations. Ignoring the thought, he took another step closer and growled again.

"Yes," Dante breathed against her slit. "Yes…" Abruptly, the man called Dante stopped, slowly lifted his head and locked eyes with Jake. A predator's gaze, Jake thought.

Leaning up on her elbows, she swung around, turning toward Jake and screamed, struggling to flee. But with little effort, the man pressed a hand to her chest and she remained motionless. Jake could smell her fear. Again she attempted to move but the man used his magic, raising his hand seemed to put her to sleep. Eyes closed, she collapsed on the blanket. Her breasts rose and fell with deep breaths, so thankfully she wasn't dead.

Jake studied him for a moment. He wanted to make sure there was no mistake. The man's face changed to Coyote's again. Rainbow colors continued to spiral above his head. No doubt this was the enemy his grandfather described.

*Hate to end your evening but your mate has to die,* Jake thought as he prepared to lunge.

Jake arched his back as he saw Coyote's image change back to human form. The hackles rose on the back of his neck, his muscles twitched as a powerful desire to kill swept through him.

The man continued to watch Jake as he crawled away from the women on all fours, mirroring the mountain lion's sleek movements. Firelight caressed the woman's naked curves. She lay peacefully, unaware of the war about to begin. If he failed, would the creature return to continue his rape and murder?

The woman didn't seem opposed to the sexual attentions of this inhuman creature. Conflicting thoughts battled in his mind. The man apparently sensed a moment of doubt in his opponent because he shifted into complete Coyote form and darted past the fire and out of sight.

Jake's muscles went rigid. He dug his paws into the earth and leapt several yards into the air and barely missed the creature.

Coyote pivoted and ran off in the opposite direction. Jake followed, kicking sand and breaking dried branches as the two zigzagged around low brush and cacti.

Coyote didn't look back. Jake suspected his prey could hear him closing. A few more yards and Jake would have him. With his tongue he felt the long canine teeth that would plunge into the neck of his prey. He'd destroy the threat and wouldn't have to wear the mountain lion skin again.

Jake hardly felt the burning in his animal muscles pumped with adrenaline as the death of his enemy was only a few paces away. Close, so close. A few more feet…

Then Coyote misjudged a turn and ran directly into a large saguaro cactus.

And disappeared.

Stunned and still running full speed, Jake could not stop or slow down as he plowed into the plant with a sickening thud.

The sting of dozens of cactus spines pierced his face, shoulders and legs. He howled in pain and rolled on the ground.

Jake willed himself out of the mountain lion skin. As the skin fell away, many of the spines fell away. Damn. Hooking the fur over his arm, he rolled up the sleeve of his work shirt. Dots of blood on his arms showed where the spines had nailed him.

Fuck. He examined the cactus, pressing in places where he thought he saw Coyote enter, careful to avoid the spines. How did he escape? Where did he go?

He turned to walk back to where the woman was. What would he tell her? Did she know she was involved with a demon?

But when he got back to the fire, the woman was gone. Lights glowed in the adobe house. It was the only house nearby so she must live there. When the creature returned would he come after her again? If she was to be his first human victim, he needed to stay close to her, warn her.

Slipping under the fur again, he willed himself to become the mountain lion.

Heart heavy, defeated, he limped home. He'd have to tell the old man he'd failed.

Sighing deeply and stretching her arms overhead, Amy opened her eyes and gazed up into a star-filled sky. She felt as if she was drifting up a dark tunnel without sound or sensation. Finally a breeze skimmed over her damp skin and she shivered. The sounds of the desert seemed to turn back on. Damn him. He did it to her again. Or rather, he didn't do it. "Dante, what is it with you? Why won't you—" Amy reached out to him and opened her eyes. Remembering the mountain lion, she leapt to her feet.

It was gone and so was Dante. The fire that had been roaring moments ago, or what had seemed like moments ago, was now glowing embers. She scooped up the blankets, shoved on her moccasins and ran toward her house, her flashlight illuminating her way.

* * * * *

Dawn painted golden streaks across the desert plain by the time Jake vaulted over his grandfather's wire fence, still in the mountain lion form.

Bill, who had been sleeping in the lounge chair, was startled by the movement of the lion. He jumped to his feet, legs apart, fists raised as if to ward off an attacker. He sighed and lowered his arms. "About time. Welcome back."

Jake willed himself back to human and the mountain lion skin slowly dropped away, almost as easily as slipping out of a coat. The reformation was not as difficult or painful as the transformation.

He slammed the skin onto an empty lawn chair and the chair collapsed. Bill took a step back.

Jake checked his watch. "I have to go to work. Don't ever put peyote in my drink again, old man. It makes me hallucinate." He marched toward the back door.

"You wouldn't have accepted the skin or the task any other way," Bill said. "How did it go?"

Jake crossed his arms.

"Did you find the demon?"

Jake spun around, glaring at Bill. "I found two people screwing out in the desert."

"And you killed him," Bill said as if it was a simple chore like weeding the garden.

"Kill someone I know nothing about? I don't know if what I saw was real or all in my imagination."

A smile came to Bill's face but it was cold. "He's killing the animals and soon he'll come after humans. He's not human. He's not of the true Coyote myth. He's something else. This has happened before, over fifty years ago."

"Well, apparently this demon has a girlfriend. They were having sex."

Bill squinted one eye, considering. "Sex? You sure he wasn't trying to kill her with pleasure?"

"If he was, she was having a good time."

"Hmmm. Maybe she's a demon too."

"Come on, old man. You and your superstitions—"

Bill picked up the skin and held it out to Jake. "Not superstitions and you will see." When Jake didn't take the skin, Bill continued to hold it in his arms. He glanced out into the desert, then turned back. "What happened after they finished? Their sex, I mean."

Jake didn't want to answer because it would prove his grandfather was partly right.

He let out a breath. He wouldn't be able to leave until he finished telling his grandfather everything. "At first the woman screamed, then seemed to go into a trance. She looked at me but didn't respond. Then the man shifted into the Coyote form and ran away. I chased him but he disappeared into a saguaro." Jake laughed. "I told you I was hallucinating."

"A mountain lion should be faster than a coyote." Bill shook his head. Jake could tell his grandfather was getting frustrated with him. "You had the chance to kill him. Why didn't you?"

"I told you. I tried. But he ran into a saguaro cactus. Straight into it and vanished."

Bill nodded. "Right. The portal into the Otherworld. What happened to the woman?"

"I don't know. I think she went inside a house."

"You remember where this saguaro is?"

Jake nodded. It didn't matter, he wasn't going back.

"Then you'll know where to find him. A good thing because this woman will probably be his first victim."

That's what he'd thought but Jake didn't want to think about this anymore. This curse had brought nothing but grief down on his family. His father's murder, his mother abandoning him and his brother Brad. "Forget it. I'm not shifting again to rip out the throat of some mythological creature because you say he's evil. How do I know I'm thinking straight when I'm in animal form?"

Bill raised the skin again. "You retain your free will and human logic."

"I won't chance that with someone's life," Jake snapped back. "I have to go." He stormed to his truck, raced out of the driveway and down the road. He knew no matter how fast he drove, the heritage he so desperately tried to deny would follow and take over his life.

# Chapter Three

ꕤ

The next morning Amy stuffed a slice of buttered toast into her mouth, grabbed a cup of instant coffee and checked the time—twenty minutes late. Even if she saw Dante at work, she wouldn't confront him about why he left her alone in the desert before he finished his game of seduction. That was one discussion she'd rather not get into at work because of how angry she was. At the moment, she could frighten away the biggest, meanest guard dog with a glance. Great sex or not, Dante was exasperating and she intended to tell him they were through.

Exhausted and frustrated, she yanked open her front door, stumbled over a cardboard box on her porch and spilled her coffee. At first the small object inside looked like a discarded ball of orange angora yarn. Crouching down, she poked it with a finger. The fluffball moved and meowed. A kitten, a very young one from the size of the thing, was curled up on a pile of rags. It raised its tiny head, blinked and meowed again.

"You've got to be kidding me," she said to the cat.

Glancing up and down her street, she looked for the culprit who'd abandoned the creature. The kitten looked only a few weeks old and could fit on her palm. If she left it behind it would die. She swore. She'd have to bring it to work.

"Come on, let's go, we're late," she groaned. "Just for today, then you're going to the animal shelter."

Setting her coffee cup down, she reached out to the kitten. It hissed and ten needlelike nails sunk into her hand and sharp teeth gnawed at her knuckle. She jerked her hand back. "Wow, monster, I'm trying to save your life. Don't blame you for being pissed but I need to get to work." The offensive odor coming from the box made her go search for a clean one. Grabbing the kitten by the scruff of the neck, she avoided additional attempts at clawing and biting and brought the animal inside.

Several packing boxes were left over from her move to Arizona, so she lined one with a plastic garbage bag and paper towels, then brought the box to her car.

"Okay, orphan, after work you're going to the animal shelter unless someone at the lab wants to adopt you." *Now I'm really late.*

Chemistry lab technologist Truly Duly was blessed with free-spirited parents. Unfortunately, Truly claimed they'd smoked a bit too much weed in the sixties and seventies and were in an altered state when they were picking baby names.

When Amy walked into the lab carrying the cardboard box emitting sounds of mewing, Truly got up from her computer and rushed over to the box. "What do you got there?" She peered inside. "Oooh. Kitten. What a cutie." She yanked off her nitrile gloves and washed her hands in a nearby sink, then readjusted the narrow glitter hairband holding back her wavy red hair. Truly was only thirty-four, a couple of years older than Amy, but her sun-worn skin and lack of makeup both aged her a bit and gave her a healthy glow.

Amy placed the box on the floor next to her desk. "Someone abandoned it on my porch this morning. I need to drop it at the animal shelter after work."

Truly laughed. "Good luck. They won't take a kitten that small. You're going to need to feed her every six hours by hand. We can get some milk from the cafeteria and use a syringe until you stop at the pet store for formula." She crouched down beside the box and picked up the kitten, her long ivory linen skirt pooled around the floor as she nuzzled the tiny thing. Her turquoise and silver bangles clanged together. The kitten meowed loudly. "Aw, she's hungry."

"I'm not getting pet supplies, because I'm not keeping it." Amy didn't want to tell Truly she expected to be moving out of Arizona within the year so she didn't want to commit to a pet that would be a hassle to move across country to Florida.

"Here, hold her. I'll get the milk and a syringe." Truly stood and passed the kitten to Amy. The kitten hissed and bit her again.

"Ouch." She dropped the fluffball in the box. "She doesn't like me. Why don't you take her home?"

Truly crinkled her nose and pressed her lips together as if thinking about it. The fluorescent lighting brought out the pale sprinkle of freckles across her nose and cheeks. "Can't. I already have two and they would eat her alive." Reaching inside the box, Truly lifted the kitten out and cradled her in her arms as she stroked her. "Now I know why you were late. I thought it was because you had a hot date." Truly didn't make eye contact.

Amy decided not to mention the encounter with Dante. Truly was the only one in the lab who knew Amy and Dante had been seeing each other but since Dante was a lab director at Drake Diagnostic Laboratories, she thought it was best not to publicize it. Their relationship was temporary, gratifying and bizarre. She wasn't about to write home about him or start hanging photos in her cubicle. And she certainly wasn't going to talk about their sexual adventures with her coworkers. "It took me a while to find a clean box for the cat."

"I started the chem run," Truly said as she slipped the kitten back in the box. "Looks like we'll have another busy day. Micro says they're swamped too."

Amy would check with the microbiology department later. They must have acquired new accounts for the increase in workload. "Thanks. I'll take the kitten to the storeroom if you get the milk and a syringe. Maybe after we feed her, she'll quiet down."

In the storeroom, Amy gave up trying to feed the kitten and let Truly do it.

"She doesn't need much but you need to feed her on her stomach." Truly held the cat on her palm and aimed the syringe with milk into her mouth. More dribbled down onto the paper towels but the kitten managed to get her fill. "Try it. You'll have to feed her again at six and at midnight."

Amy groaned. "I'm calling the animal shelter anyway. Maybe they'll take her."

Truly glared at her. "Feed her."

"Okay." This time the kitten didn't attempt to sink teeth or claws into Amy's arm and took a few more drops of milk, then rested her head in Amy's hand.

"Awww, see? She likes you. She was ornery before because she was hungry. What are you going to name her?"

Amy shot her an icy stare.

Truly ignored her. "Hmmm. She has dark orange and brown coloring. A tiger mixed in there. I think you should call her Sienna."

"Whatever." Amy found a pack of paper towels on one of the shelves and added more to the box. Sienna was curled up, eyes closed and purring. "Asleep already. Back to work."

Back in the chemistry department Truly tugged on some gloves and sat at the chemistry analyzer and loaded another tray of patient blood samples. "Hey, aren't you going to tell me about why you were really late? I mean, you're the boss and you don't have to but I'm dying to hear about your hot date."

"Yes and no. I did see Dante last night. But he couldn't stay." Amy didn't look up from the stack of reports she was signing. And he had done the same to her before. *Where the hell does he go and why can't he ever finish making love to me?* What worried her more was that she never remembered him leaving. How could he do that? Was he hypnotizing her? His eagerness toward sexual encounters seemed obsessive.

"He took over Lisa's position months ago. There's something wicked sexy about him. He doesn't say much but you know it's there smoldering beneath the surface..." Truly raised her eyebrows as if waiting for Amy to tell all.

Amy picked up the quality control files and carried them to her desk, turning her back on Truly.

"Those administration people on the second floor don't usually converse with us lab rats," Truly persisted. "So, did he stay over? Was he good?" She went over to the computer to review the results on the instrument.

Amy caved, a little. "No, he didn't stay over. And, yes, he's hot." She didn't feel like mentioning she'd had about enough of Dante and his games but to tell Truly would only bring on more questions. "I need to call the animal shelter." She pulled the phone book off a shelf above her desk.

Truly gave her a disapproving look. "Maybe it's synchronicity that brought the kitten to you."

Amy groaned as she flipped through pages but didn't look at them. "Someone just dropped the poor thing off instead of bringing it to the shelter."

"A cat could be just what you need to adjust to your new home."

"I'm adjusting."

Truly wheeled her chair away from her computer and rolled over to Amy's desk. "Oh yeah, then what's this?" She opened a file folder that was lying on top of Amy's desk. Inside were Amy's résumé and a list of companies in Florida. "You've only been in Arizona eight months. Why don't you give it a chance? Don't you like it here? Don't you like working with me?"

Amy sighed. "I'll have to watch what I leave on my desk in the future."

Truly grinned, apparently not at all remorseful.

"It's not that I don't like it here," Amy began. "I miss Florida. My family's there and I left behind some good friends."

"Boyfriend?"

"Not really. I was seeing someone but it wasn't going anywhere." Amy pursed her lips in disgust, remembering the evening she'd told Erik about her job transfer. He'd said she should go to Arizona. It was a great opportunity. His lack of emotion stung more than moving away from her parents.

Truly crossed her legs under her long skirt and leaned forward in her chair. "What did he say when you broke the news about Drake Diagnostics consolidating all the laboratories in Arizona?"

She shrugged. "It wasn't a big hardship that I left." Four months after she moved to Arizona, Erik got engaged. Had he been seeing her before Amy left? Amy didn't know and wasn't going to explain the gory details to Truly.

"Well, you'll find someone special here."

Amy shook her head. "I don't want to get serious with anyone because I don't plan on staying. If I can do a good job here, I hope they'll consider me for a management position in the main office in Florida. If not, I'm looking into other companies."

"Then why didn't you apply to those companies before you moved?" Truly rolled back to her computer.

"The management position wasn't available then and I couldn't find another job soon enough. The raise and relocation reimbursement was too good to pass up."

"Well, you can still adopt the kitten," Truly said, sounding hurt as if not liking Arizona and the kitten was an insult to her.

"Why? I don't want anything to tie me here in case I get a job offer. No pets, no year-long lease—I had to pay extra for month-to-month rent on my house—and no serious relationships."

"No ties or friendships whatsoever," Truly snapped back.

Now she had hurt her feelings. "I didn't mean it like that."

Truly typed on her computer and the printer nearby began to print out reports. "Of course you did. How often do your Florida friends phone you now? Email you every day?"

Amy crossed her arms and leaned back in her chair. "I still get emails, occasionally. They're busy."

Truly gave a self-satisfied smile but there was no pleasure in her expression. "Right. And the emails will become fewer. You quickly fade out of their lives and routine. You can't live your life as if your current arrangement is temporary. The nomad life becomes lonely. I know, I've lived it, Amy."

"I see what you're saying. But I think I'd be happier in Florida," Amy said, hoping that explained her feelings and would ease the tension.

Truly sighed and shook her head. "You don't see. You can't find happiness in a place or with a person. You can only find happiness here inside." She pointed to her heart. Then she stood, grabbed the reports and slammed them onto Amy's desk. "Sign these, please. I'm going to lunch."

Grabbing her coffee cup, Truly left the department and didn't ask Amy to join her.

Leaning her forehead against her hand, Amy signed the reports, then scanned through her inter-office email. One was from Dante Akando asking her to come to his office.

She groaned. Heat rushed to her face. She was not going to jump at his beck and call.

"Amy, here're two more racks," Tina, the lab assistant from Central Processing, said as she dropped off the tubes of blood and requisitions.

"Wow." Amy blinked at the petite blonde wearing an oversized lab coat and sneakers. "We've already had a triple run this morning. Did we get new accounts or something?"

"No, same accounts, just a ton of sick dogs, horses and several cows."

"Cows? Since when did we start testing cows?" Amy picked up the forms and searched for some clue as to why there was such an increase of sick animals.

Tina shrugged her shoulders. "Last week, I think. I guess there are a few, huh? We're logging in more so don't complain when I bring you more work." She strode out of the lab. Looked like Amy was going to work some overtime tonight. Plunking her elbows on her desk, she massaged her forehead with her fingers.

She skimmed through the forms. Most of the veterinarians didn't fill in the area that asked for symptoms. But a few stated listlessness, weakness, loss of appetite—vague symptoms that could be caused by many illnesses. The vets were ordering blood work and microbiology studies—across-the-board studies. In other words, they didn't know what was wrong.

After lunch, Truly returned and still wasn't talking to her. Amy received more work and another email message from Dante. "Urgent. Please come to my office concerning a new project."

Project, my ass. Was this another game? She would have to go see him. He had captured her attention when she first started working at the lab. And there had been an awareness, a pull that she thought he felt too by the way he looked at her. When Dante had approached her at work, she had turned him down several times because she didn't want to get involved, especially with her supervisor. But his dark handsome looks were too compelling to refuse. Now she realized what a mistake it had been to start up anything with him. "Truly, I need to go to Dante's office. I'll be right back."

"Sure," Truly said sarcastically, obviously still annoyed. "Have a good time. I'll hold the fort."

* * * * *

Amy resisted the urge to kick the door to the administrative offices instead of knocking. Physical gratification. That was all she and Dante were to each other. He shouldn't infuriate her so. She wasn't romantically involved with him, so why should she care?

With the realization of her empty love life, a big, dark hole grew in her heart. Even in Florida, she'd had plenty of dates but at thirty-two she had never been married. Most of her friends had kids, had husbands, divorced or on their second. What was wrong with her? Growing up living a nomad's life with a father in the navy who had to move frequently didn't help her when it came to making long-term friends.

Amy knocked at the door to Dante's office. She'd save their personal discussion for later.

"Come in," he announced.

She opened the door and walked in. The office was small but large enough to hold an ample commercial-grade black desk and a tall black leather chair. Two smaller burgundy leather chairs faced the front of his desk. Against two walls stood floor-to-ceiling bookcases, stacked with books, notebooks and audio-visual items. "Hello, Dante. What do you need?" Crossing her arms, Amy strolled in and stood by his desk.

"Hmmm. I have a few things in mind," he said with obvious innuendo.

"I have to get back. We're very busy."

"This won't take long." With a wave of his hand he offered her one of the two seats. She sat and realized the seats were much lower than his chair. A power play to show his dominance? He stood and she began to do the same.

"No, sit, please." He came between the desk and her chair and sat on the desk.

"Right. What about a project?" Despite her plans to break it off, her body heated up thinking about last night, thinking about what his hands, what his mouth had done to her.

"We're getting a new account that's going to mean some PR for the community so I want you assisting with the sample collection," he said formally but she could tell he was looking at her mouth, at her breasts and lower.

"Who's the account?"

"Saguaro National Park. We'll be running some tests on the wildlife. Apparently a number of animals in the park have died recently." Dante met her gaze, a piercing look that unsettled her.

Her head swam for a moment. "I'm sorry, tests for whom?"

His smile was humorless and fierce. "Park service."

"Of course." She squeezed her eyes shut and reopened them but Dante's face still looked blurry. And that damn self-satisfied smile of his. "What do you need me to do?" Resisting the urge to tug on her black skirt, she crossed her legs. His scrutiny tightened her nipples beneath her bra and sent a throb to her pussy. It was maddening how this man could arouse her with just a look.

"Take charge of the project."

She frowned as she studied him to see if he was serious. He wasn't smiling, he remained professional straight-faced but something didn't seem right. Something was going on and she didn't understand what. Determined to stop her hands from shaking, she gripped the armrests. "Is that all?"

"I have a meeting shortly. I'll call you in if we have any questions." Then he leaned forward, pressed his lips to her ear and whispered, "Amy, unbutton your blouse."

"What? No, ar-are you crazy?" Her eyes met his and she wondered if she had the power to resist him. What made her think of such a thing? Of course she could resist him.

She pulled away, her hand pushing at his chest. Big mistake. She caught the slight scent of him, musk and smoke and urgently wanted to dig her fingers into his shirt and pull him down onto her. Grasping her hand, he guided her down to his erection, bulging beneath his trousers. She rubbed and pressed his hard length, aching to free his straining cock. With shaking hands she attempted to unzip his pants. How did he manage to do this to her? And how many more times would he tease her before she felt his rigid shaft pulsing inside her? Wasn't she going to end her relationship with him?

His face moved close, lips a fraction of an inch away. Then he gazed into her eyes without blinking. "Unbutton your blouse," he whispered huskily. This time, his voice had a demanding edge that sent an electric jolt to her pussy.

The air in the room grew dense and she couldn't move, couldn't draw her eyes away from him. Like a dream where her legs became lead and she couldn't run.

"You're safe," he breathed.

Her hand went to the top button of her yellow silk blouse and undid it. Heartbeat racing, she continued unbuttoning the shirt down to her waist.

"Yes," he hissed, tossing the folder on his desk. Dante's heated gaze focused on her breasts as he slid his hand down her lace bra.

Amy arched her back to meet his hand, hot and rough. She whimpered.

"Oh yeah. You respond so quickly." He pulled the top of the bra down, exposing her breasts and pinched her nipples hard until she jumped. The jolt of sensation rippled to her cunt. He chuckled under his breath then bent over and took one stiff peak in his mouth.

"Someone could barge in," she whispered.

"Don't worry about it."

His hand reached under her skirt. "Ooh, thigh-highs. Nice." His fingers danced at the edge of the lace top, brushing the bare skin above. "Spread your legs," he demanded. She did without argument. The building desire between her legs already ached for his touch. After a few moments she'd tell him to stop and that she had to go.

When he reached her panties, he tugged on them. "Take them off or I'll rip them off."

"No."

"Last warning."

She lifted her hips and reached under her skirt, sliding the lace panties off. What was she doing? Every nerve in her body cried out for his touch. She had to stop but she couldn't. Was she out of her mind? Anyone could walk into his office. She dropped the panties on his desk.

"Sit," he instructed. "Hook your legs over the arms and hike up your skirt."

Shamefully, she complied. The thought of resisting him had faded like morning mist. With her legs spread wide, she hooked them over the chair's arms and realized her pussy was fully exposed to his view. Her breasts were hanging out over the top her bra.

She was panting now. Surely they could be heard by someone walking by. "Dante."

"Hush."

"This is for you, because I left you alone in the desert last night."

Was this supposed to be an apology? The man lived dangerously. At least he acknowledged leaving her alone. "Where did you go?"

The roughness of his tongue laved at her sensitive nipples. He captured them between his teeth. "I bet you're wet." Between her legs, he circled her entrance with the tips of his fingers, then plunged one finger into her moist channel. Amy nearly cried out.

"Very wet," he said, as he captured her moans with his mouth. "Shhh. I want to taste you again. Just for a minute."

"No, Dante. We should stop."

He ignored her and knelt between her legs. His tongue licked her slit and she bucked her hips. The sensations were so intense her body shuddered with every touch.

Grabbing his head, she pulled him down toward her swollen bud where her body ached for his attention but he licked, sucked and nipped everywhere but that one spot she needed him to touch most. The hunger tormented her and swept deep inside. "Dante, you're torturing me."

He hummed against her pussy, which sent another wave of sensations to her core. Then he captured her clit between his lips and licked it with his tongue, which sent her over the edge.

She bucked against his mouth while the orgasm pulsed through her, gripping the arms of the chair and biting her lip to keep from crying out.

He raised his head and smiled, then picked up his folder. Checking his watch, he said, "Get yourself squared away, I need to go to my meeting." His tone was cold after their intimate encounter and she felt cheap. She had agreed to no commitment. She hadn't agreed to being treated like a whore.

She glared at him. "What was this?"

"I don't understand. You didn't enjoy yourself?"

She growled under her breath. "Dante—"

A knock at the door made Amy swing her legs down and pull down her skirt. Too late to try to button all the buttons, Dante handed her the file to cover her open shirt and slipped her panties in his pants pocket.

Seated on the desk, he calmly said, "Come in."

Amy felt a jolt of terror. *My God, what was I thinking? I could get fired.* The door swung open.

In the open doorway, Phil from administration stuck his head into the room. He was in his forties, with dark, short-trimmed hair and business casual dress. "Sorry to interrupt. Dante, you ready?"

"Be right there, Phil. Just finishing up."

"I'll wait outside." The door closed.

Amy quickly buttoned her blouse, straightened her skirt and walked with Dante to the door.

"I'll call you later," he said. "Another night in the desert."

It was a statement not a question. "No," she answered. "I think it best we don't continue." As he was about to open the door, she realized he had her panties.

Giving her a sly grin, he slipped his hand inside his pocket. Thank God, he remembered her panties. But he pulled out a piece of gum, unwrapped it and stuck it in his mouth.

Turning toward the door, he frowned for a second, then put on his professional persona the moment he opened the door. "We'll finish this later," he said to Amy as he smiled at Phil standing in the hallway.

"Let's hustle, buddy. We're late," Phil said.

"Sorry, I'm playing catch-up today. End of the month stuff."

Phil nodded his sympathies as the two men marched down the hall toward the conference room. Still dazed, Amy felt her heart hammering inside her chest. As she strode toward the ladies' room, she swore silently. Good grief, she would have to work the rest of the day without panties.

# Chapter Four

ஐ

After Amy got back to the lab, she walked straight into the storeroom to collect her thoughts and check on Sienna. A good excuse. She wanted to hide until her pulse settled down so Truly wouldn't know what had happened with Dante. She squatted next to the box and peered inside. The kitten bobbed her head, blinked her eyes and meowed the tiniest sound. A little pang twisted inside Amy's chest.

No. There was no way she could keep this cat. Or could she? Reaching into the box, Sienna hissed and clawed at her. Jerking her hand back kept her from getting sliced with needle-sized claws.

"What's wrong with you? Hungry again?" The cat howled like a mountain lion cub, not a house cat. "Boy, are you ornery when you get hungry." Amy picked up the syringe and drew up milk from the pint container and placed it by Sienna's mouth. The kitten's head swung around and tried to bite her. Fortunately, Amy yanked her hand away in time. "Damn it, Sienna."

"What are you doing to your kitten?" Truly asked, the question sounding accusatory as she walked into the storeroom and crouched down by the box.

Amy glanced over her shoulder at Truly, refusing to look guilty and stood, waving the syringe in her hand. "I told you this cat doesn't like me. When I went to feed her, she made a fuss and tried to bite me again. Here, you try." She handed Truly the syringe.

"That must have been some meeting," Truly said with a wink. "You're all flushed."

"Stop it. I am not." Amy felt her cheeks. Was she flushed? "It's the cat. I'm calling the Humane Society and see how late they're open 'til tonight."

"I called them. They'll take a kitten that young if they have personnel available to give it twenty-four-hour care and if they have room."

"Great, thanks for—"

"They don't have either," Truly interrupted. "They said you could try a vet but they were doubtful. You could try back in a few weeks when the cat was older if you still didn't want it. They gave me information for recommended care."

Amy raised her arms then let them drop to her sides in defeat. "How am I supposed to take care of a kitten that hates me?"

Truly laughed and came over and hugged her. "Sienna doesn't hate you. She just hasn't gotten to know you yet."

Feeling the same stubborn determination and resilience that got her through college and through two long-term relationships that went sour, Amy wasn't going to let this kitten get the better of her. "Will you come and have dinner at my house tonight? I want to make sure I can feed Sienna. You seem to be the only one who can get near her without getting torn to shreds."

Truly glanced down at the kitten. "But I was supposed to dance naked in the desert tonight. The waxing moon is almost full."

Knowing Truly never missed her Earth rituals, she asked, "Well, can't you do that at my house? I have four open acres in back with no houses around and beyond that is the Sonoran Desert."

Truly swayed side to side, her skirt swooshing around her ankles. "That'll work. I'll bring prickly pear juice for margaritas if you're cooking."

"Are you trying to manifest anything special this month?"

Truly smiled wickedly. "Of course. A hunky guy."

"Great, thanks." Amy peered into the box. Sienna was sleeping again. She looked harmless when she was sleeping.

As they walked out of the storeroom and back to Chemistry, Phil from administration, who was at Dante's door earlier, was jotting a note on her desk. A knot tightened in her stomach. Could he know what had happened in Dante's office? It was not a good idea to be messing in one's own sandbox. What had she been thinking? Never again. What had Dante been thinking?

"Give me all the gory details later," Truly whispered as she walked past and got back to the autoanalyzer.

Straightening her back, she approached Phil with her best professional manner. "Hello, Phil, are you looking for me?"

"Amy, yes. Do you have a moment to come to my office?" He didn't smile. Phil always smiled.

*Oh God, he knows.* "Of course. What's this concerning?" Her throat constricted to the size of a swizzle stick.

"We just finished a meeting with a representative from the park service and I'd like you to come to my office to discuss a project."

"Project?"

He grimaced. "I know. It'll mean an increase in workload."

"Normally we would welcome the work but I hear our accounts have been ordering excessively high numbers of tests."

"A little unusual but we're fine." She crossed her arms over her lab coat, hoping to give a professional appearance. "We may need to do some overtime if it continues."

"I understand. Shall we?" He led the way toward his office on the second floor, a few doors down from Dante's. She wondered if Dante would be in Phil's office too.

Then she began to panic. She was so going to get fired. Was this a ruse to get her in his office to talk to her about her and Dante's indiscretion? She took a breath and tried to relax. Guilty conscience, that's all.

When they entered Phil's office, a man was seated in a guest chair in front of the desk. His hair was not as dark as Dante's and much shorter. The man turned and stood as they entered the room, his wide-brimmed park service hat in his hand.

"Amy, this is Jake Montag from Saguaro National Park. Jake, this is our lab supervisor, Ms. Weston." Phil pointed to a seat for Amy and began to flip through a file on his desk.

The first thing she noticed was Jake's cowboy boots beneath his tan park service uniform. Cowboy boots were something she didn't see often in Florida but she thought they looked very sexy on a guy.

Amy shook Jake's hand and welcomed him. Looking her over, he smiled and his eyes widened as if he recognized her. She didn't think she had met him before, although her mind raced through memories while her eyes were locked with his, trying to remember. Clear blue eyes, nearly the color of Truly's deepest turquoise, shone with subtle sensuality and ruggedness. Shit. As if she didn't have enough trouble she was getting hot for a new client while Dante wasn't quite out of the picture yet. What was wrong with her?

Jake had that rugged strength that made her think of backpacking trips, scaling mountains and horseback riding. Then she realized she was still holding his hand. *Idiot.* She pulled her hand away and stuck both hands in her lab coat. The realization that she had no underwear beneath her skirt did not help to keep her cool.

Jake's mouth curved in a smile, his eyes shone with an appreciative, knowing glint. She felt heat rise to her face. They both sat and stared at Phil, who seemed to have forgotten they were there. She gave Jake an awkward smile, wishing Phil wouldn't waste a client's time like this.

"Would you like me to explain what's been happening at the park, Phil? While you finish with what you're doing?" Jake asked in a calm, professional tone. "I don't want to keep Ms. Weston from her work."

He was sharp. Phil's eyebrows rose. He looked up from his file. "Of course, Amy, I don't want to keep you."

She smiled at Jake and thought she caught a slight wink. She guessed he was in his early to mid thirties, about her age. He had dark close-cropped hair with a few highlights. He probably spent extended amounts of time under the desert sun.

Unlike Dante, who was always edgy and moody, Jake had a calm demeanor and unmistakable sexual magnetism that probably smoldered beneath the surface until the right woman came along…

Phil closed the file and sat straighter in his chair. "This won't take long. I'll get right to the point," Phil said. "Normally, the park service has the state lab handle animal testing like rabies for park animals in cases when a visitor gets bitten. Rarely does the park service need to run tests for other reasons. But this is an unusual circumstance…"

Jake turned to Amy. "We're not sure what's killing so many animals."

"What kind of animals?" she asked.

"So far mostly mammals—deer, coyote, rabbits. The tests we send to the state lab are timely and costly. We'd like to run a series of tests locally to rule out a few things," Jake added.

Amy nodded. Her mind raced as she thought about the infectious agents that could infect a wide range of mammals. "I get worried when I see something jumping the species line." Amy looked at Phil. "CDC will need to be contacted if we come up with anything. And WHO tracks zoonoses diseases."

Jake frowned like he wasn't quite understanding. Amy translated. "Centers for Disease Control needs to know of diseases that are transmissible from animal to human. World Health Organization also tracks these diseases."

Nodding in understanding, Jake rubbed his forehead. The concern was etched in his brows. "We want to rule out insecticide or chemical poisons too."

"I have the list here of what we'll be screening for." Phil pulled some pages out of a file folder. "I'll make a copy for you, Amy. I've contacted a veterinarian to collect blood for toxic screens. And you and Jake will be collecting specimens for parasite, bacteria and viral studies." As he flipped through more papers, Amy noticed Jake's questioning glance at her.

Amy tried not to show her disbelief. "Out in the field?" she asked. Please, Phil was not asking her to collect animal shit with this hunky guy. He couldn't be that cruel.

"Yes, of course," Phil answered. "The fresher the better. And as many varieties as possible. I'm sure Jake will help you identify which animal left the sample. Unless you can differentiate—"

"No, no. Not my expertise," Amy interrupted. "I know microorganisms. Not animal droppings." She glanced at Jake and he was smiling. Her face felt hot.

"I'll be glad to help," Jake said.

"I'll put in an order for supplies but we should have enough in the storeroom to get started," Amy said. "When would you like to get started, Mr. Montag?"

"Tomorrow morning. If that's possible. And call me Jake please, ma'am."

"I'll get the supplies together. Where and when should I meet you?" Amy asked calmly but her hands became fists inside her pockets. She was going to spend the day with this guy. The idea was very appealing.

"I'll pick you up here at eight. We can load the supplies in my Jeep. We'll need to drive up in the high country. That's where I saw most of the dead animals."

She glanced at Phil, who seemed pleased with the plan, then back at Jake. "I guess I should wear hiking clothes then."

He smiled. "Might be a smart choice." Jake stood and shook her hand. Amy's stomach tumbled and she smiled up at him. *Stand up, idiot.* She did. Okay, any woman would be a bit flustered by the outdoorsy hunk. The guy was gorgeous.

"I'll be there." What was she going to do with the kitten tomorrow?

* * * * *

"So dump the guy, if he's weirding you out, Amy," Truly said as she added prickly pear juice, tequila and ice to Amy's blender and hit the liquefy button. The roar of the appliance drowned out Amy's retort. She nodded in agreement and continued chopping onions, slicing cucumbers, wedging tomatoes and cutting up chunks of mango. She arranged a bed of fresh mixed greens, vegetables and mango on two large dinner plates, then seasoned the thin flank steak for the grill.

"I did. At least I think I did but I don't think Dante realizes it's over yet."

Truly poured her frozen concoctions into two margarita glasses. "Make it clear, put it in writing or something. Here, try my prickly pear margaritas. I got the recipe from this guy who works in a bar in Sedona." She handed Amy a green glass with the orange drink. Amy took a sip.

"Yum. Can't drink too many of these. I have to go out in the mountains tomorrow and collect wild animal doo-doo. With Hunky Forest Ranger, I might add." She put the glass down as she set the table in the small dining area between the kitchen and living room.

"Good. I hope Hunky Forest Ranger helps take your mind off the old flame." With margarita in hand, Truly strolled around the living room, examining the few desert scene prints on the wall and grinning at the misplaced wicker furniture.

"Early miscellaneous with a Southwestern flavor and hint of Floridian beach cottage."

"Cute. Since I'm planning to move back to Florida, I didn't want to part with my furniture. It's almost new and the company paid to move all my stuff."

"Good Lord, I don't imagine that's yours." Truly pointed to the bearskin rug in front of the fireplace, head and all. "Yuck, look at the eyes and mouth." She kneeled down and stuck her finger in its mouth and rubbed its tongue. "Ouch!" She yanked her hand away and Amy dropped a fork.

"Damn it, Truly, you scared the heck out of me. Very funny." Amy held a hand over her chest and felt foolish that her heart was racing like she'd run a marathon.

Truly stretched out on the thick brown fur, using the bear's head as a pillow. "Big bear, I'm five nine and the fur is longer than me. This would be great to get laid on."

"No thanks. The landlord said to put it in a closet but it takes up all my storage space." The rental house had two bedrooms and two baths with an option to buy and the price was right. She had no intention of buying it but she hadn't told the real estate agent that. While looking for an apartment in the paper, she came across this listing for a single family home with four acres, and she was intrigued. The Southwestern style with stucco walls, Spanish tile and a beehive fireplace had personality.

The harsh scenery of the Sonoran Desert, its foreign landscape, shifting colors and wild nature, stirred something inside her. Although she missed the lush tropical beaches of Florida and her friends and family, being close to nature eased her loneliness.

"Mmmm. I'll buy it," Truly said with eyes closed and arms behind her head. "So, are you still moving back or is Dante keeping you here?"

"Dante wouldn't have any influence in my decision in staying here," she snapped.

"Whoa, touchy." Truly opened one eye for a minute. "What would keep you here? I'd like you to stay." It seemed that by keeping her eyes closed Truly could talk to Amy on a personal level and still keep her distance.

Amy didn't say anything for a long moment. "I don't know. Arizona just doesn't feel like home yet. And I don't know if it ever will."

Truly sat up and shot her a concerned look. "Oh, Amy. It takes a while, sweetie, to make friends in a new place. Give it time. You can't make a decision about an area in only a few months. When you know all the hiking trails by heart, when you can drive home from work on automatic pilot and don't remember making all the turns but you still make it home and when you go into a supermarket and someone recognizes you and says hello, then your new place is now your old place. But right now, this is home."

Amy felt a lump forming in her throat. She picked up her margarita and took several swallows. She wasn't sure where she belonged anymore. Florida didn't feel like home, although she missed her parents, her friends. When she called them, their lives continued on as if her moving had left no void. By the time she moved back to Florida, she would feel like a stranger there again. "Get up and help me with the steaks," Amy called over her shoulder as she brought a platter of meat out her sliding glass door onto the patio to grill.

"On my way." Truly unfolded an Indian blanket on a redwood lounger and stretched out with her margarita in hand.

Amy stabbed the steak and tossed the meat on the preheated grill. It sputtered and sent up flares from the juices. "Dante bought me that blanket you're sitting on." She didn't want to tell Truly that blanket was the one she and Dante nearly made love on.

"Nice." Truly narrowed her eyes and studied Amy for a moment. "Are you going to tell me what the guy's problem is? You know, I've dated some creeps in my day. I'm sure I've heard it all before. Too kinky for you? Wanted to do a threesome?"

Amy laughed. "Threesome? He didn't even want to do a twosome." The margaritas were loosening her tongue.

"What?" Truly laughed.

Amy sighed. "I mean, things got hot between us. He…pleasured me but he never completed the act and then he disappeared. I mean really disappeared. I think he knows hypnosis or something, or I fell asleep."

"Maybe he wasn't that good if you just fell asleep." Truly held up her empty glass and jumped up. "Refill?"

"No, I'm good for now." Amy turned the steaks. Dante was good but disconcerting. Truly was right. She was smart to break it off with him. After Truly left, she'd try calling him.

Truly came out of the house with a full glass. "You sure you don't want—oh, look. We have company." She pointed out toward the desert. "He must smell the steaks."

A coyote stood about fifty yards away, his nose in the air. His golden color blended in with the buff colors of the sand and dried grasses. Most of his body was hidden by scrub brush. "Oh my, I never saw one get this close before."

"They'll get into your garbage if you don't have a secure lid," Truly said as she sipped her drink.

"Is he dangerous?" Amy took the steaks off the grill and shut off the gas.

"Not really. I wouldn't leave Sienna out here alone though. He might decide to have her for lunch. Wildlife is beautiful, isn't it?"

"Yeah." Amy took the meat inside. She couldn't help the uneasy feeling she got with the coyote watching her. She wondered if she had left the steaks out there unattended, if he would've come closer, even stolen them right off the grill.

Amy mixed up her Thai peanut sauce in a bowl and sliced the beef into thin strips. She arranged the meat on the salad plates and drizzled the peanut dressing on top. "Dinner's ready." They sat at her dining room table that looked out of her sliding glass door. The coyote had gone.

"You left your drink outside," Truly said. "I'll get it." She went out for a moment and came back with the glass, stopping at the kitchen to pour the last of the concoction from the blender into Amy's glass. "Looks like our lone friend is gone."

"Sure, because we took the food inside." The kitten was making mewling noises.

"Sienna's hungry," Truly said. "After dinner, we'll feed her."

Amy dropped her fork and looked up at Truly, remembering her schedule for tomorrow. "I can't take Sienna with me tomorrow. Can you bring her to work with you?"

"Amy, I'm off. I'm going to Tucson to visit my mom for the day."

"Oh crap, I forgot. This is why I don't have pets. What am I going to do? She needs to be fed every few hours, poor thing. I have no idea how long I'll be out collecting specimens."

"I'll call my mom and cancel," Truly said.

"No, no. The cat is my responsibility. I'll figure out something. Maybe I can leave her at the ranger station, or at Betty's, my neighbor."

"What neighbor? You're in the middle of nowhere out here."

"Betty lives down the road about a quarter mile. You'll love her. She's retired and from New York. She loves cats. Wait 'til you see her gun collection."

* * * * *

When they pulled into Betty's driveway and got out of the car with Sienna's box and supplies, Amy heard three gunshots from the backyard. Truly let out a yelp.

"What the hell was that?" Truly froze.

Amy hooked arms with Truly and dragged her along. "Betty must be around back." With the box in hand, Amy walked around the side of the house, Truly tugging at her arm.

"You sure we should go back there?"

Another three shots. "Hello, Betty? It's me, Amy," she yelled as she came around the corner.

"Hey, Amy, come have a seat." Betty pointed to the picnic table where boxes of ammunition were stacked. "Who's your shy friend?" Betty held her stance, legs spread, arms outstretched, both hands gripping a pistol. She wore jeans that snugly fit her petite figure, with an oversized Disney tee shirt with a picture of Cinderella's castle. Betty stood only about five feet tall and was barely a hundred pounds. She squeezed off a couple more rounds and knocked the empty soup cans off a log about fifty or sixty feet away. Opening the chamber of the gun, she placed it on the picnic table and brushed her short brown hair out of her face. "Hey, I'm Betty." She reached her hand out to Truly.

Truly shook her hand and introduced herself, rather meekly for Truly, Amy observed.

"Can I get you some iced tea?" Betty noticed Truly eyeing the gun. "It's just a pellet gun. I take the serious hardware down to the shooting range."

Truly's eyes widened. "How serious is serious?"

"Well now. I have an old Colt .38 that was my husband's. Mel died ten years ago. My favorite is my .357 Magnum."

Truly's mouth dropped open. "You have a .357 Magnum?" She looked Betty up and down and Amy knew she was wondering why a little old lady who looked like she barely weighed a hundred pounds would own a .357.

Betty nodded, unloading the pellet gun and putting it away in a case. "Believe me, I can hit the silhouette targets pretty well at the range too. You bet your ass, a .357 can do serious damage." She made an outline of a human figure with her hands.

Amy shivered at that image even though she knew Betty was harmless. She laughed. "You should see the holster she crocheted for it too."

Truly opened her mouth and shook her head. "That I've got to see."

The sun had set, washing Betty's backyard, the desert and distant Rincon Mountains with golden and purple shadows. Sienna began meowing inside the box.

"Damn, you do have a little one in there, don't you? Let me see her." Betty picked up Sienna and the sometimes cat from hell curled up in Betty's arms. "Just tell me how often you want me to feed her."

"Thanks, Betty, I appreciate it. As soon as I get home, I'll stop by and pick her up."

"As long as it's before six because I have a hot date," Betty said. "With a younger man," she added with a wink.

"Whoa, Betty. How'd you meet this guy?"

"At the Las Olas Café." Betty crossed her arms and shifted her weight to one hip as if expecting to get a lecture.

"Betty—"

Betty put up a hand. "I know, I know. What would a young fiftyish guy want with old me?"

"That's not what I mean. You remember the last guy you picked up in a bar?"

She looked away, pursing her lips. "That was different. He said he forgot his wallet at home. I've done the same. It could happen. The mind forgets things as you get older. I only bought him dinner."

Truly groaned. "He made you pay for dinner?"

Betty nodded.

"And he tried to get her to use her credit card to pay for other things," Amy said softly.

"What things?" Truly looked horrified.

Betty rolled her eyes. "Hells bells, I ain't that stupid. I caught on to his act when he asked for a ride to pick up his car at the repair shop. He wanted me to pay the garage, said he'd pay me back. The guy had no class. I pulled the car over and told him to get the fuck out of my car. When he started to argue, I pulled out the .357 from under the seat. He got out."

Truly covered her face with her hands. "Did you call the police?"

"Hell no. I didn't want to look like no fool."

Apparently Betty hadn't learned her lesson about picking up strange men. Amy heard she had two sons who lived in New York but they didn't visit very often. She was worried about someone taking advantage of Betty even though she was one tough bird. "So how is this new stranger different?"

"He has a job and didn't ask me for money, for one thing. He's a college history professor, he showed me his ID card. His name is Lupi."

"Lupi?" both Truly and Amy asked at the same time.

"It's his last name but that's what everyone calls him. Distinguished looking and handsome. Slightly gray, goatee and glasses. I think he's in his late fifties."

"Just stick to public places for a while until you get to know him better. There are a lot of scam artists out there," Amy said. She took the kitten out of Betty's arms and placed her back in the box. The cat didn't attack her this evening. Maybe it was finally getting used to her.

"Don't worry, I can take care of myself."

"It's getting late. I need to go, Amy," Truly said as she stretched her arms out and twirled around. "Dancing naked in the moonlight tonight, remember?"

Amy glanced up at the twilight sky and saw the pale outline of the moon. "Yeah, we should go. I want to get a good night's rest. I'll be hiking all day tomorrow."

"What are you conjuring?" Betty asked Truly. "I know for a fact the naked dancing ritual works. I've never tried it though."

Truly smiled. "A man, a really hot man."

# Chapter Five

ꟻ

Amy awoke on her hands and knees. She was not in her bedroom where she'd gone to bed. Was it hours ago? She was outside in the desert and had no idea how she'd gotten there. Dreaming? Yes, dreaming by the way the scenery continued to shift in colors. And the cactus and bushes were moving as if she had spun around in circles and then stopped.

A cool breeze teased her bare skin, sending chills up her arms and legs, along her back, drawing her nipples in to taut points. She was completely naked. Blinking several times, she tried to clear her head and vision. Drained and weak, she doubted her legs would support her if she tried to stand.

The ground swayed and the ten-foot-tall saguaro cactus in front of her blurred, sharpened into view, then blurred again. The woven material beneath her came into focus. It was the Indian blanket Dante had given her. Searching her memory, she couldn't remember when the dream began. Was this a dream? Did Dante summon her? Did he hypnotize her? Or was it something more ominous?

Trying to move was like swimming in molasses. What did Truly put in those margaritas? She forced her muscles to respond so she could get up but her wrists and ankles were staked to the ground with ropes.

A hand pressed on her back. "Don't move," Dante's husky voice said. "This is a new game."

Fear hardened her muscles into petrified wood, then fear was replaced with anger. Not dreaming. She yanked on the nylon cords, feeling the ropes burn her skin. The restraints wouldn't budge. "Untie me," she demanded through gritted teeth.

"Don't you like to be tied up?" he said. "Didn't you say that was a fantasy of yours?" He sounded calm, annoyingly so.

Her mind raced through her foggy thoughts, trying to remember if they had discussed her fantasies or not. "Maybe I did but I don't remember coming out here and that bothers me."

He stroked her hair, her back and then slid his hand down over her ass. Her pussy responded, a traitor to her better judgment. She shuddered. His hand slipped between the crease of her buttocks and she resisted the urge to spread her legs wider for him.

"My hypnosis skills are better than I thought. I didn't mean to scare you, Amy. This was all for your pleasure and fun." He started to untie her wrists.

She sighed heavily and tried to sit back on her heels but her ankles were too far back. "I don't understand you," she snapped as she reached over to undo her ankles but couldn't reach. "Dante, finish untying me!" Glancing over her shoulder to shoot him a look, she noticed he was naked too. He looked away from her, staring far away, his brows in a deep frown.

He stood up and moved toward her ankles but hesitated to release her. "Don't I please you?" he whispered with a sad tone. He sounded hurt.

Rustling in nearby bushes made her jump and tug against her restraints. "What's that?"

"An owl or a raccoon. Nothing to worry about." Dante kept staring at the bush. "You don't like how I—"

"Dante, I'm finished with your games. As I said in your office, it's best we end this. Now let me up."

He didn't move or say anything. Fear flooded her thoughts again. Then she realized why he must be hesitating. His reputation at work. Should she be concerned for her immediate safety? "If you're worried about work, I can keep my professional and personal life separate. I wouldn't say anything about our relationship."

Still no movement or words.

She glanced up at him over her shoulder. He seemed miles away. For a moment, his body blurred and shrank down into the form of a coyote. The animal raised his head as if sniffing the air, then the form blurred and he was Dante again, naked and bronzed and muscular. He turned and looked down at her as if seeing her for the first time. "Dante, you're scaring me now. Please untie my ankles."

Her heart rate, which had been somewhat calm considering she had been staked to the ground, jumped to an alarming pace. Was she hallucinating, or had she been drugged?

"Sorry, Amy." His words sounded forced and insincere.

Her body shivered, more from fear than the cold. He hadn't made a fire this evening. She missed the warmth, the glow. She missed the warmth and playfulness of his body. The fire had summoned her before. What had he used to draw her out there? Something had changed between them, something had changed in him. He'd crossed a line and she knew she wouldn't feel the same about him. He was creeping her out. Defusing the heavy atmosphere might help to keep the situation from getting out of hand. "It's okay, Dante. Some women don't do well with surprises." She tried to keep her tone light.

He groaned. "Oh, Amy, I did scare you. I'm so sorry." He untied her ankles, then leaned close to her ear and whispered a rapid stream of foreign words in a preternatural voice. Amy caught her breath. The next moment she was flat on her back and Dante was perched above her on hands and knees, her body was humming with need. "Do you want to go now?" he said, smiling and breathless.

Her pussy throbbed. "What? Go? No, not yet," Amy said. Her eyes squeezed shut then opened in an attempt to clear her mind. What had they been talking about?

"You think I don't want you?" Dante asked. "Here." He took her free hand and wrapped it around his thick penis. "You don't know how much I want you, Amy." His cock twitched in eagerness in her hand.

"I'm aching for you." She shook her head. Her thoughts were fuzzy. Hadn't they agreed to stop seeing each other? Leaning onto one arm, he lowered himself onto her. He grasped her hand and stretched it above her head. With his aroused cock he rubbed the smooth end against her slick pussy. She inhaled sharply and raised her hips to increase the pressure of his cock.

Groaning, he took her mouth, kissing her hard, plunging his tongue deep. Between gasping breaths he said, "I'll give you what you want, Amy." Was it desperation or arrogant control? She wasn't sure.

This was what she had wanted for weeks and now she felt like he was forcing himself to do something he didn't want. He straddled her. His erection hard and tight against his flat abdomen. The moonlight defined the curved of his biceps and chest muscles, a thin sheen of sweat glistening on his tanned skin. She was about to remind him of protection when she noticed his jaw clenching. "Dante?"

"Mmmm?" He didn't look at her.

"You look awesome in the moonlight," she said and at the same time felt like she was forgetting to tell him something else, something important.

He smiled and palmed her breasts with both hands. His cock was hard and she was ready to suck it or have him fuck her and soon. Gliding her hands over his shoulders and arms, she resisted the urge to pull him down on top of her. "Dante. It's okay if you're not ready for this. Besides, we should use protection anyway."

He didn't say anything. Instead he leaned up and slid his hand between her legs, stroking her clit. She moaned and shuddered as sensations rippled through her body.

"You're beautiful," he said in a raspy tone. "Don't worry, I want this and I have protection." He swung his leg over her and stood up, walking over to a pile of clothes. As he dug into his pockets, she took in a deep breath. This whole evening seemed surreal like she was drifting through a sexual dream. Her body and her needs were overriding her objections and common sense. Maybe she and Dante weren't meant for each other but they both wanted release tonight. Tomorrow might be the end but for tonight, she would have him.

The desert wind stirred the dried brush, then Amy heard a strange sound. "I must be losing my mind but the wind tonight sounds like the ocean. Maybe I'm homesick."

Dante jumped to his feet, staring out into the desert, his hand fisting just beneath his nebula stone pendant.

"What is it? What do you see?" she asked. She breathed in the night air. Sea salt. She chuckled. "I am crazy. Now I smell the ocean. What is—"

"Shhh." Dante held up a hand. "Sorry, Amy." He rushed over to her and knelt beside her, kissing her mouth quickly then whispered those strange words again. Amy closed her eyes and opened them to the blaring alarm clock. She was in her bed. It was a dream, after all. The images of the sexual dream bounced around in her mind. Although turned-on by the memories, she was relieved it had only been a dream.

As she reached out to turn off the alarm, she noticed the rope burns on her wrists.

* * * * *

Dante ran along a dried creek bed, following the sound of crashing waves. Damn her, he still had time. And by interrupting him, Gwyllain wasted the valuable chi he was in the middle of collecting. Didn't she understand his predicament?

Without Amy, he would have a difficult time meeting the demoness's needs. Finding another with an aura as strong as

Amy's would be nearly impossible with so little time left. Amy was rare. He didn't think she knew how much chi she radiated. The chi given off during her orgasms had kept him from killing humans. Only a week and a half left and his cycle of offerings would be up and another of Gwyllain's minions would be the Drone and Dante could continue his life on the Earth plane. Damn Gwyllain. She could've waited.

When the creek made a ninety-degree turn, he saw the shimmering disturbance between two large boulders on the far riverbank. The rift looked like heat waves rising in the desert but it was too cool a night for that to happen here. As he approached, he felt the pull. In a last-minute desperate decision he backed away and zigzagged around the area, looking for creatures, large or small, to draw more energy upon. He managed to find a couple of bats, a field mouse and a rabbit. All four dropped as he touched his stone. They were dead and he had a fraction more chi. Better not to come back empty-handed.

An unseen force yanked him off his feet and dragged him through the portal before he had a chance to take a breath. He was plunged into a reeling darkness.

When the dizziness faded, Dante opened his eyes. A sickening free-fall sensation clutched at his gut as he stared over a rocky precipice at skyscraper height above crashing ocean waves, his feet just inch away from the crumpling edge.

His muscles froze into stiff knots. Damn Gwyllain. The demoness knew of his fear of heights, which could only mean her disappointment. Unless her lover, Tarik, was responsible for his abrupt appearance into Anartia.

Slowly he reached for the nebula stone pendant around his neck. It was gone!

He glanced down to the jagged rocks below and bile crept up to his throat. Without his pendant, if he fell…

He didn't dare turn around. One slip on the loose stones and he'd be an unrecognizable mess, chum for the fish, as the tide took his broken remains out to sea. In Gwyllain's world, immortality would end if he died a mortal's death. *Move. Take one step back and the rest will be easy.* But Dante couldn't force himself to move.

Gwyllain and Tarik's affair was discovered by her jealous husband—the Ruler, called Cragen. Cragen sought a unique punishment for such betrayal. Tarik was the ruler's lead engineer who was designing an alternative universe—something small about the size of a large island where he and Gwyllain could meet for their secret affair.

Cragen had another engineer finish the design so that the secret hideaway became the lovers' prison and an eternal exile. His wife and her lover were bound to this exile, having to maintain the stability of the artificial universe with acquired life energy transferred through sexual encounters—frequent sexual encounters.

Immortality was a gift that Gwyllain had given Dante but although he could live on Earth for long cycles, he was as much a prisoner to this exile world as Tarik and Gwyllain.

Glancing around at the once-beautiful island world surrounded by a calm sea, Dante frowned at Anartia's awful state. The sky roiled with violent storm clouds and the wind assaulted his naked body so hard his skin stung and his eyes watered. Of course Gwyllain would summon him here, naked and vulnerable. It was her way of exerting her domination, her control and if she felt it was deserved, a little punishment. His instincts told him he was in for some behavioral modification.

With great effort he avoided looking at the ocean below. Hell, he hated heights and hated that she had such control to yank him out of the Earth plane into her fragmented dimension. How was he supposed to supply her with the chi energy that she craved and needed to maintain her world when she pulled tricks like this?

He breathed in the damp, salt air, wishing he was back in his desert, his domain. What was Amy thinking of him right now after he left abruptly in the middle of their rendezvous?

Despite his technique for clearing her short-term memory, he wondered if he'd rushed and if she could remember anything.

Before Gwyllain arrived, he was going to get off this cliff. He twisted slightly, forcing himself to step back a fraction of inch, but the stones slid beneath his bare feet. *Move, damn it.* He swallowed but it felt like he was trying to force down a walnut. Carefully, he shuffled his feet back a few small steps. The gravel rolled down the incline and disappeared over the edge. Images of his body tumbling over the cliff flashed in his mind. He forced himself to look at the horizon and not at the crashing waves. Then a hand gripped the back of his neck. His sphincter tightened.

"Don't you like the view?" Gwyllain asked. Her shrill laughter pissed him off. He bit off a retort. She wouldn't push him over this edge, would she?

"I liked the view of where I was a few moments ago. The chi draw was high on this subject, would've been, except my fucking was interrupted." She tightened the pressure on his neck and shoved him closer toward the edge. *Stupid move. Don't piss off the demoness while standing on a cliff.*

Still holding him with one hand, she dangled his nebula stone necklace in front of his face. "Looking for this?" She laughed a wild, evil laugh.

"What am I supposed to do without it?" Dante tried to keep his voice level and without an edge of anger. Show her anger and Gwyllain knew how to punish and put an end to her minions. "I can't go through the portal without it and I can't transfer the chi I've assimilated."

"Time is running out. My sun sets soon." She pointed to the low-hanging red sun, mostly covered in black clouds. "That's less than two Earth weeks left and you've been diddling with this woman when you could've killed her for the largest take. And you've been collecting miniscule chi amounts with animals. Such a waste of time." Her other hand began to stroke his buttocks, sliding her fingers along his crack. Still, she wouldn't let him move away from the edge.

Below, the waves crashed on the sharp rocks, salty spray licked at his skin. This was not the time to ask why she had summoned him back to be a Drone so early. He wasn't due to give his offering for another fifty years. He didn't even know how many Drones lived as he did on the Earth plane—immortals whose only task was to provide life energy to Gwyllain every one hundred years.

She laughed that shrill laugh again and pressed her body against his back. He felt the whisper-thin material that covered her voluminous breasts and probably clung like a skin to the rest of her body. She either wore a bodysuit outfit or a long tight dress, neither leaving anything to the imagination. The material shimmered like eelskin in blues, greens or reds. He wondered what she wore right now and felt his cock twitch.

Once she absorbed his collected chi, all would be well for a time, the sea of Anartia would calm, the skies clear and the land again yield a profusion of vegetation. Then he could return to the desert. Appease the gods. An offering of chi to propitiate the gods.

"If you don't collect enough chi at the end of this moon cycle, then I'll make you my slave, or I may choose an abrupt ending to your immortality. The Drones are needed to maintain the balance on Anartia but I can find others to replace those who do not yield what is needed."

Killing mortals was looking like a reasonable alternative. "Don't worry, Gwyllain, I'll fulfill my service in time. But aren't you wasting my chi now, or your chi, by holding me here? I can think of something more interesting we could be doing." He reached around and slid his hand to her pussy. She was wearing the dress today. The silky material allowed him to feel every fold of her mound. He rubbed at her slit. She sucked in a breath and moaned her approval.

Gwyllain let go of his neck and wrapped her arm around his waist, pulling him away from the ledge. "Tell me why you don't just kill that mortal woman and go on to the next one?"

"Amy has a substantial amount of chi and as long as I don't complete the sex act, I can absorb that energy and transmit it to your world. The more frustrated she gets that I don't make love to her the more chi she gives off."

Gwyllain sighed, annoyed but somewhat satisfied with his explanation. "So the survival of my world is just a sexual game for you?" Her voice became shrill and her body pressed him toward the edge again.

Straightening, Dante grabbed her arm. If she was foolish enough to push him over the edge, as powerful as she was, she couldn't stop him from taking her over with him.

Twisting around, he crushed his broad chest against her breasts and ground his hips into her, knowing his erect cock prodded her pussy. "Fuck you, Gwyllain. I'm doing my duty. My immortality depends on the survival of your fucking fragmented world. I find killing humans offensive. If I can acquire the needed chi a different way, I'll do it. And if I run out of time, I'll resort to killing. Either way your world will be safe." He preferred to collect his offering of chi through human sexual interactions alone.

Killing animals was an alternative. His shapeshifting powers enabled him to stalk and capture animals for chi, also to travel quickly and inconspicuously. The Native American culture and mythology always fascinated him, especially the Coyote Trickster myth. Gwyllain said Tarik could incorporate a form during the merging. Many Drones used other forms as a disguise.

While holding on to one of her arms, Dante slowly trailed his other hand just beneath her breast and hoped she didn't notice he was shaking. Partly from anger and partly from nerves at standing three hundred feet above jagged rocks. But he willed himself to give her an admiring gaze. Seducing her was a better idea than challenging her, especially at the moment.

Gwyllain's back arched, her head tilted up, allowing her straight black hair to stream behind her in the wind. Her eyes glowed a midnight blue with inhuman intensity. The blue dress she wore matched her eyes and showed the details of her areolas and taut nipples. The breeze had spread the hip-high slit, revealing most of her long legs, the small dark triangle of hair between her legs. The image of Gwyllain in her dress reminded Dante of a snake shedding its skin.

Stroking his chest, she smiled wickedly. The tip of her tongue darted out and she licked her upper lip. She nodded. "Of course. You have not failed me in over one hundred fifty years. I see no reason for you not to be faithful this cycle."

Reaching up, he palmed her breast with his other hand while he continued to grind his cock between her legs. Her body quivered beneath his touch. Sucking in a breath, she watched him with heavy-lidded eyes. Yes, he had her in his power now, for however brief this moment would be.

She studied him a long moment, then as she glanced around her face hardened. "Look at my world." She raised her hand, swinging her arm out. "I have barely seen the sun, quakes have shaken the ground, fissures have formed. My home has aged too." Her voice cracked. Beneath their feet the ground rumbled and heaved. She gripped Dante's arms, leaning into him as if for protection.

In reflex to comfort a woman in distress, Dante slid an arm around her shoulders and pulled her close. "Don't worry. I have an offering now." He squeezed her breasts and waited to see her eyes soften, then asked, "Why was I summoned early to be a Drone?" He wondered if he dared be so bold. "Why is Anartia in such a state?"

She rested her palms on his chest, eyes downcast. "If I lose one of my Drones…" She stopped, then began again. "Tarik is working on a project to free Anartia and he needs more bio-energy." As if she realized she let him see too much of her vulnerable side, she jerked out of his embrace. Dante pulled her back into his arms. At first she resisted his attentions, then finally responded, melting into him. Her hands slid up his back.

"Did something happen to one of the Drones?" Dante asked. Could Tarik's jealousy move him to kill the very subjects that kept Anartia intact?

Anger flared in her eyes. "A Drone didn't make his offering in time. I dealt with him."

Dante swallowed. "Why didn't you make him Throng? Couldn't you use another servant?"

She glared at him, ignoring his question. "You have an offering." Her hand slipped down to his cock, wrapping her hand around its engorged length. "It's time we entered my temple."

# Chapter Six

ജ

Gwyllain, in her all-business mode, was ignoring his question. And her business was sex, hot and intense, addicting and bewitching, its sole purpose to fuel and maintain her realm.

She motioned for Dante to follow on an angle away from the ocean. "Let's get out of this weather and find comfort in my temple." The open field of coarse sea grass sloped up to a wide knoll. At the top was a single-story structure with designs similar to the Greek Parthenon with its Doric marble columns evenly spaced around the entire building.

Dante barely managed to suppress his look of shock. The temple had lost its once-pristine luminescence. The stones now appeared gray and crumbling. Although completely intact, the temple looked more like the ruins of the Greek Parthenon. No wonder Gwyllain was pissed. Another quake rumbled like an underground wave. The structure vibrated, sending bits of dust floating to the ground.

"See, see what has become of my beautiful temple? Without the bounty of my chi, my temple and my realm suffer. Hurry, Dante, inside." She grasped his hand as large raindrops pelted the dry stone steps, flattening her dark hair and cooling his wind-burned skin. They climbed the steps and passed through the massive colonnade.

The sound of the rain pummeled the roof. Two women servants in white robes scurried to her side, awaiting orders. Gwyllain ordered them to bring dry towels, clothing, food and wine. Turning to Dante, she smiled and welcomed him into the main room. A dozen young women lounged around the pool, some completely naked, others dressed in white tunics.

They barely gave him a glance when he entered. The slave women were to serve Gwyllain and Tarik, no others.

He caught a whiff of smoky copal from an incense burner and lemon oil from the polished carved wood furniture. Dozens of enormous pillows were scattered on the floor around a fireplace at one side of the room. On the opposite side, brocade lounges, chairs and tables created a cozy seating area. In the center of the room was a colossal bath, large enough for twenty or more. The brief time on Gwyllain's world did not allow him opportunity to meet the slaves or other Drones but he suspected there were other Drones giving the mistress her offering.

Surrounding the main room were many smaller Drone and servant rooms. How many people did she need to maintain her dimension? When she lost one or two what were the consequences to her realm? How many losses before Anartia would collapse? Or would she find new subjects to be her immortal slaves and workers?

Gwyllain slithered up to him, wrapping her arms around his neck and brushing her lips over his. "Would you like to bathe or eat first?"

Dante felt the throb in his groin. No man could resist Gwyllain. His fingers tangled in her damp hair, holding her head back as his gaze held hers and his other hand stroked her cheek, her lips, then moved down between her breasts.

The price of immortality was to pay his debt with chi energy, then live on the Earth plane for another one hundred years as a human.

"When are you going to tell me where Reilly is?" Dante asked. He didn't know when he'd have another chance to ask her. Once his cycle with Gwyllain was over, he wouldn't see her for another hundred years. During the California Gold Rush in the 1850s, while Dante lay dying in the desert, Gwyllain sent a Drone to bring him to Anartia. Gwyllain had promised him immortality and revenge, but on her terms. A wealthy prospector, John Reilly, had stolen his wife, taken his gold claim and arranged for Dante's murder. Apparently, Gwyllain thought Dante and Reilly would make worthy Drones.

"When I don't have any use for him." She picked up a glass of wine that the servant girl had poured and left on the stone table. Slowly she took a sip. "If a Drone doesn't acquire the chi I need or if I grow tired of his attentions, I will…replace him."

"It's been over a hundred and fifty years." Dante tightened his fists. "I want my revenge."

"You'll get your revenge, in time." She peered at him seductively over the top of her goblet. "Bath or food?"

Dante looked away and took a deep breath, trying to calm himself. What could he do? The Drones received new identities periodically. He didn't know John Reilly's name, where he lived or what he looked like now. How could he find him?

"You didn't answer me," she said, then gasped as his hand skimmed over her breast and found the fastening under her arm. The dress dropped at her feet.

"Shall we skip the bath and food and just enter your chamber?" He stroked her hair.

She drew lazy circles on his chest. "What's the rush?"

He grabbed her hand and gently pushed her away.

A shadow passed over her face. Her eyes flared for a moment then cooled. Her lips pursed together as if he'd hurt her feelings. "Aren't you pleased to see me, Dante? Or are you in that much of a hurry to get back to your world?"

He groaned inwardly. Share his true thoughts with a demoness, not a good plan. He walked to the edge of the pool and examined a collection of vials and crystal pitchers. He uncorked one and poured a drop in his hand and inhaled the spicy wood scent that reminded him of a pine forest in autumn. Massage oil. He re-corked the bottle and held it up. "Massage?"

She glared at him and didn't answer. Actually, he had something else in mind. It was time he held the reins for a while, for a change. "Your realm is a mess. Looks like the energy drain is extensive. Maybe we shouldn't wait." As she stepped out of the dress, his gaze moved down her body, over her breasts, which were full and teardrop shaped. The erect points of her nipples were a deep bronze, her skin a shimmery olive tan. Dante focused on the trim triangle of dark hair at the juncture of her legs. A glint of gold sparkled from her clit ring—the only piece of jewelry she wore.

She regarded him with a smoldering look. "Are you ready to replenish Anartia?" Her voice was a seductive lure.

"In a moment. I'm enjoying the view." He wanted to make her ache for him. Bring her down a few steps and she would be more amiable.

She huffed her impatience, then slid her hands over her breasts, down her belly, between her legs, then back up to her breasts. "Don't take too long. You know how restless I am." Her tone was edgy.

"And you know how I don't like to be ordered," Dante snapped.

A flicker of anger passed over Gwyllain's face. "My world, my rules."

He spun around and started for the entrance. Gwyllain gasped, then laughed. "You can't leave." She ran after him. "Dante, wait."

He knew he wouldn't get far if she sent her guards after him. He wanted her to think he was angry enough to fight her guards. Encounters with Gwyllain were exercises of will and psychology.

Before he reached the doorway, Gwyllain caught up to him and placed a hand on his arm. "Dante, I forget how much you resent—"

Then he made his move. He grasped her wrists and pinned her against one of the giant marble columns, her arms raised above her head. His hard chest crushed her breasts as he lowered his mouth over hers in a brutal and heated kiss.

She groaned and one leg hooked around his thigh to draw him closer. Crossing her wrists, he held them with one hand. His other hand dropped between her legs and a finger thrust inside her channel. Using his thumb, he flicked the ring pierced through her hood. The tiny bud beneath it swelled. She drew in a breath and stood up on her toes.

"I think I'm ready now." He chuckled as he tugged at her earlobe with his lips.

"Bastard," she said, with a smile. "You take much risk."

Dante swept her off her feet and strode down the few steps into the steaming bath.

She squealed, which brought out three of her muscled guards in white tunics carrying swords. Gwyllain waved her hand in dismissal. "Mistress?" they shouted.

"It's all right. You may go." The men retreated, disappearing behind the columns. As Dante stepped deeper into the water, a rumble vibrated underground, sending a tremble through the columns and a seismic wave over the surface of the water.

"Maybe we should skip the pleasantries and get down to business," he said.

She groaned and looked longingly at one side of the Roman tub where her servants had placed thick white towels, bowls of fruit and cheese. An opened bottle of wine and two glasses stood on a small stone platform. Another rumble passed though the hall and Gwyllain gripped his shoulders. "Maybe you're right. I can take from you what I need and we can enjoy the bath and eat later." Her mouth widened in a sensuous smile. "Besides, I sense your body needs to release all the delicious chi you've saved for me and my world. I'm ready for you now."

An incredible body and sexual skills, she had. Charm and tact, she didn't. Picking up the vial of massage oil, he scooped her up in his arms and hurried into her bedchamber. He climbed up on the massive bed, then dropped her among a pile of pillows. She scooted backward toward the middle of the bed, tossing pillows aside.

He placed the vial of massage oil on the bedside table for later.

In the shadowy light of the room, she stretched out, touching her breasts, tweaking her nipples into hard points. All along, her gaze watched him as if measuring his response. His cock twitched and he saw her smile.

Outside he heard the waves crashing on the cliffs and the spattering of rain on the stone balcony. A jolt of icy fear seeped into his bones. They both had the power of destruction right now.

She could destroy him with a flip of her hand. But if he withheld his chi, could he destroy her world? Did her other minions supply enough or was it a delicate balance? He had the power to destroy creatures and humans on the Earth plane. Knowing he might have the power to destroy Gwyllain's world gave him a rush and made his cock grow harder.

Worth living on the edge, if he thought he could destroy her.

"Lick me," she demanded as she raised her hips.

A smile tugged at the corners of his mouth. "Oh, I intend to." He moved up her body, sucked her nipples and rocked his hips so his cock skimmed her pussy. He wanted her to ache for it, beg for it. Maybe he was a slave to immortality but here while exchanging the valuable offering of chi, he could be the master, he could take control.

She arched her hips in an attempt to increase the contact on her pussy but he lifted himself away. Groaning, she gripped his shoulders. "Stop teasing me." Her breathing roughened.

He rolled her nipple between his tongue and teeth and made her body quiver.

Struggling beneath him, she tried to wrap her legs around his hips and draw herself to him but he pulled away again. She groaned and writhed beneath him, tossing her head from side to side. "Dante, what are you doing?" she rasped, clearly frustrated. This was just where he wanted her. He would get her much more frustrated. The demoness, who could destroy him with a wave of her hand, he would make beg for his attentions.

He chuckled, low and huskily. "Mmmm. Fucking. Isn't that what you call it?"

She glared at him. "Well, get to it. I want you inside me now."

"I'll say when. You must be patient." He reached down and slid a finger inside her and she cried out.

"Enough. Dante. Patience I don't have. Fuck me, now."

"Gwyllain, do not speak," he commanded.

Her breath caught, eyes flashed. Before she had a chance to argue, he tilted his head toward her windows while he fingered her clit and tugged on her ring. "Your world is disintegrating as we argue." Wind howled across the balcony through the open French doors, whipping the sheer draperies like ripped sails in a storm. "Enjoy the pleasure and let me pass my chi in the means that heightens my pleasure."

"I forbid you to—" A bright flash of lightning and sharp crack of thunder silenced her.

"Not another word," he warned. "It ruins my concentration," he lied. Nothing she could do or say would turn him off. She could recite poetry or threaten to kill him and he'd still be able to climax.

Beneath his hands, her skin warmed and her body leapt when he stroked her most sensitive places—nipples, navel, clit, the crease at the top of her thighs, behind her knees, her feet.

She moaned. He knew she wanted to speak but wouldn't. When her hands fisted in the sheets, he lowered his mouth onto her pussy.

She cried out and bucked her hips. Spreading her outer lips gave him better access to her clit, which he drew circles around with his tongue.

Then flicking the ring, he made her groan louder. His tongue passed over her clit and she grabbed his head and cried out as her body convulsed violently in orgasmic ecstasy.

Before her moans died down, Dante got up on his knees and rolled Gwyllain onto her stomach, slipping a pillow beneath her hips.

Snatching the vial of massage oil off the nightstand, he removed the cork and drizzled the amber fluid between the crease of her ass.

"Dante, no." She squirmed beneath him but he held her down with his hand between her shoulder blades and massaging the oil around her asshole made her twitch and gasp. He ignored the demoness's protests. He would be in command for once. "Dante," she breathed but it wasn't in protest.

He slipped in a finger. She moaned and he felt her muscles relax. He added a little more oil and Gwyllain hissed, "Yes."

He removed his finger and prodded her hole with the tip of his cock. "Get up on your knees."

Surprisingly she didn't object, she rose, exposing her buttocks for his entry. Gripping her hips, he spread her and slipped gently inside her hole.

She groaned and slowly pumped back and forth to take more of him. And that did him in. Sensations in his body rose in tempo as he reached orgasmic oblivion. The wave of an intense climax exploded in him and he shot his juices into her. Drained and shaking and relieved to give up the chi he had been collected over the last several days, he collapsed at her side. Afterward, she attempted to curl into his arms like a lover, when all he wanted to do was get up and leave. If she had been Amy, then maybe he would've drawn her to his chest. Tightening his jaw, he slipped an arm around her shoulders and pulled her to him—bedding a demoness, the price to pay for immortality and revenge.

When his breathing and heartbeat slowed, he opened his eyes and saw that servants had entered and left bowls of soapy water and towels next to the bed. Damn, they were as silent as ghosts. He'd never seen them enter or leave.

"Don't move," he said.

"Ordering me again," she moaned.

He laughed. "I'm going to wash you." He got up and rinsed a cloth in one bowl of warm water and cleaned between her legs and her buttocks, then dried her with a towel. He freshened himself as well, then climbed into bed, next to her.

The one rare time the demoness was almost human was after she received chi.

Eyes closed, she snuggled against his chest and slept. Now he could slip away without listening to her protests. Outside the wind had died and the rain stopped. The moon shone silvery over a calm sea. And the stars—the stars of Gwyllain's fragmented dimension—shone brightly and peacefully.

The chi he'd given her was only the equivalent of one half a human life. He needed a total of three lives if he was going to make it through this cycle. Less than two weeks to go and he was running out of time.

# Chapter Seven

ಖ

Truly was off to Tucson for the day so Amy didn't get any winks from her when she brought Jake through the lab for a quick tour of Drake Diagnostic Labs before they headed up to the park to collect specimens. Wearing a gray and green park service uniform, hiking boots and carrying his wide-brimmed ranger hat, Jake received plenty of admiring looks from the female lab techs. Amy heard a few murmur, "Who is that?" as he walked by.

"I hope this isn't an inconvenience taking you out of work," Jake said as he followed her into the storeroom. He crossed his arms over his chest.

"No, it's fine. I look forward to the chance to do a field project and get outside. I also think my boss wanted to be more involved as a community relations thing." She felt him watching her while she added supplies into boxes and heat flickered over her skin.

"PR, you mean?"

"Yes, it is good public relations in a way. He's an avid backpacker and a fisherman, so I'm sure this project carries some personal weight." She closed up the box, not making eye contact, fearing he would read the other reason. Her boss saw dollar signs and didn't want the park service to send these tests anywhere else. A little handholding and special treatment might keep the account local.

Amy had her own personal reasons for wanting to do this project. Jake was the kind of man you felt instantly attracted to even before you knew anything about him. Chemistry? Charisma? Whatever they called it, she felt the tug deep inside. Spending some time with Jake Montag was just what she needed to distract her enough to get Dante out of her mind and out of her system.

When she finally did look up at him, he was smiling. He bent over to pick up the box. "Here, let me."

*Damn, those blue eyes could distract her from a tornado.* She averted her gaze. "Besides, I've wanted to do some hiking since I moved here. I haven't had a chance." She had donned khakis, a tee shirt and hiking boots instead of business casual.

"If you wanted to do some hiking, why didn't you say so, Amy?" Dante was standing in the doorway.

Amy stiffened. Thoughts of what had happened last night flooded her mind. Did it actually happen? Or had she been dreaming? She opened her mouth to speak but Dante interrupted.

"I got your message last night. Sorry I didn't get a chance to call you back," Dante said to her.

Had it been a dream or was this more of his games? He was never this attentive.

Dante stepped into the storeroom, offering his hand to Jake. "Jake, how are you?"

"Good, thanks."

"Well, I won't hold you up," Dante said. "I have to get to a meeting. Good luck on your field study today. Give me a call when you get back. We can do dinner."

Amy cringed. "We'll probably get back late. It'll be too late for dinner." She didn't want to get into this with him here.

"Of course. Give me a call anyway when you get in to let me know how things went." Dante turned around and left. Not giving her a chance to argue.

Amy clenched her teeth. She didn't have time to go to his office to ask him about last night and whether or not he had summoned her out to the desert. If she had dreamed it, would she sound unstable? Not something she wanted on her personnel record while she was job hunting. No doubt about it, for personal and professional reasons, ending their relationship was the best way. She sighed and realized Jake was watching her. "Ready?" she asked, forcing a smile.

"Let's hit the road," he said as he left the storeroom with the box of supplies.

It took about forty minutes from the lab to reach the end of the gravel road at the trailhead. Amy hopped out of the Jeep and loaded up her backpack with the specimen containers and bags from the box in the back of the Jeep. Jake carried extra water and food in his pack. The early morning air was still and cool for April, the pale blue sky dotted with tuffs of clouds.

"Shouldn't we have a map?" she asked.

He smiled. "Map? I know all the trails. I work here."

"Oh."

"Something wrong?"

"I just hear stories about hikers getting lost. I don't know these mountains."

Jake slipped on his backpack and helped Amy on with hers, then locked up his Jeep.

She hooked her thumbs in the straps of her backpack, trying to look casual as they started up the trail.

"If you're not familiar with an area, a map is a good idea, or GPS or radio." He held both instruments up and then hooked them to his belt. "I always have to carry these. You haven't gone hiking in the park, have you?" His tone wasn't condescending.

She didn't want to mention she'd lived in Florida all her life and hadn't done much hiking. "Not yet."

He smiled over his shoulder. "When we get back, I'll get you a map and give you a private lesson in orienteering."

"Thanks."

He chuckled a little then ran a hand through his short brown hair. "I have to ask this. If it's not my business, just say so."

"Ask me what?" Amy walked with arms crossed.

"Is Dante Akando a boyfriend or something?"

She laughed a little.

"I mean, I think he was worried about me taking you into the mountains alone. Or the guy was staking his claim before we left."

Amy stopped walking. "Dante has no claim on me," she said sharply.

Jake turned and put up his hand in a motion of surrender. "Sorry, Amy. I stepped over professional bounds here."

She sighed in frustration. "It's all right. We should keep moving. We have a lot to do today."

"Right." He didn't take his eyes off her and appeared to look right through her. There was no sense in explaining her personal problems to this man. She hardly knew him. Predictably, Jake found signs of animals, pointing out droppings and tracks for rabbits, raccoons and deer right away, explaining their habits, and helping her to collect specimens. The man knew his way around the wilderness, and she found that very appealing.

As she followed him down the trail, her gaze skimmed over his body. Good lord, he was built. Unless he did hard-core mountain climbing he had to work out in the gym. Broad back and shoulders, biceps taut in his uniform and nice butt. The pit of her stomach did a little dance as her imagination went wild, thinking about spending the day in the woods with this gorgeous man.

Then her brain synapses finally began to fire and jolted her back to reality. She was working and she had an important project to do. Had Dante's sex games gotten her so frustrated she was ready to screw the first hot guy she met?

They walked in silence for several minutes along the foothills of the Rincon Mountains, passing knee-high growth of scrub brush, cactus and dried grasses. Climbing onto a rocky ridge, Jake reached a hand out to help her up. "Thanks, I got it," she said.

Unlike the humid, salty air she was accustomed to in Florida, the wild rawness in Arizona had its own beauty. The muted colors, the earthy scents and lapis-blue skies so eloquently revealed the magical allure of the landscape. Amy was beginning to understand why people loved the desert.

The trail twisted up the mountain, around boulders and leveled to a grassy flat area where saguaro and mesquite were alternately placed like pieces on a chessboard. Several tiny birds flitted in and out of the tangled brush and hopped along the reddish dirt.

"Up here is where I've found a number of the dead animals. Deer, raccoons, fox and those wild piglike animals called javelinas."

Sniffing the air again, she detected the faint odor of decay. She walked around the area, looking for evidence, and decided she didn't want to see anything to spoil the scenery but this was what they were up there for. "We need to collect the freshest specimens," she said with a somber tone. "Just tell me what animal the scat belongs to."

He nodded then stared at her feet. "You didn't wear bells on your boots."

"What?"

"Bells. There are mountain lions up here, you know."

She sucked in a breath. "Really." She frowned. "So what are the bells for?"

"To scare them off."

Amy narrowed her eyes at him, pointing at his boots. "You're not wearing bells."

"I don't need them, I can run fast."

"Right," she said sarcastically. "Now about the animal droppings."

He nodded and continued walking, searching on the ground. "Yes, coyote scat has bits of hair and juniper berries."

"What about mountain lions?"

He considered for a moment. "Looks similar, a little larger. Hair, juniper berries and sometimes little bells."

She punched him in the arm, laughing. "Cute."

"Ow."

"Is this the line you give all the visitors that come into the park?"

"The gullible ones." He took a drink from his water bottle and continued up the trail.

"Now you're calling me gullible?" she teased. Walking behind him, she got another nice view of toned body and powerful leg muscles. If she did more hiking maybe she'd get into better shape.

"No, just messing with you." He glanced over his shoulder and gave her a wink. "Most of the visitors get a laugh and are a little more cautious about the wildlife after that story. You'd be surprised how many hikers and campers approach wildlife like a raccoon or fox. They think they're cute."

"Well, they are but it's common sense not to handle wild animals," Amy said.

They walked along the trail a little farther and Jake stopped. "Deer. This is pretty fresh."

Sliding off her backpack, she dug inside for a screw-cap container, a specimen bag, spatula and latex gloves. After slipping on the gloves, she labeled the container with the animal type, location and date and used the spatula to scoop a sample into the cup. She sealed it and placed the container and spatula in a Ziploc bag. Then placed that in another larger plastic bag. "All set. That makes six different animal types and fifteen specimens so far." She stood and they continued up the trail. "Next time we go hiking I hope it's to enjoy the scenery and not to collect animal scat," she said in a teasing tone.

He glanced over his shoulder and the look he gave her sent a thrill to the pit of her stomach. "Let me know. I'd be happy to show you a few trails with the best views."

"That sounds great." Was he being nice, treating her like any other tourist, or did he really want to spend time with her? She rolled her eyes to the crystal blue sky. Stop reading things into his words.

"Damn it." Jake stopped abruptly and Amy almost ran into him.

"What is it?" She saw a brown mass of fur under a spiny, greenish yellow palo verde tree.

"Deer." He pulled out a notebook and jotted a few notes. "That makes a dozen in two weeks," he said as he rubbed his forehead.

"Did an animal get it?"

"Doesn't look like it." He studied the animal closer. "No visible marks, so it wasn't attacked or shot."

"You're keeping a log of the animal deaths?"

"It'd break your heart if I read off the list. I've not seen anything like this before and I've worked in the park for ten years." He left the deer behind and continued up the trail. No doubt predators would eventually get to it. "I can't tell you what this park means for people around here, especially my grandfather," he continued. "He's lived here all his life. It's a constant fight to protect the land."

"The park wouldn't close because of this, would it?"

A moment of anger flashed in his eyes, then he softened. "Not likely." He frowned. "Animals get sick and die but it's rarely harmful to humans. Rumors of an unknown deadly disease might keep visitors away without the park closing. Understand what I'm saying?"

"Of course, Jake. Confidentiality applies to patients and clients. I can't discuss this project with anyone outside the lab who isn't working directly on this project."

He sighed in obvious relief. "Good. Don't need the media getting a hold of this." He stood and continued up the trail.

After several hours, she had to admit watching how Jake moved with ease, confidence and pride up the trail was a hell of a lot more interesting than the breathtaking scenery. They had about all the specimens they needed for an initial study but she didn't say anything, and she didn't want the day to end.

As a park ranger, he probably knew every inch of these trails, had traveled them a hundred times and could name every plant and prickly thing they passed.

He'd been walking at a steady pace for the last hour and didn't look out of breath. Beads of sweat trickled down her back and between her breasts. Several times she wiped perspiration from her forehead with the back of her hand. He didn't even look like he had broken out in a sweat, damn him.

Was this a race or something?

"This is a little out of our way but I'd like to take you up on this one trail to show you the view. It's…well, you've got to see it for yourself. Then we'll stop for lunch."

"Lunch sounds good," she said, doing a poor job of not huffing and puffing. She really needed to get back into shape.

His face lit up as he glanced back at her. "You okay back there? Need a break?"

"No, I'm fine." Her heart felt like it would burst out of her chest and her lungs ached but she didn't want to admit it.

"Keep drinking water or you'll get dehydrated."

She took a swig of water and slipped the bottle back in its carrier and took a few deep breaths before speaking, hoping not to sound winded. "How far?" She resisted the urge to say, "Aren't we there yet?"

"Not very." Glancing back at her again, he slowed down and smiled. Maybe he finally realized she'd reached her physical limit but wouldn't admit it. "It's a little steep here. Give me your hand." She took it and he half pulled her up the narrow path covered with loose fine gravel. Her boots slipped and he grabbed her by her waistband to keep her from going down to her knees.

"Thanks, I'm not much of a mountain goat," she said, laughing.

"No worries, it's a bad spot. The view is worth the climb."

At the top, he released her and grinned like a boy with a new bicycle. "What do you think?"

She turned 'round in a complete circle and whistled. "Oh my." From this viewpoint she couldn't see any houses or signs of civilization in any directions. "It's like we stepped back into the Old West."

He smiled. "So how long have you lived here? I can hear the slight Southern twang in your accent."

"It slips out now and then. I moved here eight months ago when my company merged the labs."

"Quite a change."

"Arizona is not Florida."

He must have noticed her hesitation because he asked, "You miss Florida, don't you? Why did you leave?"

"I couldn't find another job before my company offered the transfer, and the pay increase was good. I thought I'd give it a shot."

He glanced back over his shoulder at her and the serious look he gave her sent a heat wave undulating through her body. Images came to mind of the two of them curled up naked on Dante's Indian blanket making love in all the ways that Dante hadn't. It had been so long since she felt a man filling her, thrusting inside her. Amy blinked the images away and sucked in a deep breath.

"That must have been hard for you to move away from your friends and family. I'm sure you miss them." He didn't give her a chance to respond, just pointed to a large flat rock for her to sit on as he slipped off his backpack. "We can stop here."

She wriggled out of her backpack, dropping it beside the rock. When she sat, she tried massaging the ache and stiffness from her fatigued muscles. She wondered if she would be able to get up after lunch. "Great, I'm getting hungry."

"You're going back," he said, more as a statement, not a question.

If she was planning to leave Arizona why should she get interested in this man? And why not tell him right off? "I've put in for a management position." She glanced at him but saw no response. Just as well.

"I know I couldn't leave the Sonora Desert," he said, "not only for me but I keep and eye on my grandfather. He'll never leave. Hope the job works out for you. You need to find a place you can call home."

His words sent a little thrill through her. How long had it been since she met a man who cared anything about another's well-being? And he was considering hers too?

Did Dante care for her? He cared about his gratification. Amy was just as guilty. If she and Dante could've had a casual affair and still cared and respected each other she would've been fine but their encounters had become very shallow and crude. "Sounds like you and your grandfather are close."

Jake nodded. He sanitized his hands with antibacterial gel, handed her the bottle and retrieved sandwiches from the pack. "My grandfather is quite a character. He lives by the old Indian ways."

"What does that mean?"

"He's part Navajo. He believes in spirits, the traditions, folklore and mythology of the Navajo Nation."

"Are you Navajo?" She didn't think he looked Navajo.

"No, I call him my grandfather though." He stared at his sandwich and didn't say more. Standing up, he excused himself for a call of nature break.

Jake walked several yards out of sight before stopping to relieve himself. Amy had been great all day. She'd kept up with his pace, been pleasant company, collected specimens with scientific professionalism and had seemed eager to learn about the different animals of concern in the study. She seemed as worried as he was about the animals, about the park and how this would impact the visitors.

Smiling to himself, he thought how he'd managed to keep the excursion on a professional level, although several times his mind wandered to what would've happened if they'd met under other circumstances and were hiking to enjoy each other's company instead of working on a field project. He'd been pushing her at a steady pace too without a word of complaint from her.

His grandfather always said he was too hard on his dates and that was why they never stuck around for long.

She wore little makeup which he liked. Most of the outdoorsy kind of women he met or dated went a bit too far with the natural end and never wore makeup or anything feminine. Not that women didn't look sexy in jeans and tee shirts but he had a thing for women with nice legs. Shorts or skirts did it for him. Most guys liked women with huge breasts. Large or small, didn't matter to him but if he had to make an assessment, he would say Amy's breasts weren't too large or small, just perfect. Nice, very nice. Best to keep his thoughts off her legs and breasts if he was going to get through the rest of the day.

Instead he remembered the gold hoop earrings she wore and a gold dolphin pendant that hung on a chain and swept her cleavage. She didn't wear any perfume which was a good idea when walking in the woods since animals can detect scents at great distances.

He wondered if the Dante character was out of her life. And if so, when would be the appropriate time to ask her out? He hadn't been out on a date since Alison left him. If she hadn't panicked, he might not have hurt her. Damn it, he wasn't sure. He retained his human thoughts when he was in animal form but the animal instincts also prevailed. Did he dare risk getting close to someone again?

A surge of desire flowed southward and if he returned now, he would look very unprofessional. *Okay, Montag, cool your jets.* Bending over slightly, hands on hips, Jake took a few deep breaths to regain control.

Damn, she was hot.

He couldn't determine if she was sending all kinds of take-it-slow signals. After all, she had a boyfriend, whether or not he was on the outs. He had the impression they weren't on the best of terms at the moment. If the opportunity arose, he would see if she was available. After they dropped off the specimens—

"Jake! Jake!" Amy screamed from several yards away.

He felt the adrenaline rush as he tore off in Amy's direction.

# Chapter Eight

By the time Jake reached Amy, she was holding a fist-sized rock in her hand, ready to throw it at the coyote that was perched on top of a boulder. The animal seemed to be facing her off, daring her to make a move.

"Jake!" Her eyes were wide with terror, her chest heaving with each breath.

He strode over to her, gently removing the weapon from her grip. "Easy. He won't hurt you. You probably scared him. Tell me what happened."

She turned and pointed at the coyote that had lowered his head and peered at Jake, still not moving. Why hadn't the thing run away? Maybe he was hungry and smelled their food. "That coyote came after me."

"What did he do?"

"It was in the bushes and jumped out at me." She rubbed her face. "Sorry, I didn't mean to scream. It startled me. I think it's the same one that's been around my house."

He couldn't help but smile at that. "Amy, there are lots of coyotes around here."

She made a face and planted her hands on her hips. "But this one is missing part of his tail. I'm sure he's the same one."

He looked around but the coyote had taken off. Damn, the thing was quick. "Well, he's gone now. Come back and have something to eat." He rubbed her back. "We have more ground to cover and should head back before it gets dark."

She groaned and put her hands to her face.

"What's wrong?"

"I'm supposed to pick up Sienna from Betty's house by six. I don't think I'll make it back to the lab and to her house in time."

"We can stop at Betty's first," he said. Her quick smile was unexpected, considering what she had just witnessed. "But we need to have something to eat first."

"Thanks."

Her straight blonde hair was a bit tangled from the breeze.

Facing her, he was standing very close, only inches away. Glancing down, he couldn't help but notice that the coolness of the late afternoon had hardened her nipples to fine points, showing though the thin tee shirt. Waves of heat rippled through his groin. His cock stiffened. Ignoring his aroused state and his urge to check out her ass, he asked, "Who's Sienna?"

"The cat from hell." Her gaze held his and she made no motion to leave.

He chuckled. "Your cat?"

"Mine until I can find her a home."

"Can't wait to meet this hellcat."

They returned to where the backpacks were. Amy cleaned her hands and plopped down on a rock. "How are you holding up?" Jake asked as he offered her a sandwich.

"Good," she said a bit winded, wiping sweat from her forehead with the back of her hand. She didn't want him to think he had pushed her too hard. Every muscle ached and was fatigued and by tomorrow she wondered if she would be able to walk. "I'm feeling my legs. Good exercise." She took a bite of sandwich and several swallows from her water bottle.

"What don't you like about Arizona beside rogue coyotes?" He didn't take his eyes off her while he chewed.

She smiled at that. "I like Arizona. The landscape is mesmerizing but I miss the ocean and my friends and family. I don't feel like I belong here."

"Eight months isn't long enough to decide about a place."

She felt her face flush. The intensity of his gaze sent her pulse racing. She took another bite of her sandwich and stared at her boots. Maybe she was responding to Jake because she saw something in him that she hadn't seen in other men, something she craved. Was it his down-to-earth attitude and rugged strength that she felt? Did being around nature make him more aware of people's feelings? "You could be right about that. You and your grandfather have lived here all your life?"

He nodded. There was much more that he wasn't telling her but she wouldn't pry into his personal life. "Do you know if an illness like this has occurred in the past? Would your grandfather know if he remembers a similar event of an animal epidemic? It might help if I ask him some questions."

Jake pursed his lips. He didn't look convinced. "You can talk to him but he already has his theories as to the cause of the animal deaths."

"He does?" Amy stiffened. Why hadn't he said anything about these theories before? Any history of a similar outbreak would be significant. "So this has happened before?"

Jake's shoulders slumped. "I didn't mention it, because according to Bill, my grandfather, it happened over fifty years ago and it was caused by a mythological being, the Trickster."

Amy blinked and then stared at him, unsure of what to say.

"Right. That's why I didn't say anything. It's hard to confirm events that happened in this area more than fifty years ago. Records aren't that good. And then there's the metaphysical aspect of the story. I don't…it doesn't hold water for me."

"How is a mythological being killing the animals?"

Jake sighed in annoyance. "It's not. It's superstition," he snapped.

"Some myths are based in fact," she persisted. "It couldn't hurt."

"Suit yourself but you're wasting your time. My grandfather has his own twist to the Trickster myth. It's unlike any Indian folklore story."

"I don't mind." She smiled, trying to ease the tension that had formed between them. "If it doesn't help me, I'll learn something about Indian folklore. But if you're sure it's a waste of time, I won't bother him."

"No, he'd love to get a chance to tell his story." Jake leaned his foot on a rock, staring off in the distance.

A crunching sound made Amy turn her head.

"Shhh," Jake whispered. "Don't move. Let's see what it is."

Amy could hear the animal's footfalls and snapping branches as it ran up the hill. Gripping the rock kept her from jumping up and startling the creature. Then it appeared—a coyote. It stopped when it saw Amy and Jake and appeared to study them warily. It paced back and forth twenty yards in front of them as if expecting them to move and then it stopped again.

"That's the same one. See his tail?" Amy whispered. "What's he doing?"

"Checking us out. Just curious." Jake studied the animal with interest. She expected he knew the normal habits of every living creature. The coyote made a bold move by approaching closer and Jake took a few noisy steps forward. The coyote stopped, holding his head high as if in a defiant pose.

"He doesn't seem afraid of us," she whispered.

"He's acting a little odd. I don't like it. He might smell the food." Then the coyote charged toward them. "Watch out, Amy."

She put her sandwich down on her backpack and stood. Jake stomped his feet but the animal sped straight for him. Jake glanced around, looking for a branch or rock, she thought, to fight off the animal. In an instant, the coyote leapt up onto Jake, like a dog. But he didn't bite him and Jake managed to shove the animal aside with his knee. The coyote yelped and then ran toward Amy.

She stumbled backward, falling over the rock as the coyote pounced on top of the boulder, snatched her sandwich and perched there with it in his mouth. He glared down at her as if triumphant with his victory.

Amy froze in disbelief, then heard Jake shout.

Swinging a dried branch, Jake charged toward the coyote while yelling, "Hey! Hey! Hey!" The coyote leapt off the rock, scrambled down the trail, a golden ghost moving among the sage and cactus. He soon was out of sight.

Jake crouched down beside her and helped her sit up. "Are you okay? He didn't bite or scratch you, did he?" He lifted each arm and rubbed it, examining it closely from her hand, to her wrist, then up to each shoulder apparently for bite marks or scratches. Then he began at her legs.

"Really, I'm fine. I fell before he got to the rock. He didn't touch me." She rubbed her elbow. She'd banged it when she fell backward. "What the hell was that? Do coyotes normally act like that?"

Jake shot her a worried look and made her stretch out her legs. "They can be bold when they're hungry. Are you sure you weren't scratched or bitten?"

"Yes, I'm sure," she said impatiently. She slid up her pant legs to her knees, which was as far as she could get them to go. Rubbing her shins and calves, she let him take a closer look. "See? I'm fine. No puncture holes. Do you want me to take the pants off to make sure?"

He bowed his head, dropping his chin to his chest and smiled. "No, a tempting thought, I'll admit, but not necessary."

She glanced down the trail to see if she could see any sign of the coyote. "We don't have coyotes in Florida. I never knew they would act like that." Did her voice just go up an octave? Hard to concentrate when a gorgeous guy was manhandling her arms and legs. Every nerve ending was on fire now, even her nipples had tightened as if it was twenty degrees and freezing outside. The ground was hard and she thought she might have a cactus spine poking her in the butt but she didn't want to move. At the moment, she was indulging in a little fantasy of pulling Mr. Ranger Man on top of her just to feel all the marvelous weight on her.

Served Dante right. The man had gotten her so worked up by teasing her over the last few weeks, then leaving her hanging partly satisfied, it was no wonder her sexual appetite was in overdrive.

"It is unusual and that's why I'm concerned. Rabid animals behave strangely but I've never seen a rabid animal act like that coyote just did. I'll have to write up a report and have the other rangers keep an eye out."

"He wasn't acting sick," she said. "More like he had an attitude problem. Maybe he was just hungry."

"I hope that's what it was."

* * * * *

Amy was his, damn it! That son of a bitch had to pay. Coyote limped down the canyon on a parallel course with the humans' trails. He'd stumbled on the boulder, skinning his paw when he snatched the food. Ignoring the sting, he stayed off the man-made trails. The scents were overpowering and confused him when he was hunting.

A jackrabbit darted out from under a sage bush and raced in a zigzag pattern through the grass. In an instant, Coyote pounced and had the jackrabbit between his two paws. The heartbeat of the trapped creature fluttered between Coyote's paws. He smiled at his small conquest. Opening his mouth, Coyote let the rabbit's fear increase, which also increased its chi. The darkness flowed through Coyote's body, its seductive stream filling him and taking him to yet a higher level. Here he had the power to control, to kill, to extract as much chi as his mistress needed. The rush he got with each conquest was like a drug, better than the most intense orgasm.

Images of Amy came to mind, her naked on his red blanket, writhing for his touch, reaching orgasm. Amy's cunt slick with her juices, her clit swollen and sensitive to his touch. He wanted her, unlike any women before. To have her as any man would have a woman. If he fulfilled his offering on time to Gwyllain could he have her then?

The torment of taking Amy to the edge of dark sexual pleasures but not fucking her completely was more than he could bear sometimes. As his heart rate picked up, Coyote leaned toward the animal, his mouth brushing against its fur, then the chi energy surged from the rabbit in a gushing electrical stream that entered through Coyote's mouth.

The chi flowed though every muscle and nerve like waves on a pond and then all was calm again. The jackrabbit was dead. Lifting his head, Coyote scanned the area and sniffed the air. He listened and heard a sidewinder snake skim across the dried earth. The snake slithered out beneath a creosote bush, then disappeared in a hole under a rock. If Coyote had time, he would dig for it but he didn't want to waste the time.

Late afternoon, the nocturnal animals were beginning to move again. Swiftly, he sped across the open field and killed several more animals from the smallest field mouse to a deer. The brief encounter earlier with Amy and the ranger had drawn some chi. Fear and sex were the greatest modes for retrieving chi aside from the life energy of death itself. As he stood on that boulder he could feel Amy's fear, even taste it, the energy trembled down to his bones. Her aura and their sex games would sustain him on the Earth plane after he satisfied Gwyllain's offering.

He must make his apportionment, go to Anartia and worship Gwyllain.

Once his offering was made to the demoness and the portal closed, he could have Amy the way he wanted her and the way she wanted him. The ranger wanted her too, lusted for her. He could smell the guy's arousal from a mile away, the bastard. What got Coyote's hackles up was that he could smell her arousal from being around the ranger. After the cycle, he would have her back.

Coyote found the place in the desert behind Amy's house. The prickling along his fur told him it was time to go to Anartia, time to shift. Salty air and the heather meadow filled his nostrils. He could hear the rushing water as it slammed against jagged rocks. These were not scents typical of the desert and no body of water anywhere near here could make similar sounds.

He looked from side to side and found his clothing beside the saguaro cactus. Walking around the twenty-foot-high cactus, he found the vertical blue line running from the base to its tip.

The portal.

The twenty-foot circular area surrounding the saguaro was the egress point. As long as he held the nebula stone to his chest, he could travel to Anartia here.

He willed himself to shift and became the man, then put on the clothes at the base of the cactus. The chi surged through his veins. His cock grew hard.

In his experience, women emitted higher levels of chi during sex or when they were afraid and a few like Amy expelled an excessive amount. He preferred to use sex rather than fear or killing to acquire the needed chi. But he would do what was necessary. And right now it was necessary to fuck Gwyllain.

The cool nebula stone pendant rested against his skin. He lifted the stone and was instantly propelled through the portal.

Cautiously, Dante stepped away from the edge of the cliff in Gwyllain's world, trying to adjust to the wave of dizziness that followed the portal passage. Once his head cleared and his steps were sure, he strode across the field of heather toward the temple. He glanced back over his shoulder and swore. The sun was a lot closer to the horizon than he had expected. He had no time to waste if he was going to meet his debt.

The sunlight shimmered golden on the ocean and streaks of pale yellow radiated from behind gray-purple clouds. The sky was mostly calm and clear. Much improved from his last visit but still not pristine enough to meet Gwyllain's standards.

Could his previous offering have been more than he thought? Maybe he wasn't that far behind in the chi.

As he approached the temple Tarik came out and jogged down the stairs with what looked like a large stone in his hands. His chest was bare and he wore wide black pants. The stone he continued to pump up and down over his head, accentuating his developed chest and biceps. Was Tarik in a good mood or bad? In the demoness's hierarchy of lovers, Tarik was her favorite and his power far exceeded any Drone. This was one dude Dante didn't want to have to fight with and considering the guy's size, Dante probably would get his ass kicked. If Tarik wasn't tending to Gwyllain and her demands, he was in the chambers beneath the temple running his experiments. Part mage, part scientist, Tarik was trying to find a way to break their exile. A thousand years' worth of Tarik's experiments and Anartia was still a prison for them. No wonder Tarik wasn't the most pleasant person to be around.

He gave Dante a quick once-over, obviously sizing him up as a poor opponent.

"How are you?" Dante asked, trying not to have his question sound like a challenge.

The guy smiled. "Superb. Being Gwyllain's eternal sex slave? Don't you love it, bro?" he said with a hint of sarcasm. Tarik wasn't a Drone and didn't have to exchange lifeforce energy with the demoness, but after a thousand years was Tarik also getting tired of fucking Gwyllain?

The tension in Dante's shoulders relaxed a bit. He told him his name. "You just finish with her?" Cocking his head toward the entrance of the temple.

"Oh yeah." She's good and primed for you. Probably in a tolerable mood now. I think I wore her out."

"I'm impressed." Dante laughed. "That ain't an easy feat, and I've been here a long while."

"Come and run with me." Tarik glanced out across the field. "I'm doing a workout."

"I need to give my offering."

Tarik laughed. "Let her rest. She'll be out for a while. Your chi won't be lost in a workout, man."

Dante took off his shirt and tossed it on the steps. "Lead the way."

Of course Tarik aimed for the cliff, traversing the edge. Keeping as far from the rim as possible, Dante matched Tarik's pace. "How are the experiments going?"

"I think I've found a key to break Gwyllain as the conduit to Anartia and at the same time free Anartia from its inter-dimensional connection to Earth."

Dante had heard this over fifty years ago and still he remained a Drone, serving Gwyllain and maintaining Anartia. Tarik passed Dante the stone. The weight made his arms ache. His lungs burned from running. He felt good though, alive and in control for once.

Why did Tarik have to run so close to the edge? "What kind of key?" Dante would humor him anyway.

"Sha Warriors." Tarik shook out his arms. His breathing was labored now. "There are mortals with an excess of chi energy. They emit massive amounts of white light. If I can bring at least three of them here, on Anartia at the same time, I might be able to create a power surge. The power should break the resonant ties to Earth and Anartia will be free to travel anywhere—its original design and purpose intended."

"When will you do this?" Dante asked.

"The Sha Warriors need to be found and brought here first. Someone with enough life force energy to knock you on your ass."

He hadn't been collecting chi for the demoness's offering for long but Amy had more energy than anyone he'd met. That was why he hadn't gone after too many other victims. "A Sha Warrior shouldn't be killed like other prey?"

"Hell, no. And not changed into Drones. Bring them to Anartia."

"Is this why Gwyllain summoned me back about fifty years early?"

"Partly. My experiments will require extra energy, and she may demand your service at any time. Keep an eye out for a Sha Warrior. We'll make them slaves on Anartia until we have three to use for my test." He waved his fingers for Dante to hand him back the stone for his turn.

Dante wanted to finish his cycle and return to Earth to be with Amy. He didn't want her trapped on Anartia while he was on Earth for his next cycle—for however long that would be. According to Tarik the promise of hundred-year cycles of freedom had just ended. He'd have to finish his quota of chi for this cycle as soon as possible and keep his suspicions about Amy possibly being a Sha Warrior a secret. "Do you think she's awake yet? I should be getting back. I have a quota to fill."

Tarik ignored the question and studied the sky. "Interesting. What's she up to?" Pointing at a gray-blue cloud, he said, "See that formation? See how it swirls like the portal stone?"

They stopped running and Dante looked up. "Looks like a tornado forming."

"The eternal storm. Yes, that suits her. She's awake now. We should head back."

They turned around and began a slow jog back to the temple. "She controls the weather?" Dante asked.

"She's connected to everything. She can't leave and neither can I without dying and destroying all those tied to Anartia. We are rulers and prisoners of our own kingdom. She would ravage an entire planet if she could be free."

"Only a truly evil demoness would care little about destroying another world to free herself from exile."

Tarik shot him a cold stare while he lifted the stone chest-high.

Dante's body stiffened. "Demanding and irritable, a royal bitch at times but destroy another world?" Dante shook his head. "I don't see that in her. She saved my life."

"Ha! To see that with my own eyes would've been a delight. And how did she accomplish this heroic act?"

"My wife and I had left Philadelphia and traveled to California during the 1849 Gold Rush but our stake yielded little gold. The hardship was more than she could endure and she left me for a wealthy ranch owner from Sacramento."

"Why didn't you just kill the bastard and take back your woman?" Tarik asked as if that would've solved all the problems.

The pain still twisted deep in Dante's gut. "The rancher had power and money. Even if I had killed him, my wife wouldn't have come back. So I decided to return east and open a mercantile business in Philadelphia, make my profits then come back and get her. But while crossing the desert, I..." Dante hesitated. Did he want to admit to this man his failings?

Tarik arched a brow. "What? You were ambushed by enemies? Became seriously ill during the journey?"

Dante rubbed his forehead and stared at his cowboy boots. "No. It was stupid."

"Can't be worse than getting caught screwing your ruler's mistress. How do you think I got exiled here with Gwyllain?"

"I never asked, and I never hear the Drones speak of it."

"I was the ruler's engineer and I was working on fragmenting dimensions, creating independent worlds—"

"I have no idea what you're talking about."

"Doesn't matter. I was in the middle of creating an alternative universe for Gwyllain, a little private self-contained paradise where we could escape to and where Cragen couldn't find us."

"But he found out," Dante said

Tarik nodded. "Before I was finished. Cragen had other engineers complete the project to his specifications, combining magic and science. Our paradise became our prison for eternity. We need to maintain its energy source or it'll collapse and become nonexistent and so will we."

"Her generous offer of immortality was to save her own neck." Dante shook his head.

"And mine," Tarik added.

"That explains a lot. She's not the easiest woman to please."

"Can't argue with you there." Tarik narrowed his eyes. "What's your alter ego?"

"I don't follow."

"Your altered form or skill. Drones are given a power or skill to aid them with their quarry."

"Coyote. At least for the last couple of cycles."

Tarik nodded. "Interesting. I don't use my animal form very often." Tarik's body and face instantly changed to a slim young man about twenty with long blond-streaked hair. He looked like he was a surfer minus the board. Then he morphed into a man about his original age of early thirties but with dark mahogany skin, lean and handsome in business clothes and next, about ten or fifteen years older as a distinguished-looking man wearing a ski jacket and holding a pair of downhill skis. Finally, the guy was back in his original form. "I like variety."

Dante exhaled forcefully, he waited a few moments, expecting Tarik to change again and feeling inadequate with his simplistic shapeshifting skill. "Why do you change form if you don't go to Earth?"

"I like variety and so does Gwyllain." Tarik shrugged. "Don't piss her off, put in your time, a lot of time, and maybe she'll let me create a new form for you."

Dante wanted to know how long but somehow it didn't seem right to ask. "You have an animal form?"

Tarik's mouth slowly curved into a smile. "Tell me how Gwyllain saved you and I'll show you my non-human form."

The wind howled over the crest of the cliffs and whispered through the heather, stirring up the sweet, grassy fragrance. Dante would have to tell Tarik. The man would find out eventually. When you spend eternity with someone trapped in a universe the size of an island, secrets are hard to keep.

"On my way back east, I had stopped over in Tucson and overheard two men talking in a bar," Dante began. "They said gold had been found in the Rincon Mountains and not many people had heard because of the California rush. They also mentioned that prospectors were staking their claims and only a few areas remained."

A smirk formed on Tarik's face. "I see the conclusion of this tale."

"Yes, I was a fool. Many men suffered from gold fever and dreams of wealth back then. I traveled to the Rincons. They were on my way anyway. I was ambushed in the desert by a group of men who stole my horse and belongings. They beat me up, left me for dead. That's when one of the Drones arrived. I thought he was a mirage or I was hallucinating. He looked like an Indian."

Tarik narrowed his eyes.

His jaw tensed at the horrific possibilities but realized there was no graceful way out it. And he still had the business of worshiping the demoness. "He showed when I was near death. He had been watching me and said John Reilly, the man who stole my wife, had also found gold in my claim and had arranged for my murder. I passed out and came to on Anartia where Gwyllain made her offer. I agreed to her terms—immortality and revenge on John Reilly—but I had to provide her with the needed chi at her command."

"She made an offer you couldn't refuse. But why the coyote?"

"I've always had an interest in Indian folklore and I can travel fast and inconspicuously in animal form. Helps me to capture the chi energy of animals more easily."

Tarik nodded and glanced behind him toward the entrance of the temple. "She'll be wondering where we are. I'll show you my beast and be on my way."

Despite his curiosity, Dante suddenly didn't want to see Tarik's non-human form. Stalling, he said with a bitter edge to his voice, "The price is high for eternal life. I'm still her sex slave."

"The price is high to maintain Anartia and all who dwell here," he countered. "She could've left you in the desert for the vultures."

"True."

The severity of Tarik's expression didn't soften. "I only use this when I need to exhibit a little power and strength over her."

"Fear also draws in more chi on Earth," Dante said.

Tarik stepped to the edge of the cliff, an inch away from plunging to his death. The wind whipped at his hair and pants. The sound of the waves crashed against the jagged rocks below.

"Wouldn't all those of Anartia die if you fell?"

Tarik glanced at Dante with a wicked grin and stepped away from the edge. "After we were exiled here over a thousand years ago, I developed a fascination with Egyptian mythology. I selected my form from their mythological creatures, Horus, with a minor alteration."

Dante breathed normally again as Tarik moved farther away from the precipice. He searched his memory, trying to recall what sort of beast Horus was as Tarik began to change.

His solid form wavered and flowed into an indefinable mass, then grew taller to about eight feet. Dante stepped back as the creature took shape. From the shoulders down was a more muscular form of Tarik, wearing a loincloth that came down to his knees.

Jerking in surprise and partial fear, Dante backed down a few more steps when the form of a huge falcon's head replaced Tarik's head. When the bird of prey turned its head and looked at Dante with one white eye and one golden eye, Dante's blood ran cold and he froze like a rabbit about to be attacked.

The falcon head turned to the side and opened its mouth. It took in a wheezing breath and exhaled a stream of fire to Dante's horror. The form of Horus wavered again, shrunk and Tarik again was in his original form, smiling.

"Like the minor alteration? The fire-breathing Horus? I designed that myself. It took me over four hundred years to perfect."

Dante felt nauseous. He needed to get to the Earth plane soon.

"You look like you have a full load of chi and I want to make a run around my kingdom. Gwyllain should be ready for you by now. Don't keep her waiting." He lifted his head as if he could hear. "Yes, she's moving about. See ya 'round."

Tarik gave Dante a mischievous grin as he turned and ran down the coastline away from the temple. Dante gripped his nebula stone pendant in his right hand and charged across the grassy field toward the temple.

Dante didn't envy the ruling demon—at least Dante could live as a man on Earth. He probably had a couple more visits before his offering was sufficient. What did Tarik do while his mistress was *maintaining* their kingdom?

* * * * *

Gwyllain was furious.

Dante strolled into the small alcove to the left of the sunken bath. Gwyllain's deep blue eyes followed him as he approached. She was completely naked and not alone.

"You kept us waiting," she said with annoyance.

A man in the process of tying her up was solid and about four inches taller than Dante and wore a short loincloth and a gold band around his forehead. Wavy dark hair hung over his brow, nearly hiding exotic blue-gray eyes. Intense emotion smoldered in those eyes but Dante couldn't determine if the man was evil or merely amused. He nodded to Dante and continued with his wrapping and tying as if it was an art form. The rope crisscrossed tightly around her breasts, making them jut out, the skin taut. Then he wound lengths around her upper arms, pulling her arms behind her back and securing her wrists. He twisted the rope and looped it through a large metal ring hanging from the ceiling.

"Am I interrupting?" Dante asked. "I could always wait outside." He gave a mischievous grin. His cock was hard, watching Gwyllain, naked and vulnerable and in a submissive role getting tied up.

"No, we've been waiting. Decided to start without you. Would you like to join us?"

He nodded, while the man tied a few more knots, and connected chains. Dante studied the elaborate collection of chains, pulleys, rings and ropes hanging from the ceiling, walls and columns. Funny that he never noticed all this before. But then he hadn't been in this particular room before. He didn't know this side of Gwyllain. This would be interesting. "I guess. Does he have a name?"

"Zorian," Gwyllain answered. "He's a servant and a trainer. He doesn't travel to the Earth plane yet like you do. He's here to protect and please me as I request. My personal slave as you will be if you don't complete your offering on time."

"Ah. I see." Dante smiled. *Not a job I care to have.* "Trainer?"

Zorian studied Dante with an intense gaze. "The Drones sometimes need assistance with their duties."

*Great. Another reason to stay in Gwyllain's good graces.*

Her legs spread as Zorian tugged on the ropes. Her clit ring glistened in the firelight burning in the sconces. He smelled sweet, spicy incense but it wasn't the torch. On a marble table a thin coil of smoke rose from a censer. A large carafe of red wine and goblets were also on the table.

"Tighter," she ordered.

The ropes creaked as the servant tugged the ropes and looped them several times around a cleat on the wall.

She closed her eyes and groaned, gyrating her hips. "Yes, that's good."

Finished with the shackles and ropes, the servant dropped his loincloth, revealing an engorged penis that curved upward, nearly touching his hard abs. He slipped a hand between her legs and stroked her pussy for a second or two, then withdrew his hand, teasing her. Gwyllain groaned. Her head lolled to the side and her mouth opened. "Dante, get naked and come here. Touch me."

"No, she's not ready to be touched," the servant said firmly.

Dante removed his clothes anyway while he considered the situation. He had the chi he needed to give Gwyllain. Was this bozo going to hassle him? "Hey, this is your party but I have chi to give her. It can wait if she wishes, though time is short."

"My servant is acting through my wishes. I don't always have to be the dominant one, Dante. I can be very obedient and enjoy a good amount of pain and bondage." Her body was quivering in her bonds. Was she in pain or anticipating pleasure?

"Come here," the servant demand. "I will show you. Hold this a moment and don't touch the tip." He handed Dante a long rod with a cone-shaped object and a metal loop at the end.

Gwyllain giggled as Zorian secured a silk blindfold over her eyes and tied it behind her head.

"Do you remember your signal words for me?" Zorian asked Gwyllain.

She smiled and nodded, rotating her hips again.

"Good. We'll get started. I'll take the boltstick."

Dante tried to hand it to Zorian but Zorian held up his hand, making a sign not to say anything. He showed Dante how to turn it on and tiny blue sparks shot out of the metal loop, crackling with electricity.

Hearing that, Gwyllain sucked in a breath. "Oh yes, touch me with it, Master Zorian."

"Was that a request?" Zorian asked in a scolding tone.

"My mistake, Master Zorian."

"I'll forgive you one mistake," he said.

"Thank you, Master Zorian."

Dante looked at Zorian as if to say, "You've got to be kidding."

Zorian placed his hand over Dante's and guided the boltstick loop over Gwyllain's inner thigh. Her body jerked, then quivered. She moaned with pleasure. Letting go of Dante's hand, Zorian crossed his arms and smiled, then cocked his head for him to continue on his own.

"Does that please you, Gwyllain?" Zorian asked.

"Oh yes."

"Yes, what?"

"Yes, thank you, Master Zorian."

Zorian smirked. "That was a second mistake. I think a punishment is in order." He pointed to her nipples.

Dante brought the loop to her nipples. Blue-white sparks danced around the peak like tiny stars, bringing the tips to fine points. Gwyllain arched her back and twisted as if she ached for the other breast to have equal attention but didn't dare ask. Dante then brought the electrified loop to the other nipple and that peak hardened to a point too.

"Yes, thank you, Master Zorian." She moaned and rocked her hips a few moments more then cried out, "Oh, edge, edge." She breathed heavily.

Zorian pulled the boltstick away from her nipples. "Very good, Gwyllain. I did not give you permission to have an orgasm yet."

Dante had to bite his lower lip to keep from laughing. Damn, she was so turned-on by this freaking sex toy that she could come by teasing her nipples? Zorian guided Dante's hand with the boltstick along her arms, her abdomen, her legs. When her breath slowed, he eased it up to her pussy. Gwyllain's breath caught.

"Yes, thank you, Master Zorian."

She cried out as the loop made contact with her swollen clit. Dante's cock pulsed at the same time, as he imagined the sensations. He didn't know how much longer he could hold off his own climax. Saying "edge" was not going to be a magic word for him. With his free hand, he took himself in hand and slowly stroked his cock.

"I think your Drone is getting turned-on, Gwyllain."

"Yes, Master Zorian." Gwyllain sounded pleased.

As Gwyllain cried "edge" again, Zorian took the boltstick out of Dante's hand. "Take her now," Zorian ordered.

Dante nodded and almost said to himself, *Yes, thank you, Master Zorian.* He hooked Gwyllain's legs around his hips as he thrust his hard and aching cock deep inside her.

"Edge," Gwyllain screamed.

"You may come as you wish," Zorian said.

"Yes, thank you, Master…" Gwyllain never finished. She climaxed and arched against her binds. Spreading his legs wide for balance, Dante thrust harder and his orgasm consumed him, pulsing and straining, draining him of chi. Gwyllain clung to him while he gripped the chains for several moments more while their heartbeats returned to normal.

# Chapter Nine

ဢ

When Betty didn't open her door, Amy and Jake went around to the back of the house. "She target-shoots back here," Amy told him.

He blinked, the corners of his mouth twitched in a slight smile. "How old did you say she was?"

She shrugged. "Early sixties. She looks good for her age."

"Oh boy, a Grandma Moses type. Should we give her a warning that we're coming so she doesn't shoot us?"

"No, it's only a pellet gun. She saves the .357 for the target range." She grinned as Jake rubbed his face with his hand and stared at her in shock.

"Is she any good?" He frowned, walking slower.

"She seems to think so. Even crocheted a holster for it."

Jake burst out laughing. Amy didn't think she'd ever heard him laugh like that and she liked the sound of it. And she liked the look of honest joy in his eyes.

"I think I like her already." As they rounded the corner of Betty's house, Jake froze. The smile tightened to a fierce look of dread.

Amy scanned the backyard for her neighbor. Several yards past her fifty-yard bull's-eye targets mounted up on a stand, Betty was crouched down on one knee.

She had her hand out toward a coyote who was sniffing her hand, its tongue licking the tips of her fingers.

"Betty!" Amy shouted but Jake hushed her by raising his hand. He didn't run but swiftly walked out to her.

Calmly, he spoke to her as he got close. "Betty, slowly pull your hand away from the coyote and stand up."

Betty didn't move.

She frowned at Jake. "Who are you?"

"A friend of Amy's. That coyote may seem friendly but he can bite and may have rabies. You can't take a chance."

"Oh, I doubt that. Rabid animals are usually vicious or behave strangely. He's just tame. Must be use to people around the park."

To all appearances the coyote was friendly but after Amy's experience with the coyote up on the mountain earlier, she was worried.

Amy moved closer and noticed the coyote eyeing Jake, its eyes narrowing as if in warning as it continued to lick Betty's hand.

"Betty," Amy whispered forcefully. "You should know better. He's a wild animal and unpredictable."

She pulled her hand away and rested it on her knee. "Oh, for heaven's sake. You two are worrying for nothing." She stood up. The coyote took a step back but continued to glare at Jake. The intelligence in his eyes made Amy's skin crawl.

"He wasn't going to bite me. He's been here before and I will wash my hands." Betty folded her arms and glanced at the coyote. "Sorry, buddy. See you later."

Jake approached the animal, Amy thought either to scare him or test to see how it would react.

The coyote trotted back several paces then stopped next to a saguaro cactus as if it would give it protection. "Go on, git," Jake yelled, then ran toward the animal and stomped his feet.

The coyote ran a few more steps back then stopped and turned to stare at Jake. "Crazy. It's almost like he's being defiant."

"Could that be the same coyote that attacked us earlier? Look, his tail is short too."

"Not likely," Jake said. "It's too far for him to travel in a short time."

Betty strolled past Amy, heading toward her house, arms crossed, her shoulders taut. Amy followed.

"Attacked?" Betty asked, making a face. Obviously she didn't believe it. "A coyote attacked you today?"

"Charged us. Jumped up on Jake like a big old dog would, then snatched my sandwich. We think he was after our lunch."

"I doubt it's the same one. Too far away." Jake followed. "They often get their tails caught in fences or bitten in fights or shot, not unusual to see more than one like that."

"I didn't shoot it," Betty said defensively. "He was hungry, is all," Betty said, standing up for the animal. "This one's come around here before."

"How was Sienna today?" Amy asked, changing the subject.

"Oh, she's a sweet thing."

Amy spied the kitten's box sitting on the picnic table and her heart tightened. Didn't Truly say that a coyote could go after kittens for prey if it was hungry?

"I fed her an hour ago, so she should be good for a while." Betty reached into the box and the kitten hissed and snapped like a tiger cub. Betty yanked her hand away. "Yeow. What's got into her?"

"Don't worry, Betty. Sienna can be a bit manic."

Jake picked up the kitten and she purred and curled up into the crook of his elbow. Amy glanced at Jake and shook her head in disbelief.

The look Jake gave her was unmistakably scorching, lustful and made Amy catch her breath.

"Lupi will be here in less than an hour. I have just enough time to shower and change."

"I'm a little worried about you going out with this guy after that hitchhiker," Amy said.

Betty rolled her eyes. "I should never have told you that story. And he looked so young, like my grandson who's thirteen." She looked at Jake to explain. "How was I supposed to know he had a gun? He just wanted money."

"Did you report it?" Jake asked.

Betty huffed. "This happened years ago and no, I didn't report it because I didn't want anyone thinking me a fool for picking up a hitchhiker. After that, I bought a .357 and started going to the range."

Jake gleamed with a smile he was holding back.

"If you're so worried, why don't you come out to the Los Olas Café tonight and meet him, both of you."

"I'm sure Jake has other plans tonight."

"No, I don't. Mexican sounds good to me."

* * * * *

At the lab, Jake helped her carry the boxes of specimens into the specimen receiving area. On the way in she'd noticed Dante's car was still in the parking lot. *Terrific. He rarely works late.*

The thought of facing him made her cringe. She wasn't sure how he was handling her breaking up with him and she would rather not have a battle with him at work and in front of Jake. Considering Dante's possessiveness, she expected he was not going to handle it well.

"I reckon we'll want to clean up and change before going out."

"So how did it go?" Dante asked from behind them.

Amy spun around. "Very well. Collected thirty-two specimens from various animals along three park trails."

"You must be exhausted," Dante said sympathetically.

"A little," she said, not meeting his eyes.

"She did great," Jake said, smiling with a professional manner. "We covered a lot of ground. I'd like to try another area in a few days when it's convenient."

Dante nodded. "We'll have some results for you in a couple of days," he said to Jake then turned toward Amy and cracked a wide grin. "Can I see you in my office?"

"Can't it wait until tomorrow? I'm ready to head out and get something to eat. The evening shift will take care of these." Amy pointed to the specimens. The sooner she got out of there the better. She had an idea what Dante had in mind by calling her into his office. Flashes of him yanking up her skirt, ripping off her panties and finger-fucking her came to mind but she was turned-on. She was embarrassed. And he had opened her blouse too, exposing her breasts. Anyone could've walked in. She could've lost her job, they both could've. Stupid.

Dante stood straighter and examined them both, first glancing at Jake then at Amy, then back at Jake as if he suspected something was going on that he didn't like. Nothing was going on. She didn't think, not yet anyway.

"This won't take long." Dante persisted.

Amy cursed to herself. After all his speeches about being a free spirit, not getting serious, dating other people—he even bragged about the other women after him—he had to pull the possessive crap tonight. But since he was also assigned to oversee this project, she couldn't tell him good night and leave. "My cat's in the car. Jake was kind enough to invite me to dinner. We have to clean up first."

Dante frowned slightly and smiled at Jake. "I won't keep her long. You don't need to wait, Jake. I don't want to inconvenience you." His condescending tone flowed like an undercurrent in an ocean.

"Not a problem. Go have your meeting." Jake didn't rise to Dante's attitude.

Although Amy tried not to reveal any emotion to either of them, she was fuming. "Thanks, Jake, I'll see you at my house," she said.

"I'll be there." Jake left for the parking lot as Amy followed Dante to his office.

When Dante closed the door behind her, he locked it. Her stomach jumped. "Why did you lock the door?"

"So we won't be disturbed." He pressed her up against the wall, pinning her arms over her head.

"Stop it." She jerked free and hurried to the other side of the room. "Is this why you called me into your office?"

"You've been leaving messages on my phone. I thought you wanted to see me."

She sighed and looked at her shoes, then looked up at him, stiffening her back. "That's not why I've been calling you."

"Oh? Then why? Should I start another campfire? That teasing, kinky routine always got you so aroused." Dante reached out to take her hand and she pulled away again.

"I didn't want to do this here but you won't answer your phone or call me at home. You rarely did in the few months we were seeing each other. Seeing. That's a joke. We were fucking. Fucking that's a joke too because we never actually fucked. Why was that, Dante? Don't you like to fuck?" She was pissed now. She didn't like being backed into a corner. How did she let herself let this go on for so long? What was it about him? It had been more than the sex. It was never love, it was more like an obsession. Now she wanted to be free of him.

"I told you I dated others."

"So you do this with other women?"

He didn't answer at first. "Sometimes."

"Then no great loss when I'm gone," she said as she walked to the door.

"What happened between you and Nature Boy today? You two hit it off awfully fast."

Still holding the doorknob, she spun around. "Oh, we had a very romantic time on the trails today collecting animal feces. Great first date. And what if I had? You don't want a committed relationship, you're dating other women. Why would you have a problem with me seeing other men? Grow up, Dante."

She unlocked the door and flung it open. "Good night."

"No more campfires?" he asked, smiling.

"No. More. Campfires," she said between clenched teeth.

"Got it. Enjoy your dinner," he said as he sat down behind his desk as if they'd just finished a discussion about the budget for the next fiscal year.

* * * * *

After Jake picked her up at her house, Amy kept reminding herself that this was not a date, this was a business dinner. Although she wished it was. For a Thursday night, the Los Olas Café was unusually packed with patrons. Jake and Amy entered the restaurant and Jake gave their name to the host. Tall arched ceilings and walls artificially made to look like crumbling plaster and old brick. Cozy booths surrounded the main dining area with stained glass lamps hanging low over each table. Other wooden tables were scattered around the rest of the room. The smells of grilled beef, onions, peppers and Mexican spices filled the room.

"Two for dinner," Jake told the hostess standing at the small lighted desk.

The hostess's eyes lit up when she glanced at Jake.

"There's a fifteen-minute wait," the hostess said. "We have a live band in the bar this evening. I'll be giving some line dancing lessons. I do hope you'll stay around." She gave him her sexy cover model smile. A twinge of jealousy hit Amy, and she shrugged it off. The guy was a hunk, what did she expect?

"Thanks." Jake turned to Amy. "Want to wait at the bar?"

"First let me see if Betty is here with her date. She did say to come over and say hello. I want to check him out, make sure he's not a serial killer or something."

Jake laughed. "And you think you're going to figure that out just by saying hello?"

She crossed her arms and raised her chin. "I'm a pretty good judge of character." Hadn't always made the best choices concerning the men in her own life over the years but she didn't want to admit to that.

"There she is." Jake pointed to a booth at the far wall, partly hidden by decorative fountain surrounded by tropical plants and Aztec pottery.

Amy walked straight over to their table with Jake right behind her. Betty's face lit up when she saw them. "Amy! Jake! You made it. We're almost done eating but we're going to the bar to dance later." Amy made introductions. Lupi stood to shake hands, smiling warmly. He was much shorter than Jake, probably late fifties, a bit stocky but not heavy. The trim goatee might have looked threatening on another man but Amy saw kindness and intelligence glinting in his eyes. He was like the college professor who all the students loved and often saw in the hallways with armfuls of books, oblivious to his untied shoelace.

"Please sit," Jake said. "We only wanted to say hello."

"Their tortillas are homemade, try the fajitas," Lupi offered.

"And the house margarita. Yum," Betty added.

"Sounds great." Lupi seemed friendly enough but Jake was right. How could she really know if this guy was okay? "Betty says you teach at the University of Phoenix?"

"Yes, I teach history. Only part-time though. I'm semi-retired."

"I miss working with the kids," Betty said.

"You were a teacher too?" Jake asked.

Betty shook her head. "No, no. I was only a teacher's aide for third graders."

Jake frowned. "Don't say only a teacher's aide. You had a very important job. You were in charge of the duct tape." He smiled.

Betty burst out laughing and slapped her hand on the table. "I like you, Jake. You're good people and cute too."

Lupi chuckled too and sipped his water. "Hey, I could use that duct tape on some of my students. Even though they're young adults, they sometimes act like they're in third grade."

Jake had been holding his hand at the small of Amy's back for the last couple of minutes and she didn't want to move away. The heat of his hand penetrated through her burnt orange top.

His hand moved slightly and her body responded by sending goose bumps along her arms and making her nipples pucker. A slight throb reached between her legs. *I'm turned-on, damn it. But I just met this guy today.*

"Jake?" a small, sexy voice said from behind them. "Table for two? I found one a little early for you," the hostess said with a dump-your-date-meet-me-after-work look.

"Ready?" Jake asked Amy.

She nodded. They said their goodbyes to Lupi and Betty and followed the hostess to their table.

* * * * *

He hadn't been looking for anyone in his life at the moment. The last romantic disaster taught him to keep his private life and history to himself. After Alison left for California months ago, he had been too busy to date—a good excuse. The average person couldn't deal with his issues.

Alison had been the first woman he confided in and she didn't want to have anything to do with him after that. The scratch on her leg that his mountain lion form had made left a scar but the internal wound was much deeper. She'd left so fast, it was like a magic trick. *I can make them disappear but they don't come back.*

He wouldn't make that same mistake twice. He'd managed to disown his past, his heritage. He didn't need to share details of his shapeshifting abilities with every woman he met.

After the waitress took their drink and food orders, Jake leaned back in the booth, his arm stretched over the back of the seat. "Tired? It was a long day." Amy had been staring across the room as if she was miles away. She looked a little sad too.

Blinking, she shook herself and straightened. "Sorry, daydreaming a little. No, I'm not tired."

"Want to share your daydream?"

"If I was back home in Florida, I would be out with my friends tonight."

"Thursday night is ladies' night out?" he asked as the hostess brought them their drinks.

"You'll love these margaritas. They're my favorite too," the hostess said. Was it his imagination or had the hostess unbuttoned a button or two since she sat them at the table?

"What happened to our waitress?" Jake asked.

She blushed. "Oh, she's tied up with an order so I offered to help out."

"Great that you all work together like that," Amy said with a hint of sarcasm, her chin in her hand.

Just then the waitress arrived with chips and salsa. She glanced at the drinks and frowned. "Something wrong?" she asked the hostess.

"No, no. Your drinks were up and I happened to be there," the hostess said as if she did it all the time.

The waitress furrowed her brows and shrugged as if to say, "Whatever." Both women left.

Amy started giggling. "I think the hostess has the hots for you." Her cell phone rang. She apologized, glanced at the screen, frowned and pressed the ringer off.

He didn't comment. Instead, he smiled and changed the subject. "What would you and your friends be doing tonight then in Florida? Since it was ladies' night."

The smile slipped from her face, replace by a sad loneliness.

"It's not ladies' night." Her mouth pressed tight in a grimace. The phone began to ring again with a different tone. She groaned. "I'm sorry, I thought I turned it off. It's…a text from work."

"Maybe you should check it then," he said.

She pressed the keypad on her phone, studied the screen and frowned. Glancing up, she met his gaze as she flipped the phone closed and tossed it in her purse. "It's work but it's not work related. Dante was wishing me happy birthday." She rolled her eyes.

Jake was beginning to get the picture. "Did you two have plans this evening?"

"No."

He nodded and wondered if he was crossing a line. "Is this a jealous boyfriend issue?"

Amy gave a nervous laugh. "No, he's not a boyfriend."

"It's none of my business." Jake raised his hands as if trying to wipe away his last question.

"It's okay. There was something between us but it recently ended."

"I'm sorry."

"Nothing to be sorry for." She sighed and looked away, then sipped her drink.

"Something else is eating at you." He sipped his beer, never taking his eyes off her.

"It's nothing, really."

"Oh no, after what we did today, I think you can confide in me. What gives?"

She let out a breath. "It sounds silly but I've only been away from Florida eight months and none of my friends called me today. I didn't receive any cards either." She looked a little sheepish. Her hands cupped her margarita glass.

"Your friends forgot your birthday."

She shrugged. "We always went out on each other's birthdays. One of my friends recently got engaged and I didn't get invited to the wedding. It's like I fell off the planet when I moved."

"That sucks." He reached across the table and took her hand, squeezing it. "Happy birthday, Amy. And I'm sorry your friends didn't call you."

"Thanks but that's not the whole problem. I'm thinking that if they've forgotten my birthday in only eight months, how is it going to be when I finally do return to Florida? Will I feel like a stranger moving into a new area again and starting over?"

"You could stay here."

"Arizona is nice but my home is in Florida. At least it was."

"That's too bad." He wanted to say he'd hoped to get to know her better, much better. The band had started playing already, the country western music wafted into the dining room. "Since it's your birthday, I'll have to treat you to a dance to two before we leave."

"You'll probably have that hostess after you to give you lessons," she warned.

"Not a problem. I don't need lessons. Can you two-step?" he asked as the waitress brought them their dinners still sizzling on the cast-iron serving skillets.

"Since I don't know what two-step is, I'd say no," she laughed.

"Not a problem. I can teach you." Dinner couldn't get over fast enough because then he'd have her in his arms and begin persuading her to stay in Arizona.

"One dance," she said. "I have to work tomorrow. And it better be a slow one so I don't tumble onto the floor."

"Very slow." The slower the better. His cock stirred with the thought of holding her close, his hand pressing at the curve of her back just above her buttocks. Her breasts crushed against his chest. He groaned inwardly. Damn, it had been too long. He was turning into a horndog. He ate his fajita dinner but didn't remember how it tasted.

*****

"This is it. We're up." Jake took Amy's hand and drew her out toward the dance floor. Several other couples began to move in a counterclockwise direction.

"That's the two-step?" she asked.

"It's not as hard as it looks. Watch their steps. Quick, quick, slow, slow."

She glanced at the other couples as they eased around the room in perfect rhythm, making turns without missing a beat. "Everyone is wearing cowboy boots and hats—the men and the women. The typical attire in a dance club in Florida is slinky, short and low-cut."

"Don't worry about what people are wearing. Watch the steps." Jake placed his hand in the small of her back as a couple passed them doing several spins.

"Oh, terrific. Maybe this was a bad idea. I don't think I can do this."

"Sure you can." He walked her through the steps on the side, then held her closer for a dry run before going out on the dance floor. "It'll take a few tries. Everyone had to learn at one time."

She giggled nervously and looked up at him with intense sexy eyes. "I'm sure I'm going to trip and fall on my ass."

"I've got you, I won't let you fall."

He took her hand. "Come on. Don't be afraid to make a mistake. Just remember, quick, quick, slow, slow." Pressing his body hard against hers, he gazed into her eyes as the next song started. "Ready?"

"Let's do it." She smiled.

Damn, she felt good, smelled good. He breathed in the hint of citrus fragrance—her hair or perfume, he wasn't sure.

He whispered the dance steps in her ear to get her started. When she stumbled, he pressed his hand on the small of her back and started again. "That's it. You have it now."

"This is fun," she said and he thought she meant it.

"You should try hiking when you don't have to collect specimens. I can show you some great trails if you like. This is a great time of year to hike. The summers are rough in the heat."

"I may not be here by summer anyway."

He leaned back and studied her. "Oh, right. You're moving." He stiffened and chose not to say any more.

She fell silent too.

*Damn, should've kept my mouth shut. I'm pushing her.*

After a few times around the room, her body began to relax in his arms and she seemed to anticipate when he was going to move one way or the other either by the pressure of his hand on her back or the pulling and pushing of his left hand clasped around hers.

As they moved together, he wondered if she was getting as turned-on as he was. Maybe she wasn't interested in getting involved with someone if she'd just broken up with that guy.

Jake leaned close and whispered, "Ready to try something new?"

"Excuse me?"

"A spin? Like what that couple just did." He tilted his chin toward a couple in front of them.

"Oh. Okay."

"Ready, go." He pressed on her back and had her walk under his raised arm which made her lose the rhythm. "Not bad for a first try. Get the steps going and we'll try it again."

"I think I get the idea."

He wanted to ask her out to dance another night.

"Ready to try again?" This time she managed to keep her footing through the turn.

"Hey, I did it."

He gazed down at her and had the sudden urge to kiss her but fortunately restrained himself. "Yeah, you did great." The music changed to another song, a much slower one. They stood off to the side, gazing at one another and not speaking.

This was going to get complicated. If things did progress with Amy as he hoped, how long should he wait until he told her about his abilities? A heavy dread weighed him down. He pushed the thought out of his mind. Not for a long time.

The dance floor filled up again and Jake urged her out. "One more? It's just a waltz, an easy box step."

"Easy if you know how."

"Didn't any of your old boyfriends take you dancing?"

"Not this kind."

"No more lessons tonight. We'll just wing it." He took her in his arms and pulled her close, dancing in any easy, no-patterned style.

The feel of her hand sliding along his back was maddening. Was she aware of what she was doing to him? The softness of her breasts, the heat of her hand, her scent. She rested her head on his shoulder and he felt the heat of her body radiate through him.

Again he stroked her back and steered them by pulling or pushing with his left hand. He couldn't help focusing on his arousal. Hell, he wouldn't be human if he wasn't getting a little turned-on. They'd been dancing for a few songs now.

The dancing had ignited a need in him, something he hadn't dared think about since Alison. Sure, it wouldn't take much arm twisting to take her into his bed but he wanted more than one night of sex with Amy.

He was teetering on a precarious edge, wanting to slide his fingers into her hair, press his lips to her neck. As his hand continued to stroke her back, lewd and fervent thoughts paraded around his head. He longed to tease her until she was slick with juices. Then he would thrust his cock inside her to the hilt while his mouth captured her cries of pleasure. Closing his eyes, he imagined his tongue fucking her mouth as his cock was fucking her pussy. His fingers dug into her shoulder.

Jake drew her closer, their hips touching, her mound rubbing the bulge beneath his jeans. Lord, he wanted to be inside her.

The song ended and another one with a beat for a two-step dance began. The other couples fell into step. Still holding her in his arms, Jake glanced down at her. "I should get you home. You have to work tomorrow, don't you?"

She nodded. "This sounds like an easy song for the two-step. Do you have time for one more?" she asked Jake.

"Sure." He moved her into the dance. "Are you beginning to like country music?"

"Not really. I was just looking for an excuse to dance one more dance with you."

*Good answer.* He smiled and pressed her against his body.

"You don't have to work tomorrow?" she asked him.

"I do but I didn't want to stop dancing with you." He felt the vibration from his pager and groaned. They stopped dancing. "I'm sorry, my pager."

He led her off the dance floor and slipped his pager off his belt and read the screen. Frowning, he grabbed his cell phone. "I'm sorry, Amy. It's my grandfather. He's in his eighties," he said as he dialed the number on his cell phone.

"Sure, no problem."

"Come on, Bill, answer your phone." After several moments, Jake cursed under his breath and hung up. "He's not answering. He texted 9-1-1 on my pager but he's not answering his phone. It's not unusual. He's done this before. But I still worry. Would you mind if we go straight there first before I take you home? Just in case."

"Of course."

# Chapter Ten

ஐ

When Amy followed Jake into Bill Sike's double-wide mobile home, she had expected a shaman to be wearing something that represented the Native American heritage. Instead, the man wore jeans, a denim buttoned Western-style shirt and cowboy boots. He was stretched out in a lounge chair, smoking a cigarette. His hair was mostly gray with black streaks, long, past his shoulders, and pulled into a ponytail.

"What took you?" Bill said as he got up and nodded to Amy. "I see what took you." He introduced himself. He held his hand out to Amy to shake.

Amy shook it and introduced herself.

"We were in town when I got your page. What's the emergency?" Jake asked.

"Sorry to mess up your evening." The lines around his eyes became more pronounced as he squinted and studied her.

"No problem," Amy said. She didn't mention that they were dancing. She glanced around the room. The furniture was old and worn and the area rugs looked like hand-woven Indian wares. A bookshelf on one side of the living room contained several books and Indian pottery, sculptures, feathers and dream catchers. On the walls were photos from old Western movies where the backdrop used some of the common Arizona red rock formations. Amy recognized John Wayne, Debbie Reynolds, Alan Ladd and Angie Dickinson but there were many more she didn't know although the faces were familiar.

The room was neat and had a sweet aroma of fresh tobacco and strong coffee.

"Why didn't you answer your phone?" Jake said.

"Must've been outside tending the fire. Meditating."

Jake rolled his eyes. "I thought something was wrong or you were sick. Why did you page me?"

"Something is wrong." Bill paced the room for a moment without saying anything.

"Why don't you sit?" Jake placed a hand on Bill's shoulder and the old man shot him a look.

"I'm not sick."

"I can wait outside if you like," Amy offered. Maybe Bill had something personal to discuss.

"No, I reckon this concerns you," Bill said to Amy.

Jake sighed, showing his frustration. "What does?"

"I had one of my visions." He glared at Jake as if challenging him to discount them. "More than the visions… I've seen him too. Out back."

"Seen who? Where out back?" Jake frowned, glancing at Amy.

"Coyote." Bill walked to the back door window and pointed outside. "He's been standing out there waiting and watching me the last couple nights. Tonight he stared right at me as the bastard walked up to this door as confident as you please with a crow's feather in his mouth. Then he dropped the feather on the doormat, looked me in the eye and ran off."

Jake ran a hand through his hair and took a breath before commenting. "Okay, so this was your dream?"

Bill turned to face Jake, his hands clenched. "No dream. This just happened. That's why I paged you." He picked up a clay bowl with a bundle that looked like a cluster of dried wheat together. He lit the end with a lighter until the ends glowed and the herb began to smoke. The sweet woody scent filled the room as he waved the bundle around.

He dropped the smoldering stick into the bowl and handed it to Jake. "Here, you finish smudging the room while I get something for you." Bill left the room.

Jake gave Amy a worried look but complied with his grandfather by waving the stick in the air and walking around the kitchen, dining area and living room.

"What's smudging supposed to do?" Amy asked.

"To clear negative energies or rid bad spirits from entering an area. The Indians use mostly sage, cedar and sweetgrass." He held up the smoldering bundle. "I think this is white sage.

"Smells nice."

When Bill returned, he held an animal skin hooked over his arm and some objects in his other hand. He held them out for Jake to take. There was an Indian drum, a leather pouch, feathers and a few stones. The stones looked like turquoise and obsidian.

"No, old man." Jake shook his head.

"What kind of animal fur is that?" Amy was curious but felt awkward to ask what the other objects were meant for. It might have been something sacred and she didn't want to be rude.

"Mountain lion," Bill said without taking his eyes off Jake.

Jake hadn't taken the fur or the items from Bill. Neither man moved as if there was a silent war going on between them. The air in the room was tense. "Would you like me to wait outside, Jake? It looks like you two have something to discuss."

"No need, Amy," Jake said through clenched teeth. "Bill and I have already discussed this topic and he knows my view."

Bill dropped the fur and items into a worn recliner chair and turned to Amy.

He smiled. "Please excuse my grandson. He's stubborn when it comes to the old ways and facing things he can't change."

Amy smiled awkwardly and shrugged, not sure what to say and she glanced at Jake for a clue as what to do. Jake hadn't made eye contact with her during this whole ordeal. "Don't apologize for me, Granddad," he said stiffly but with respect. "She doesn't need to know about this now." He turned to Amy. "I'm sorry. It's a family matter. Sorry to bring you in on this."

She smiled. "No problem."

"Come on outside," Bill ordered them both.

Jake grimaced and shook his head. Amy grabbed his arm and dragged him outside. "Come on. It's not like I've never had a fight with my parents."

He chuckled. "I'm sure it wasn't about this."

She glanced at the fur, dying to know what it was about. "No, I'm sure you're right."

Outside, Bill had a fire burning in an old metal barrel cut down to use as a fire pit. The flames danced and crackled, sparks drifting up a foot or so, then faded out. The sky was completely clear and filled with brilliant stars so vivid in the desert sky. "You may deny your heritage but you can't deny that something unusual is haunting the land and the animals."

Jake closed his eyes for a moment as if to gather his patience. "When you say unusual, you mean supernatural."

Bill stood his ground. "I've had my visions, yes. At first I thought it was *Iktomi* but the creature in this vision does not speak the sacred language and he travels much faster than Coyote."

Jake propped his hand on his hips and took a breath to speak but remained silent.

Amy glanced first at Bill, then at Jake. "What does he mean?"

Jake placed a hand on Amy's back. "An Indian myth. *Iktomi* is the Coyote shapeshifter."

He still didn't answer her question, she thought.

"He's been here. I've seen him in my dreams. But not *Iktomi*, not Coyote, something else, something deadly."

A chill skimmed over Amy's skin that seemed to reach down to her bones. She rubbed her arms.

Bill unfolded an Indian blanket from a webbed lawn chair and draped it over her shoulders. "The desert air has a chill at night."

"Thank you." She tucked the blanket up under her chin. Bill looked into her eyes for a moment as if he could see something there. See into her mind, her thoughts.

Jake shook his head. "Don't worry, Bill. You've heard me talk about the animals dying and you're worried. It's causing your dreams. I know how you love the park. Amy's company is helping to find—"

Bill spun around to face Jake. "Damn it. You know my dreams. Don't talk to me like I'm an old man." His hands fisted at his side. "You're in danger and so is she. You know the significance of the crow feather."

"Okay, okay," Jake said. "I believe you."

Bill kicked a stone across the yard. Amy jumped at his display of rage. "Then believe me when I say you're both in danger."

"Danger? From what?" Amy asked.

"Whom," Bill said. "Coyote, or another trickster. Something evil and more deadly."

"What does the crow feather mean? I don't understand," Amy added.

"Crow is a messenger from the spirits. He knows both worlds. But a gift of a crow feather from a trickster is a bad omen." Bill paced in front of the fire.

"If this is true what am I supposed to do?" Jake said but she wasn't sure if he truly believed what his grandfather was saying.

"Use your powers—"

"I can protect her without my powers. I just need to keep her away from him." Jake glanced at Amy as if he finally admitted more than he'd planned.

"Do you know who he is?" Bill asked.

Jake shook his head.

Bill lowered his voice. "Even if you did, I'm afraid it won't be enough." He pulled a small leather pouch from his shirt pocket and removed a pinch of what seemed like loose tobacco. He tossed it on the fire. The flames blazed for a second, then died down.

She got a whiff of the sweet tobacco mixed with some other incense.

Bill then took a turquoise stone from his pocket and held in his palm toward the fire. He closed his eyes and mumbled a few words that she couldn't decipher, then brought the stone to her. "Here, Amy. It'll help protect you."

Jake sighed loudly behind her as if annoyed.

"Well, it's something," Bill said. "It will help."

"What should I do with it?" she asked.

"Keep it with you. It'll give you strength and help protect you from evil."

"Thank you, Bill."

"Stay and have a quick cup of coffee with me and I'll let you be on your way," Bill said.

Jake started to protest.

"It's okay, I'd love a cup of coffee. Can I help you?" Amy asked.

"No, no. I can get it. Sit by the fire. I'll be right out." Bill went inside and she and Jake dragged folding lawn chairs closer to the metal drum still blazing with a fire.

"You'll be sorry when you taste his coffee. It's as thick as motor oil," Jake chuckled.

"I don't mind. Does he have these visions often?"

"All his life."

"Are they prophetic?"

He studied her and smiled warily. "Do you believe in esoteric perceptions? Metaphysics?"

"I may be a scientist but I have read about a variety of phenomena like astrology, dream travel and fortune telling. I have an open mind but have not found that I have any skills in those areas. A psychic friend foretold of my move out west six months before my company informed me. She also told me she didn't see me coming back. I told her she was wrong about that part."

"So you don't read minds or tell futures," Jake said with a lighthearted tone.

"Afraid not."

He nodded while staring into the fire.

"What psychic skills do you have?" she asked.

He shot her a look.

Bill came out with three coffee mugs. "You take your coffee with milk and sugar?" he asked Amy as he handed her a mug and then Jake.

"Yes, thank you. That's how I like it," she said.

"Amy's from the lab helping the park service determine the cause of the animal deaths." Jake sipped his coffee.

He put his mug down on a metal end table and threw a log onto the fire. Sparks swirled and floated up toward the star-filled sky then dimmed out. The flames crackled and sputtered as waves of heat flowed over Amy. It wasn't that cold out but she felt cold. Bill's small backyard was bordered by a chain-link fence. Several shrubs were planted around the fenceline. There was also an old doghouse in one corner but she hadn't seen any sign of a dog. Beyond the fence was the desert. Miles of flat harsh plains, dotted with saguaro and prickly pear cactus, mesquite and creosote bushes and many other low-growing plants whose names she hadn't yet learned. Past the lowlands were the shadows of the distant mountains.

When she first moved here she'd thought the desert was dead. She was wrong. It was alive with creatures and plant life unlike anything she had ever seen.

"You okay, Amy?" Jake asked.

"Huh? Oh yes. Just staring out into the desert. It's beautiful at night. So peaceful. And it changes. Since I moved here, I've seen the desert change over the months."

"Like a work of art that is never finished," Bill said.

"So true," Amy said.

"Do you remember your dreams, Amy?" Bill asked.

"Sometimes," she said, looking at her shoes. Lately, she was having a lot of sexual dreams and had blamed them on Dante.

"Have Coyote or other animals turned up in your dreams lately?" he asked, leaning forward in his chair.

"I'm not sure I remember. What other animals?" she asked.

"Other predators—" Bill began.

"It's getting late," Jake interrupted. He stood and walked toward Amy. "We can talk about dreams another night. Amy has to work in the morning and so do I," he said to Bill.

Bill pressed his lips together, his eyes offering a warning. "This isn't finished, son. Don't abandon your gift. Sometimes you have to face your past. Her life may depend on it. She connected to what's happening to the animals and you know it." Bill looked worried.

"Don't. Stop this. It's not what you think. And I have faced my past." Jake dumped the rest of his coffee into the fire.

Amy was surprised by the vehemence in his voice. She stood and slowly folded the blanket and placed it on the chair. What would these dreams have to do with anything? And why would it make Jake so upset?

"It sounds fascinating, Bill, I'd love to talk more sometime," Amy said. "But Jake's right. It is late and I have to get up early. Thank you for the coffee and the stone. I'll keep it with me always."

Bill smiled at that and nodded. He stood. "I'll show you out."

* * * * *

They drove in silence almost all the way to Amy's house. Jake was torn between whether to apologize for his grandfather's behavior or his own or let it pass. He had no intention of allowing Amy to get a glimpse of his true nature even though Bill was certain supernatural work was necessary. Bill nearly exposed him by bringing out the fur. That ancient heritage had destroyed his family and ended his relationship with Alison. Couldn't Bill understand why he wanted to leave that behind?

What kind of mother abandons two young boys and runs off with a man fifteen years younger than she? On the surface she sounded like a heartless mother but she'd found a way out of the madness. She married into a family where the men inherited the strange ability when they reached puberty. The Norwegians called it *Eigi Einhamr*, not one-skinned. Had his mother known about the genetic trait before she married? That was one question he'd never had the nerve to ask his mother.

By wearing the skin of any animal and concentrating on becoming that beast, a man with the powers of *Eigi Einhamr* could become that animal and retain the memories and knowledge of his human self. Then he could change back at will.

His father had changed into a wolf. Jake barely remembered the thick, black fur draped over a chair in their house when he was nine years old. He only saw his father change once—the night he was shot. The transformation disturbed his mother, so his father didn't do it often. A few months after his father died, his brother Brad was eleven and

Brad had found a leopard fur belonging to their father. He wrapped himself in it, transforming right before their mother. It was more than she could handle.

Bill Sike was wise to Native American myth and legends, although he'd had never heard of *Eigi Einhamr*. Jake's mother explained her dilemma, her fears of having the same fate happen to her sons. Bill agreed to raise them and to teach them to use their powers wisely. Brad was in the armed services using his talents overseas in the Special Forces. But after losing his father and mother to the *Eigi Einhamr*, Jake chose never to shift into an animal.

Then Bill had performed a ceremony, selecting the mountain lion as the chosen animal for Jake. Usually those of *Eigi Einhamr* descent chose the animal which appealed to them most. Although an *Eigi Einhamr* could change into any animal he desired as long as he had the skin.

Jake had donned the fur and shifted into the lion with Bill's guidance. The freedom and power while in the animal's body was invigorating, climbing the mountains, racing across the plains but the fear remained. The loss of his father, the abandonment of his mother still left an open wound. He slipped out of the skin and handed Bill the mountain lion fur for safekeeping.

"Sorry, if I put you in an uncomfortable position back there," Jake finally said. He couldn't go into how much Bill meant to him. How Bill had helped him and his brother after his mother abandoned them.

"Not at all. I enjoyed meeting him."

Silence stretched for a long moment. "He sticks to his old Navajo ways. Myths and traditions."

"I got that. It's very interesting. I'd like to hear more sometime. And what your take is on all of it."

"Sure," he said uneasily.

He pulled into her driveway and hit the brakes a little too hard. Standing in front of her garage like a golden ghost was a coyote.

"Jake, it's that coyote again." Amy reached over and gripped his arm, the first time she touched him during the whole ride back.

The coyote held his head high, staring at them in the headlights.

"He could be the same one, or just another one checking out your trash. I hope you secured your lids or you'll have a mess." Jake beeped his horn a couple times as he inched his Jeep closer. The animal didn't move. "Stubborn, isn't he?"

Finally, the coyote got up, sniffing the air and backed up but remained in the driveway.

"It is the same one," Amy exclaimed. "Look at his tail. It's chopped off like the one at Betty's and on the trail."

The last quarter of the coyote's tail was missing. "You're right. He must have a den nearby."

Amy released his arm and gave him an odd look. "Could what your grandfather said have any truth to it?"

He groaned.

"Well, some myths are based in truth," she argued.

They were treading on dangerous ground and he had no intension of discussing his history with her tonight, or probably any night. "You're a scientist. Don't you think we'll have more success in helping these animals with science than delving into desert magic?" His tone was a bit sharper than he intended.

She shrugged. "I do know science. It's my profession and I haven't lived in the desert long enough to understand as well as you. But as a scientist I don't rule out any possibility no matter how strange it may seem."

"There's nothing unusual about a coyote sitting in your driveway at night," Jake said, trying to keep his voice even.

She got out of the truck and strode toward the coyote.

"Amy, don't. He's a wild animal and you need to be wary of rabies."

She continued marching toward the animal and surprisingly he didn't scare off as he would've expected.

She stopped a few feet from the animal that faced her, his head and tail down. "Shoo, go away!" she yelled at him, waving her arms.

The coyote didn't move. Then he tilted his head as if puzzled, like a dog would.

"Careful, Amy."

"Is this normal behavior of a coyote? I've lived here for eight months and chased a couple out of my trash. Never have I had one act like this or like the one did today at Betty's or up in the mountains to us."

"Maybe someone was feeding him and he's become part tame," Jake said.

She sighed. "Yes, that could be."

Jake walked closer and the coyote approached Jake, moving between Amy and Jake.

"Strange. Showing territorial behavior," Jake said. "Enough. I don't like it." He clapped his hands and the sharp sound made the coyote jump back. Jake ran toward him, yelling. The animal ran off, glancing behind him. It took Jake a few times of chasing, clapping and yelling to force the coyote on his way.

"Let me know if he continues to come around. I'll contact animal control. They can set up a humane trap to move him if he becomes a nuisance."

"I'm sure it won't come to that," she said.

"Sorry to get you home so late. I have your sunglasses and water bottle you left in the back of my Jeep. I'll get them."

She stood by him as he open the back door of his Jeep. She let out a small cry as the dome light hit the tan fur.

"Damn it," Jake muttered. "He gave it to me anyway." The mountain lion pelt along with the drum, hawk feathers and quartz stones rested on the floor next to Amy's sunglasses and water bottle.

He pulled the items out and handed them to her.

"Is that part of the desert magic you don't want to talk about?" she asked, her eyes studying him.

He rubbed his face and shook his head. "It's not a topic I care to go into this evening." When he realized how harsh that sounded he amended it. "At least not tonight. It's a very long story. Okay?"

She nodded and leaned up and kissed him on the cheek. "Yes, that's okay. Thanks for dinner and the dancing. I had a great time. And I enjoyed meeting your grandfather." Her voice was soft and sexy. She remained close and there was desire in her eyes.

He wanted her. Having her in his arms on the dance floor had provoked a desperate need to indulge in the lust that burned inside him, to quench that craving. Part of the desperation came from denying his heritage, avoiding the change. Apart from the other night, he hadn't changed in form in months and his muscles and bones ached for the shift as much as he ached for a woman's body.

"I had a nice time too." He was treading on dangerous ground seeing her now while he had two beasts to control. He wouldn't let the *Eigi Einhamr* consume him. As the desire for sex increased, so did the need to shift take on his chosen form, any form, and race into the night until his animal body was exhausted.

Pursuing Amy was a risk. How long could he keep his secret side hidden?

His body was on fire, wanting a taste of her passion, a hint to what could be between them.

"Would I be out of line if I asked you out? I know I'm a client but I'd like to go dancing again," he asked.

"Outside our professional connection?" she asked in a teasing tone.

"Right."

"I don't see a problem. Though I wouldn't mention it to my colleagues right now."

"Like Dante?"

She smiled and looked down at her shoes. "I don't think you're out of line. Give me a call. I'd love to hear the story that goes with that animal hide." She smiled but the expression quickly faded, probably after seeing his shocked expression at the mention of the animal hide.

"Right. Good night then." Damn, he hadn't meant to sound short with her. How was he going to avoid talking about the significance of the mountain lion skin without scaring her?

"Good night, Jake." She went inside her house and closed the door.

# Chapter Eleven

ꟸ

Amy leaned against her front door, hung her head and groaned. Crap. Why did she have to mention the animal skin? Obviously it was a sore spot between him and his grandfather and here she was urging him to talk about it at their next meeting. He'll think she was a nosy, prying woman with no sensitivity.

His Jeep pulled out of her driveway and the roar of his engine disappeared up the road. Her stomach gave a little flutter. Only gone a few minutes and already she was missing him like a teenager pining for a new beau. Wasn't it a little soon to get hung up on a new guy with Dante barely out of the picture?

Already Jake had begun to fill a void that Dante couldn't or had no desire to fill by asking about her family and interests. In the eight months that she'd known Dante, he'd never asked if she had brothers or sisters, if it was hard for her to move from Florida, or what she liked or didn't like about Arizona and Florida. Jake had asked her all these things in one night and they weren't on a date—not really a date. A new client was taking her out for dinner and had been kind enough to show her the Texas Two-Step.

Squeezing her arms around her waist, she blew out an exasperated breath. She liked dancing with him, liked the feel of him. It felt so good having him hold her. If she had held his gaze a little bit longer would he have kissed her? Yeah, right, she was sounding like a kid with a bad crush. And she was traveling down a road that would lead nowhere once she got a job offer in Florida. Jake wouldn't follow her to Florida. He'd lived here all his life and he had his grandfather to take care of. If there was something between her and Jake, something more than a business relationship as she sensed there was, she would have to guard her feeling from getting too serious and be upfront with him too.

Without turning on her living room light, she strode into her kitchen, tossed her purse and keys on the baker's rack and flipped on the small light above her stove.

A scratching sound made her jump. She spun around, pulse pounding and then realized it was Sienna in her cardboard box. Running a hand through her hair, she took a deep breath and willed her heartbeat to slow down, then picked up the tea kettle and filled it at her sink for tea. She placed it on the stove to heat and checked on her cat. The heating pad placed under the crate was keeping the inside of Sienna's home nice and cozy warm.

Sienna mewed and clawed inside her box. "All right already, I'll feed you in a minute." Amy replaced the soiled paper with fresh then filled the syringe with the formula she'd bought from the pet store. Sitting on the floor, she held the cat in her palm while gently squirting the measured syringe of milk into the kitten's eager mouth. Sienna took it easily without drawing blood. Amazing.

After Sienna was full, Amy put her back in her box and watched as she curled up in a ball and went right to sleep. Hard to believe that tiny fluffball had terrorized her and nearly clawed her to death just yesterday. *Don't get attached to her because you're not moving her to Florida.*

She poured hot water over the tea bag in her earthenware mug to steep and went into her bedroom to change. The hardwood floor was cool on her bare feet and the room was chilly but when she'd moved eight months ago she hadn't bought herself anything warmer to sleep in because she didn't think she would be in Arizona that long. Who would've thought the desert nights would be so cold? Digging into her dresser drawer, she reminded herself to do laundry the next day and pulled out a sleeveless silk nightshirt that came mid-thigh and slipped it on. Shivering with goose bumps covering her skin and nipples hard, she yanked the Indian blanket off her bed—tried not to think it was a gift from Dante—and wrapped herself in it. The she strode back out into the kitchen for her tea.

She dunked the chamomile tea bag several times in the steaming mug of water, then added a teaspoon of honey. Holding the cup in one hand, she grasped the blanket tightly around her with the other. Sleep wouldn't come easily tonight. Thoughts of Jake and Dante bounced around her head. Throw in her job and plans to move to Florida and she had a circus juggler attempting to keep all those images aloft in her mind at one time. Instead, they ricocheted, collided and rolled around inside. No way was she getting any sleep tonight.

For the first time the thought of moving back to Florida didn't fill her with excitement or longing as it had in the past. She hadn't heard from any of her friends in months. By now she'd be as much a stranger there as she was here. As the months passed, and the emails and phone calls from her friends stopped, she wondered what made friendships last.

She noticed the message light on her phone was blinking. Her heart lifted a bit. Maybe her friends from Florida did call her after all. Pressing the button, she dropped onto the sofa and listened to the messages as she sipped her tea. Her mother's voice came across the first message. Her mother wished her happy birthday and told Amy about her brother's two boys, bragging about how well they were doing in school. She also asked how the job hunting was going and if she thought she'd be back in Florida by the fall.

The next call was from Truly, apologizing for missing her birthday. She was still at her mother's house but wanted to go out to celebrate Amy's birthday when she returned. She had done something special for her today, a little magic to heat up her love life. Just a little ritual, very positive but she didn't elaborate. Amy curled her feet under her and smiled, shaking her head. Truly would have to explain about what she meant by "something special". Truly had danced naked in the desert on the full moon, it was her little ritual to draw in new love in her life. Amy wondered if that had been successful.

The third and last call was from Dante. She closed her eyes, preparing for the message. A wave of foreboding weighed her down for two reasons—the last call meant no friend had called her from Florida and she didn't feel like hearing what Dante had to say. She was about to get up and turn off the machine but decided she'd better hear him out. She expected to hear Dante complain and try to manipulate her somehow. He only asked where she was. Why wasn't she answering her cell phone and maybe they should talk. "I thought you enjoyed our sex games by the bonfire," his voice stiffly said. "I thought I always satisfied you. I tried to make it exciting. You said you didn't want anything serious."

She blinked and stared at the phone in disbelief. He was the one who'd said he didn't want a serious relationship. She'd agreed to it because in the back of her mind, she wasn't going to live there for long. Now he was trying to turn it around as if it was always her idea.

"If you met someone else, I understand," the message continued. "Give me a call or I'll see you at work." The message ended.

Closing her eyes, she dropped her head back against the sofa. Damn, she would have to face him again. True, she was finding herself attracted to Jake but that wasn't the reason she was ending her relationship with Dante. Dante was creeping her out. How he'd managed it get her outside with his hypnosis, she didn't know. And their sex life was beginning to feel shallow and empty.

Sex for the sake of sexual satisfaction might only be fine in the heat of the moment, or in the rare event of a one-night stand. Women are human too and maybe the guy was really hot. But to continue a relationship minus the emotion and caring made her feel cheap. She'd rather spend the night with her vibrator or a good book.

Finally she'd met someone normal and could put Dante and that bizarre relationship behind her. She took a sip of her tea and let the light herbal taste roll over her tongue, then slip down her throat.

Amy sighed and stretched. Every muscle in her body stiffened into knotted cords. Outside tranquilizers or sex, chamomile tea was the only thing that would calm her down enough to sleep.

She placed the mug on the coffee table, stretched out on the sofa, pulled the red blanket over her and stared into the black, cold fireplace, then glanced toward her sliding glass door. Outside the silhouettes of the saguaros stood like gray specters above the desert landscape. When her tired eyes blinked, they almost appeared to move closer. She snuggled under the blanket, pulling it up to her chin, unable to take her eyes off the desert and the saguaros. Were they moving? Shaking her head. No, only her imagination. She closed her eyes. *Don't look at them.*

The desert sounds of trilling, chirping insects pierced the night. A bat squealed. She would listen to the music of the desert until she got sleepy, then she'd go to bed.

She studied the saguaros suspiciously. *There is nothing frightening about the saguaros.* Keeping her eyes closed, she rolled toward the back of the sofa, pressed her face into the cushions and was asleep before she took another breath.

"Amy?" Jake's voice called from behind her.

Amy remained motionless for a moment, her mind and body moving through a sea of molasses. Finally she rolled over and blinked. Jake stood in the living room. He wore no shirt, only jeans. She blinked several times, expecting him to disappear. "Jake?"

"Yes. Did I startle you?"

"A little. You came back." Rubbing her forehead with the heel of her hand, she tried to recall if she had locked her front door when she came home.

"Is that all right? I'll leave if you want me to." There was no regret in his voice. He took a step closer and the roaring fire from the fireplace flickered shadows across the muscles of his chest and arms.

"No, that's fine. You made a fire. How long have you been here? I never heard you come in."

He chuckled low in his throat. "I know. You were asleep. I knocked and the door was open. I saw you… Are you sure this is all right?" He stuck his hands in his pockets, his mouth quirking in a sexy half smile.

"Sure. It's fine." Although in the back of her mind it seemed out of character for Jake to walk into her house. They hadn't known each other that long. "Why did you come back?"

"I didn't want the evening to end. I wanted to…"

"Tell me about the animal skin. Tell me your story," she offered. Maybe he sensed her curiosity about it and felt a need to tell her. Obviously it was something important for Jake and his grandfather to get into a fight over.

"What animal skin? What story?"

"Huh?" Now she was confused. How could he not remember? She started to get up but her muscles refused to comply as if she was trying to move through liquid lead. Of course, she was dreaming. She was having a lucid dream—the only explanation for the surreal situation.

Jake raised his hand and signaled her to lie back down.

Her body obeyed. Leaning back on cushions, she gazed up at him. "Nice for you to join my dream world this evening."

Jake smiled, his eyes ablaze with a sensual intensity that was arousing. In sleep, she had tossed back the blanket because of the heat from the fire. The Indian cover was tangled around her knees and she knew her thin yellow nightshirt left nothing to the imagination of what she wore beneath it. The thought provoked a twitch to her pussy.

He approached her and knelt on the floor. Her stomach quivered with anticipation and the extent of her arousal was evident by the warm moisture between her legs.

Venturing without hesitation, she reached out and glided her fingertips over his thick biceps, up to his shoulders, then across his broad chest. The smoldering look that sparkled in his eyes urged her on. Her fingers trailed to his nipples which stiffened and beaded when she pressed and pinched them.

Grasping her hands, he held both arms above her head as he leaned over her and gazed into her eyes. Her stomach fluttered when his lips parted and his mouth took hers, his tongue probing and thrusting deep. He groaned and she whimpered beneath the kiss. Writhing and arching her back, she tried to drink in the kiss and draw his body closer.

Finally, he released her hands and she wrapped her arms around his neck and the kiss intensified. They gasped for breath as the kiss ramped up to urgent and wild desperation.

"Oh God," she breathed, grabbing his ass and running her hands up and down his back.

"Damn, you're so hot," he groaned against her neck. Then his mouth moved down her chest and sucked a nipple through the thin material, creating a wet circle.

Amy shuddered. She groped inside the waistband of his jeans and managed to undo the button and zipper while Jake was fondling her breasts. Working her hand down the front of his open jeans, she grasped his swollen cock and sucked in a breath. "God, you're…um…impressive. Like to take these off?" she asked in a teasing tone as she tugged at the jeans.

He smiled wickedly and stood, kicking off his boots, then sliding the jeans down over his narrow hips and muscular thighs. All that hiking really did pay off, at least in her dream vision of him. His abs were ripped and hard. As her gaze traveled down, she sucked in a breath and her lips parted at the sight of his thick cock.

*Would loving Jake be like this if I was awake? Truly's magic. This was all because of Truly's magic. What did she do? I've never had dreams with such details before.*

She could feel the ache and need of her arousal and saw Jake's desire in his eyes. The smell of his manly scent was like worn leather, rain and sage.

*Touch me now.* Reaching out to him, she wrapped her fist around his shaft and began to pump him. She gently cupped his weighty testicles as she tightened her grip on his shaft with the upward stroke to the head, squeezing a creamy drop of pre-cum at the tip. Could she taste in her dream too? She wanted to lick that drop and slid her mouth over his penis. She opened her mouth and bent toward him to do just that, when he held up a hand.

"Stop. I'll come if you keep that up." He pushed her against the cushions and gathered the hem of her nightshirt in his fist, drawing it over her head in one swift motion. "We have all night," he said huskily.

She gave a dry laugh. "Really? I don't think either of us will last that long. I have supplies in my bedroom." Then realized the silliness of needing condoms in a dream.

"We won't be getting that far for a while," he said as he knelt beside the sofa and kneaded her breasts with both hands, then pinched the nipples until her body was writhing. She wanted to feel his weight on her and feel the thickness of his cock inside her. How much longer would he make her wait? It was her dream and she could lead it the way she wanted it to go, the way she knew Jake would be. Not like Dante was—good at teasing and getting her off but lousy at making love.

Her hips rocked, her clit throbbed and ached to be touched. As if Jake could read her mind, he moved from her breasts and trailed his fingers to the drenched cleft of her pussy. Then he used his other hand to expose her swollen, sensitive clit. With a feather touch, he probed her nub. Amy jerked, her body hovering at the very precipice of an orgasm.

"Oh, fuck. Please don't stop." Her hips rose and undulated, inviting his continued touch but Jake's fingers touched everywhere but where she needed to be stimulated. "You're teasing me—no, torturing me."

"Yes, I am. Don't come yet."

"Oh, Jake, I'm on the edge." Her body trembled with need. A few well-placed touches or strokes and she'd come in an instant.

"Hold off. Make it last." Slipping his finger between her folds, he slid into her channel and plunged deep. "Your cunt is hot and juicy, Amy. You're ready to be fucked."

She groaned and raised her hips off the sofa. He pressed her back down. "I want you inside me, Jake."

"Not yet. Ride my fingers." He pumped two fingers inside her. It wasn't nearly enough. She wanted to feel the thickness of his cock spreading her wide, feeling the root of his shaft rub her clit.

"Oh, Jake. Take me. Please."

"You're so wet." He ignored her pleas. Outside the sound of the insects grew louder. She glanced at the fireplace and the flames blazed higher and he hadn't added any firewood. Dream, she reminded herself, no insects and no firewood. Couldn't she make the dream go the way she wanted?

"Jake, make me come now." In the background she heard Sienna mewing but she ignored her.

He turned his head and gave her an odd look. For a moment she thought his face changed like in a nightmare. His head lowered and he sucked her clit. Almost there. Grasping his head, her fingers entwined in his hair. Jake's tongue lapped at her clit in maddening circles but for some reason she couldn't reach climax. So close…so close…but not there yet. The cacophony of insects began to fade. *No, don't wake up.* "Oh, that's good. Like that." She raised her hips.

"Yes, baby, yes," he said.

Sienna's mewing grew louder. Still Amy ignored it. The distraction was enough to yank her away from the rhythm of her pending orgasm. Fearing she might be waking from her dream, she gripped Jake's shoulders, easing him up. "Jake, take me now. Hurry. Come inside me." He complied, lying on top of her.

"Shhh. I know you're ready. I want to savor every moment," he said huskily. He took her mouth again in a kiss that took her breath, captured her whimpers.

During the kiss, she wriggled and spread her legs until she had his hard cock pressed on her pussy. He rose up from the kiss and smiled wickedly. "Impatient, aren't you?"

"Hell, yeah."

He chuckled softly. "More passion to fill the well."

Huh? Reaching down, she gripped his shaft, angling it between her damp folds to slip toward her entrance, at the same time she met his gaze.

He frowned. His expression lacked the strength, confidence and powerful sensuality only moments ago he had exuded. Making her desire known would ease the dream in the direction she wanted.

As she maneuvered the head of his cock to her slick entrance, Jake's eyes widened in panic. His blue eyes flashed and turned to brown. She knew his eyes were blue but dreams did odd things. All she cared about was the heated sensation of the tip of his cock probing the opening of her wet channel. Her stomach coiled and every muscle quivered in anticipation. Gripping his ass and raising her hip, she tried to urge his head inside. "Yes, Jake, make love to me." She felt him slip him a little more and moaned. Blissful triumph. "Oh God, yes."

Her head lolled from side to side and she glanced at the fireplace. The fire in the fireplace was fading out. She closed her eyes, rocking her hips to feel Jake's cock slip in past the head. "Jake," she beseeched.

Sienna yowled like a wildcat. Amy's head swam. She opened her eyes and blinked to clear her vision.

The fireplace was black, the room cold.

Jake stood beside the sofa. She never felt him slip out of her body. The room spun and blurred. Amy rubbed her eyes. When she could focus again she realized she was awake and naked and alone.

Not alone.

Standing in the shadows beside the fireplace was Dante.

Staring at him for a moment, she wasn't sure if she was still dreaming and if he was really there. Then Dante tilted his chin up in a defiant pose, glaring at her. He was bare-chested and wore brown suede pants. His long black hair and sleek muscular body made him look like an Indian out of an old Western movie.

"Dante?" Her words barely came out in a raspy whisper.

Not answering her, he shook his head in disgust, pursing his mouth together and raising his eyes to the ceiling.

Her heartbeat thundered in her ears. "Dante? How did you get in? What are you doing here?" Was he screwing with her mind again while she slept? Did he trick her into having a sexual dream, making her think she was having a wet dream with Jake? *Bastard.*

He pressed the heels of his hands into his eyes and groaned. Then he glared at her. "Sorry." The look frightened her and she pulled the blanket closer. Sienna hissed and yowled. Her skin crawled with gooseflesh, not knowing if what she was seeing was real or a hallucination. Amy did not like being frightened in her own home.

Covering herself with the blanket, she stood and took a breath as she gathered the courage to speak. She pointed to the front door. "Get out!"

Without a word, Dante's form faded into a ghostlike image, then changed into the coyote with the chopped-off tail.

She sucked in a sharp breath and screamed. The kitten hissed and clawed at her box as if the tiny thing would attack the coyote given a chance. Amy hoped the coyote didn't smell Sienna and eat her.

Frantically, she searched around the room, looking for a weapon to fight off the predator. Weapon, weapon. Her home was invaded, her pet was threatened.

She then spied the rack of fireplace tools, leapt over the coffee table, tripped over the bear rug and snatched up a poker. Waving the wrought iron tip at the animal, she approached it cautiously.

The coyote raised his chin, sniffed the air, swung around and walked straight through the glass door as if there was no glass.

Amy dropped the poker and let out a choked scream. Her hand cupped over her mouth. Fear kept her from looking outside to see if the coyote was there but she had to see, had to know for sure if she had imagined it.

She vaulted to the window and peered out. It was there. The coyote was weaving around scrub brush, heading toward the tall saguaro silhouetted against the star-filled sky.

Sienna mewed softly like a sweet kitten again. Scooping her up in her arms, Amy strode through her house, carrying the poker. After checking every window and door to make sure everything was locked up tight, she put her kitten back to bed. An icy chill skittered across Amy's skin. What good would locked windows and doors do when the creature could move though walls?

# Chapter Twelve

Dante changed back into his human form and spat on the ground. Well, that was a royal fuckup. He marched in giant strides toward the tall saguaro. No telling how much chi he lost in that fiasco. He glanced over his shoulder at Amy's house in the distance and saw that she hadn't followed. Then he kicked a passing tumbleweed. It floated up a few feet then slowly bounced back onto the ground. Kicking a ball of dead twigs did little to ease his anxiety.

He had no choice now. Finding mortals wasn't easy, especially with the level of life force that Amy Weston provided. He didn't have the time left to search out other partners. Hunting an animal or two on his way to the portal might help add to his offering but again, he didn't have time. He would have to find humans to kill and fast.

The heady scent of moist, sea air made his throat tighten knowing he'd have to deal with Gwyllain soon. Along the eastern horizon a hint of golden light touched the velvety black sky above the desert horizon. Dawn was approaching and he had to get to work, so the sooner he faced Gwyllain's hostility, the sooner he'd be back.

The landmark for the portal, the tall saguaro, was twenty yards away. The sound of crashing waves roared above the desert sounds. Rough seas. Not a good sign. Get this journey over with, he thought as he grasped the nebula stone pendant in one hand. Dante held his breath as the ground dropped out beneath his feet. He plummeted into darkness.

When he righted himself, the transfer through the portal was complete. Dante was in Anartia.

At the edge of the cliffs, the turbulent gray waves beat against the jagged rocks. A cold wind whipped at his bare chest and sliced through his pants. The sky had lost its tranquility since the last time he was here. Dark clouds roiled into mountain-sized thunderheads as lightning bolts discharged in violent streaks. *What the hell is going on?*

He'd never seen Anartia in such a state. A little stormy, sometimes gray but never this violent. As he understood this fragmented world, its existence depended on a delicate balance of energy. In his hundred-and-fifty-odd years as an immortal, he had the opportunity to study quantum physics, dark matter, vacuum energy, magnetic and gravitational fields, all which might explain the essence of Anartia and how it was constructed to some degree, because Gwyllain had said it was artificially constructed.

Dante's knowledge only touched the basics in those sciences and he doubted if even the most gifted scientists from Earth could grasp the alternative world's framework. All the laws of physics didn't apply here as far as Dante could determine.

But he knew in his gut that something was not right. Annihilating one member of Gwyllain's Throng shouldn't cause such upheaval. Gwyllain had told him he only had to serve her with offerings of chi one month every hundred years. The last time he served her was in 1955. The effect of Tarik's experiments had required Dante's early return, no doubt.

Moving away from the cliff edge, he let out a breath, grateful that she wasn't around to greet him this time. Who in their right mind designed the portal entrance at the edge of a precipice overlooking the ocean?

He scanned the fields of heather leading up to the temple. Many of the flowers were shriveled, the grass brown and flattened. He wondered what the temple's gardens looked like. Gwyllain took pride in her gardens and would be furious if they suffered too.

Two gardens spread out the full length of the temple, a private one off Gwyllain's chamber and one that led off from the pool area. Each mini-oasis was lush with tropical flowers—hibiscus, jasmine, gardenias, orchids—and shaded by large fruit trees. Statues of unknown people or unknown gods, marble benches, trellises and water fountains were scattered throughout. Like a garden on Mount Olympus. Dante had been curious about the statues. Were they gods of these beings? Did immortals have gods or a god that they worshiped? He hadn't asked because he preferred to spend the least amount of time on Anartia as possible. Small talk with Gwyllain might anger her or keep him there longer. Best to do his worship and leave.

Tarik had told him Anartia had been exiled around Earth for over a thousand years. And if Gwyllain had been acquiring hundreds of servants during that time, what parts of Earth's ancient mythology was molded by them? Told by various individuals who did Gwyllain's bidding?

As he walked toward the temple with trepidation, two young women and two men ran out and headed toward the cliffs, their hands on their pendants. All looked to be in their twenties or thirties and wore casual Earth clothes for cold-weather temperatures—jeans, sweaters with parkas. They nodded a greeting as they passed Dante and leapt off the cliff. They all vanished the instant their feet left the ground.

Shortly after they left, another group of three ran out of the temple. They were all men in exercise shorts and tees as if they just came out of the gym. What the hell? The swirling nebula stone pendant also hung around their necks. They jogged down the field following the four who had just passed, gave Dante a short salute and jumped into the void.

How many Throng did Gwyllain have? She usually alternated her offerings. Dante hadn't seen this many come and go during his last visit. Besides the men and women who remained at the temple as her slaves and guards, and Tarik,

Gwyllain's mate, the only other visitors to Anartia were occasional Drones arriving with their offering. Puzzling.

He ran up to the temple and entered. He was late but if Gwyllain had just entertained another Drone maybe she wouldn't care.

Scanning the great hall, he saw her stretched out, naked, facedown, on one of the cushioned lounge chairs surrounding the pool. A muscle-bound guard, wearing only a loincloth, poured scented oils from jewel-colored glass pitchers onto his palm and began massaging her back.

The man's hands worked her neck, arms and back, then moved down to her ass. After squeezing and massaging her ass cheeks, he continued to her thighs but first he slicked up his hands with more oil. Dante felt his cock twitch. He knew he mustn't speak until Gwyllain spoke first.

The linebacker with long blond hair slid his hand between her crease and Gwyllain giggled and wiggled her hips. He looked up and grinned at Dante, then continued his work on her thighs and calves. "Oh, you have wonderful hands, Valdon," she breathed.

"A Drone has come to give his offering, mistress," Valdon said as he grinned at Dante.

"I'll come back." Dante groaned to himself and turned around. He'd take a walk around outside and then return. By that time, she should be finished with Valdon.

"Where the hell are you going?" she snapped.

"You look...busy. I thought I'd give you some privacy," Dante said, trying not to show his impatience.

She raised her hand and the sound of metal chains rattling came up behind him. A cold steel collar locked around Dante's neck. Another slave dragged him and chained him to the wall beside Gwyllain's lounger.

Gwyllain rolled onto her back, exposing her full breasts and smoothly shaved pussy. Her clit ring glinted in the light from the flaming sconces. Pouring more oil into his hands,

Valdon rubbed them vigorously together while he grinned up at Dante as if saying, "Glad her wrath is on you and not me."

Valdon leaned over her head and massaged the glistening oil into her breasts and abdomen. Despite his predicament, Dante's cock twitched at the erotic sight. Gwyllain was beautiful even though she was a bitch.

"Something on your mind?" Dante asked with a slight tone of annoyance. He had an idea but thought he would wait for her words. A vibration shook the marble floor, sending a ripple across the pool water. Outside, thunder and fierce winds clashed in a violent storm. Gwyllain seemed oblivious to it.

She sighed and languidly stretched her arms up over her head, looking awfully calm considering her kingdom appeared to be crumbling at her feet. "Your sexual adventures are not the most adequate means to collect the vital chi I need to maintain Anartia," she said with a cutting tone.

Dante knew better than to argue. Killing mortals was not his favorite choice and drawing off the life force without killing wasn't an easy skill. Sexual encounters were more desirable as long as he didn't transfer his chi energy to his partner by having intercourse. His throat tightened. Now he knew why Gwyllain was pissed. Not because he was late but because of the level of intimacy with Amy. But his last interaction with Amy was not physical and he drained her chi on a subconscious level. The loss of his energy to her was still possible.

"You fucked up, Dante, and you're running out of time." She pointed an accusing finger at him. Her lips tightened, pressing all the flow of blood out of them so they looked pale. Valdon stepped away from the lounger at the fury in her voice, possibly realizing all the massaging in the world wouldn't relax Gwyllain at the moment.

"I can make my quota in time. I did last time." Tugging at the chains, he tested the strength of the bolts. He wasn't going anywhere. "If I can make my offering to you and get back to Earth."

"Your offering is tainted." She waved her hand toward a slave girl seated on a marble bench by the pool. As she approached Gwyllain, Dante could see she looked to be in her twenties. Her exotic dark eyes glanced shyly at Dante then were averted. When she stood beside Gwyllain, her head bowed, straight blue-black hair fell forward, nearly covering her face. She was small in frame but the thin blue sarong that covered her showed every outline of her round breasts and curved buttocks. "Take his offering," Gwyllain demanded. "Dante needs to start fresh. I will not accept tainted chi."

"But I acquired this woman's chi through dream travel, through her subconscious, not physically. It was her dream that I barely entered her. And it was only for a second. Such a waste of the life force."

The woman untied the golden braid holding her sarong together, opened the silky robe and let it slide to the floor. She then kicked off her golden sandals and sauntered over to Dante.

"It is a waste, isn't it?" Gwyllain glowered at him. "If you don't make your quota of offering in time, you can take Valdon's position. He's been my personal slave for about one hundred years now. I'm sure he'd like a chance to return to Earth for some recreation."

Valdon gave Dante a competitive glare. His eyes glinted with mischief.

Great, the bouncer-sized slave wanted Dante's job.

"Don't be concerned about running out of time," Gwyllain said with a soothing motherly tone as she stroked Valdon's cock beneath his loincloth. "Tarik is performing some experiments which require more energy. That's why Anartia is experiencing some unseasonable weather. I needed to call up a few more Drones before their time to assist, as I did you."

Dante nodded. The woman unzipped his pants and had them tugged down his hips. Fuck, he was getting hard. "That explains why you called me back early. I thought I wasn't due until 2055. Every hundred years you had said."

"Or as you are needed," Gwyllain corrected.

"Do you really have to do that, darling?" Dante asked the woman.

She smiled and nodded. "Believe me, it's my pleasure."

He sighed in frustration. "Great," he said sarcastically. "Are you going to tell me your name?" he asked the woman sucking his cock fiercely. He had to admit, she was damn good.

She raised her head for a moment and said, "Sakari." Her small hand wrapped around his penis with an iron grip. She slowly pumped the length of him.

He took in a breath and tried to steady his words. "And when will Tarik complete his project?" he asked Gwyllain, trying not to succumb to Sakari's expert touch. Was this a test? He knew he'd lost some chi with his dream travel with Amy but he still had a reasonable offering to give Gwyllain. As good as the slave girl was working his cock, he didn't want to give in to it. He had to save his climax for Gwyllain.

Gwyllain regarded Sakari's attentions and smiled, then waved toward her slave Valdon to continue his massage of her. He rubbed his hands with oil and began on her arms and then slid to her breasts.

"Tarik's work will be completed when Anartia is free from exile." The demoness's tone rose to a shriek. Anartia exists only as long as we remain here to be conduits of the energy to keep Anartia in existence. If either of us leaves Anartia, then this world and all connected to it will perish."

Bound in exile, Gwyllain and Tarik had been trapped in this world and had to maintain its existence with Gwyllain as the matriarch by using her collected chi energy. Her ruler husband had purposely designed her exiled universe to remain intact, depending on her numerous sexual adventures as the source of its continued existence. A jilted husband's revenge.

Dante bit his lower lip to stifle a groan as Sakari deep throated his cock again. "Aren't you wasting the precious chi by allowing Sakari to have her way with me? As much as I'm enjoying her company."

Gwyllain smiled mischievously and didn't answer. She glanced up at Valdon. "Lower, please."

Valdon moved around to her side, facing Dante as if he wanted to make sure Dante could see what he was doing to his mistress. With his huge hands, glistening with spicy scented oil, Valdon used both hands to work her mons until they were slick with oil and her juices. Gwyllain moaned and rolled her hips.

That didn't help Dante to resist Sakari's attentions.

Gwyllain sucked in a deep slow breath. "Over the last thousand years, I've acquired enough Drones such as you, Dante, to build the energy levels so Tarik could begin his experiments. We can't invite all our Drones to Anartia at once because of the energy required to maintain our small world and support a hundred servants. It's a delicate balance. And as Tarik continues with his experiments, more energy will be necessary."

She moaned and Valdon slipped his finger inside her cunt. "Mmmm. Yes, Valdon." Glancing back at Dante with eyelids half lowered, mouth parted. "And then there are those who grow tired of immortality and don't return or can't return..." She raised her brows and glared at him. "We have to replenish the Throng—I need Drones and slaves to replace them."

"Why are you telling me this?" Although he expected she was warning him.

"Don't. Waste. My. Time," she snapped. "You can be replaced. Or become my slave."

Replaced. Would she kill him? Slave? He would rather she kill him.

Dante closed his eyes, trying to fight the onslaught of sexual desire gripping him. Watching Valdon pleasure Gwyllain was beyond any mortal or immortal man's control. Sakari had his pants completely off and tossed aside. He hadn't noticed she had disappeared into another room for a moment until she returned with a pillow which she placed on the floor at his feet.

Sakari knelt down, grasped his engorged cock in her fist and deep throated him right to the hilt. "Good God, woman."

Gwyllain arched her back and groaned as Valdon pumped his finger or fingers inside her cunt. Dante didn't want to watch because it was launching him closer to the edge of his own orgasm by watching her writhing on that lounger.

"Ah, Gwyllain, I can see that you're busy and I understand your concern. But I do have a decent amount of offering to give you that is about to spill in this beautiful woman's mouth. This woman who I'm involved with has an enormous amount of chi. I can find other means to collect it. If you need energy that badly—"

"We are looking at other ways to supply Anartia as well. You'll have to work harder since your cycle is coming to a close. Once the full moon begins to wane. Kill this woman. Kill the three that you need for my offering. If you don't, I will have Sakari drain all your life force and you'll vanish into the dust of the desert, right where I found you."

The threat registered but the consequences of not performing his duties were lost for the moment as Sakari continued to suck him off with brilliant expertise.

She grasped his testicles in one palm as she rapidly stroked up and down his cock. The sensation of his pending climax coiled low in his gut. He groaned, trying to fight it, trying to pull away from her but not wanting to at the same time. Desire coiled and built deep in his groin. Too late to stop it. Clenching his jaw, he yanked on the chains as the spasms coursed through his body and the orgasm jolted him into a trembling release. He groaned louder, unable to restrain himself and heard Valdon laugh.

Dante rocked his hips, pumping his cock into her mouth and she sucked him. His seed spurted into her mouth. She took it all. Fuck.

# Chapter Thirteen

ꝏ

Determined to face Dante head-on, she marched down the hall Friday morning, preparing to barge into his office and ask what was going on but she slid to a halt when her hand gripped around the locked doorknob. Hadn't he gotten in yet? It was after nine.

Her arms dropped to her sides.

"Dante called to say he's running late," Phil said from behind her. "Something I can help you with?"

Startled, she spun around, took a breath and sputtered her response. "No, no. I wanted to let him know Micro will have a preliminary report this afternoon on that project for the park service, but nothing final until next week from the samples we collected yesterday."

Phil nodded. "Good. I'd like to see the final when you get it. My wife and I love that park. Hate to see those animals harmed, such a valuable resource."

"It is a beautiful park," Amy agreed, trying to think of a graceful excuse back to her department. She didn't want to run into Dante with Phil standing here. Maybe she could've brought Sienna to work instead of dropping her off at Betty's. Phil was such an animal lover. "I'm sure they'll discover the cause and the danger to the animals will pass."

"Let's hope they do," Phil said as he continued on down the hall to his office.

Had someone cranked up the air-conditioning? She felt like she was standing in a walk-in refrigerator. The image of the coyote walking through her walls sent a shiver through her. She had seen Dante in her house, change into the coyote and walk through her glass door. That was no dream because Sienna had woken her up. She had to talk Bill about the coyote.

When she got back to the lab, Truly was examining culture plates and casting odd looks in Amy's direction. "You ready to get some coffee?" Truly asked. "I need a break."

"Sure. Everything all right?" Amy asked as she washed her hands. "How's your mom?"

Truly removed her nitrile gloves and washed her hands too. "My mom's fine. We had a nice visit. Let's get coffee but first I have something for you."

Amy cocked her head, wondering. "What do you have? Not another kitten I hope."

"No, remember on your answering machine I did something special for you?" Truly smiled.

"Yeah," Amy said cautiously. There was something ominous in her tone.

Grinning widely, Truly slid a large paper bag from beside her chair and placed it on Amy's desk. "Surprise! Happy belated birthday."

"Oh, Truly. Wow thanks. That's so nice. How did you know?"

Her smile faded. "Dante told me."

"Oh." She wasn't sure why Dante would tell Truly about her birthday when he didn't mention it until the end of the day, when she was out with Jake. "Well, let me see what it is." She opened the bag and lifted out a cactus plant.

"It's a Christmas cactus."

The emerald green branches hung over the ceramic terracotta bowl. "It's gorgeous. Thank you." She hugged Truly. "I love plants. And I bet I won't kill a cactus."

"Around Christmastime it'll blossom with bright red flowers."

Amy felt her throat tighten and tears swam in her eyes. Truly always went out of her way to make her feel welcome in

Arizona. "I can't wait until Christmas to see the blooms." A pang tightened around her heart. Would she still be in Arizona next December?

"But there's something special about this cactus." Truly's mouth twisted in a wicked grin.

Amy studied the plant for a moment and after not seeing anything unusual turned back to her friend. "Okay, I give. What's so special?"

"I did a spell with the plant."

"What kind of spell? Do I really want to know?"

Truly held up her hands. "Oh no, it's a good spell to bring a committed love into your life. Someone special."

"Oh. And how did you do this to the poor plant?"

"I buried an apple and a fig in the soil and planted the cactus on top. The apple and fig represent the spirits of man and woman. The plant represents the relationship that will grow and become strong and everlasting. So you must water it but not too much. Tend it but give it space."

Amy tried not to smile since Truly appeared serious. "Well, that's why I broke up with Dante. The unstable, flaky relationship had finally taken its toll. I guess I'm ready for a committed relationship," she said for Truly's sake, though she wasn't sure if she believed in what she said. She had to commit to her perfect place to live first, her perfect job first, then she would be stable and settled enough to find the perfect mate. Of course, no one was perfect and she understood that. But she needed to aim for compatible.

Amy's cell phone rang and she answered. Betty was crying hysterically. "Betty, what's wrong?"

Betty rambled on for several sentences, not making sense until Amy interrupted. "Betty, slow down. Tell me what happened. Are you all right?"

Betty took a breath through sobs. "Yes, I'm okay. But Lupi's dead."

"Dead? My God, what happened?"

"He went hiking this morning. I had my yoga class so I didn't go. He was supposed to pick me up for coffee and when he didn't show I called his house. When he didn't answer, I got worried and drove over. The police were there trying to find contact information for next of kin. Another hiker found him."

"Do you want me to come over? I can leave work."

"No, no. I have a friend here. I really didn't know Lupi that well."

"I'm sure it's still—"

"It was that damn coyote," Betty blurted out.

"What?"

"Lupi said he saw that coyote with the funny tail on another hike. Something not right about that animal.

"Why did he have to die?" Betty sobbed into the phone again. "We were getting along so nicely."

"I'll stop over after work and check on you. I'm so sorry."

"Thank you, dear."

Still stunned by the news, she hung up and turned to Truly. "My neighbor just lost a friend. He died while hiking today."

"Oh, I'm sorry. Is your neighbor all right?" Truly patted Amy's shoulder.

"Not too good. I'll go to her house after work and see if she needs anything." *Coyote disappeared,* Amy mused. *Ran away or really disappeared?*

"I'm sure she'll appreciate that." Truly hooked elbows with Amy. "Come on, let's get some coffee. You look like you need a break and I need to talk to you."

A prickle swept over Amy's skin. Something in Truly's tone hinted at bad news. She didn't need any more problems today. When they got their coffee in the cafeteria, they found a table off to the side out of earshot from other employees.

"Okay, Truly, what's up? You have me worried. You're not getting another job, are you?"

Truly stared into her coffee. She seemed to have a hard time making eye contact. "No. You said you and Dante weren't dating anymore, right?"

Amy chuckled a little. "I don't know if what we had most people would call dating."

"He was kind of like your," Truly lowered her voice, "fucking buddy."

Amy rolled her eyes. "Crudely put but correct, I suppose."

"You're not seeing him anymore, are you?"

*Seeing him? That depends. In animal or human form? God, that sounded insane.* "I'm not dating him anymore."

"Good."

Amy waited for more information but Truly sipped her coffee. "So?"

"So, he asked me out."

"When?"

"Last night after I got back from my mom's. I've known him for years but we've never dated. I always wanted to. When he came over late I thought he was looking for you but he said you two weren't seeing each other anymore."

Amy scratched her head and tried to keep her expression neutral. Doesn't waste any time, does he? Then neither did Truly. "Did you go out last night?"

Truly averted her attention to her coffee cup. "No, it was late. We talked for a while, then he left. I guess he'll call to plan something later."

Talked for a while? Knowing Dante, Amy knew he didn't waste time with friendly conversation. Had Dante began his sexual games with Truly? What was he up to? Her intuition was seeing red flags, telling her not to trust him, telling her there was something ominous or supernatural about him.

Truly wouldn't believe her warnings because she'd think Amy was reacting through jealousy.

Amy was way over Dante. There was never an emotional connection between them. He'd pushed her sexual limits, helped her to explore her dark sensual side and for a while she got a rush from their encounters. Now she was afraid of him. If she didn't at least warn Truly about Dante, she'd never forgive herself if anything happened.

"Truly, word of caution about Dante. Be careful. There's something not right about him. Something—"

"Unconventional? I know. That's what makes him interesting. Kind of dark, sensual and charismatic." Truly sipped her coffee, her eyes bright with mischief.

"That's not what I mean. And I'm not jealous. The man scares me."

Truly frowned. Apparently she did think Amy was jealous. "Don't worry, I can handle Dante."

When they got back to the lab, Amy sat at her desk and shuffled through requisition slips, trying to decide what to do next. The more she thought about the coyote walking through her wall last night, the more she was convinced the incident was not a dream. She didn't understand it but there was something happening, something she was drawn into. Now he was pursuing Truly. She felt the turquoise stone in her pocket and wondered if it would protect her from Dante or any future malevolent danger.

If that job offer came through she could forget about all this craziness. The Christmas cactus made her wonder if she would be around long enough to see it bloom eight months from now. But she couldn't ignore what was happening to her, not if Truly was in danger.

She couldn't hide from Dante and had to see Jake as soon as possible. Would he understand if she dared to explain this madness to him?

Of course, she wanted to see Jake for other reasons and not to dance with the man. That strong pull in her gut and the thrill coursing through her whenever she thought of him revealed feelings she couldn't deny.

Amy touched the thick jade leaves of the plant then dug her finger into the dirt. It was bone dry. "Does this plant need water, you think?" Amy asked Truly who was entering data on the computer. On Truly's desk was a large black feather with a strand of colored beads tied to the quill end with rawhide.

Amy's hand grasped her throat and she felt the blood drain from her face. Dante never gave her a feather, only the Indian blanket. She stared at the feather as if it was an evil talisman.

"What is that? And where did you get it?"

Truly glanced over her shoulder. "What? Oh, this?" Smiling, she picked up the feather, waving it in front of her then placed it down. "A crow feather. Dante gave it to me last night." She sighed.

Amy's stomach tightened. She didn't like this at all. "Truly. A crow feather? You don't find that odd?" She didn't care if Jake thought she was crazy, she had to talk to Bill now. If Bill made sense of what happened last night, she could explain it to Truly. If she tried now, Truly wouldn't believe her.

"We didn't get around to talking about the significance of the feather." Truly blushed so Amy had an idea why Truly and Dante didn't get around to discussing the feather. "God, Amy, it's only a feather. I've been around the block. I can take care of myself. Dante is arrogant, not dangerous." Truly twirled the crow feather in her fingers.

Amy remembered the fear in Bill's eyes when he mentioned the crow's feather. Scientists like to have proof, physical evidence. She couldn't call this physical evidence or proof, only a creepy coincidence. Bill said it wasn't a good sign. She didn't know what it meant but she was going to find out.

She picked up the phone. "Hello? Jake? Sorry to call you at work." She had waited until Truly went into another room to work so she wouldn't over hear the conversation.

"That's fine. I just got in. Do you have results this soon?"

"No, nothing yet. I was wondering if you were free for lunch. I had something I wanted to talk to you about." Realizing that sounded awfully vague, she added, "Someplace quiet because this has to do with what your grandfather was talking about last night."

He paused for several moments and she thought he'd turn her down. "I can't meet you for lunch. Bill went into the hospital last night."

"Oh no, is he all right?"

"Yes, he's fine. They're keeping him another night to be sure. His blood pressure went up. After I left your place, he paged me again. I've been at the hospital since."

"Oh, then we can make this another time, of course." She drew squiggly lines on a piece of paper. Her hands were shaking.

"No, I'd like to see you tonight. Some place quiet," he said as if considering options. "I can fix you dinner at my place after I visit Bill."

"Sure, what time?" While he gave her the time and direction her stomach did a twirl. She wanted to bury her head in his chest and tell him all her worries—the coyote who traveled through walls, the psycho boyfriend who was dating her girlfriend, her neighbor's friend who might have been murdered by a supernatural coyote, and how Amy thought Bill and his Coyote myth was somehow connected. She wanted to hear that Jake could make it right or at least explain it all so this craziness made sense.

* * * * *

After work she stopped at Betty's house. Her friend was working in her garden. Betty stood and gave her a tearful hug. "I still can't believe it, Amy. He was in great shape. Worked out, hiked a few days a week."

"I'm so sorry. You two seemed to hit it off so well." She held Betty's hand. "Is there anything I can do?"

"No, no. I'm fine." She wiped her eyes with her forearm.

"I don't like you being alone." Amy looked out into the desert. Was he out there? Was Betty next? "You didn't find a crow's feather, did you?"

"A what?" Betty frowned, looking confused.

"Crow feather. Never mind. Do me a favor. That coyote we keep seeing around. If you see it, stay away from it. I think it's rabid."

With a nod, Betty picked up her garden tools and walked toward her shed. Amy followed. "Something ain't right about the animal. If I see it again on my property, I'll shoot it."

* * * * *

Later that evening, Amy stood outside Jake's house, holding her fist against the door but didn't knock. She was filled with trepidation at the thought of telling him all her strange experiences with the coyote. Last night at the restaurant with Jake, she felt the sparks flying between them especially while they danced. There was something dark and sexy about him. He was attractive in a different way from Dante—more open and approachable. Would she spoil it once she started talking about her bizarre dreams, the coyote's strange appearances and her suspicions about Lupi's death? But she had to tell him. Too many unusual things were happening to brush it off as coincidence.

If she was right, then Truly was in danger and maybe Betty too. She knocked and her stomach twisted.

The door swung open and Jake stood there, smiling. "Hi, come on in. Dinner's almost ready." He wore jeans and a brown polo shirt that fitted snugly over his muscled chest. "Beer, soda or iced tea?" he asked as he led her through the living room.

"Beer, please."

Jake went into the kitchen for their drinks. Glancing around his place, Amy walked into a great room with high ceilings and a stone fireplace that took up most of one wall. A wall of windows offered a magnificent view of the desert and mountains beyond. The décor had a very masculine and Southwestern feel with brown leather couches and chairs, terracotta tiles in the kitchen. "I like your house," she said.

He smiled, pleased with her comment. "I have chicken grilling on the deck. Hope you don't mind Mexican again. I'm making fajitas." He grasped her hand, leading her into the living room area where she sat on the leather couch.

The early evening light cast a golden glow through the windows and onto the beige walls, making the room cozy. She could imagine sitting there with him in the dark with the fire blazing, staring up into the desert night sky. "This is nice, Jake. The view is breathtaking."

"Yeah, the view sold me too. The house needed work when I bought it. I'm nearly finished."

She couldn't believe how relaxed she felt, considering that she hadn't known Jake for long. With Dante, she was always tense and on edge and not the good kind of sexual tension. How nice to feel relaxed and at ease with a man in his home. Then a realization hit her. She'd never been invited to Dante's house and she'd known him for eight months. Why hadn't that surprised her before now?

The scent of charcoal-grilled food pushed unpleasant thoughts about Dante out of her mind. She glanced outside and saw smoke rising from the grill. Motioning to the deck, she said, "I think the chicken's done."

Jake looked over his shoulder then leapt to his feet. "Jesus, don't worry, I used to be a fireman." He ran out the door, grabbing tongs and a plate as he passed the kitchen. Amy followed.

"Fireman? When were you a fireman?" Amy stood beside him on the deck as he scooped up the chicken breasts.

"In college when I was training for the forest service. I was a Hot Shot. Fought fires for the National Park Service." He brought the plate of chicken into the house, started slicing and took a bite. "Not too bad. I'll cut off the burned parts."

"It looks fine. Can I help? It smells great," she said.

He pointed to a platter of grated cheddar cheese, lettuce, tomatoes, warmed tortillas and guacamole. "You can take that to the table."

As she carried the platter she imagined him in the dangerous job of fighting fires. "Were people injured or killed in the fires you fought? Homes destroyed?"

His face tightened as if remembering some painful experience. "Let's sit and eat."

She hesitated about asking him again. Silence filled the room and the golden light from the setting sun vanished and the room grew dark. Jake stood and turned on the dimmer switch for the light over the table. He struck a match and lit a candle in the center.

"A number of houses were destroyed by the fires I fought. Fortunately only one civilian death—a man who wouldn't leave his home. The largest causalities are rarely mentioned in the news."

It took Amy a second to understand where he was going. "The animals."

Jake nodded. "They become trapped. I once saw an elk and a bear standing in a shallow creek staring up at a mountain engulfed in flames." He stopped to take a gulp of beer. Blue eyes lit with emotion as he described the incident.

She placed a hand on his. "What happened?"

"They just stood there, standing side by side, no longer enemies. Their common foe now the fire."

"Do you think they made it out?" Even as she asked the question, she knew the answer.

Jake's expression looked grim. "Probably not."

"Have there been forest fires out here?"

"Not like the ones in California or Montana."

"Still, animals are dying here," she said, remembering the coyote in her house, Dante and her dream.

"We're working on that," he said, cutting into his fajita.

"Do you miss fighting fires?"

"I miss the people, the teamwork, the experience. I don't miss the fire," he said, not looking up.

"I understand."

Jake studied her for a moment, then took a sip of beer. "Have you thought about giving Arizona a chance?" he asked.

Taking in a deep breath, she stared at him, unsure of how to answer. "My family lives in Florida. I don't know. How long do you give a place until it feels like home?"

"I don't know." He took her hand and squeezed. "I understand about family. Bill's not a blood relative but he might as well be. My mother left my brother and me with Bill when I was nine. Brad was eleven. Bill would never leave this area and he has no one. He's getting up in years and needs someone to keep an eye on him but he won't admit it."

She was tempted to ask what happened to his mother but they hadn't known each other that long. When he was ready, he would tell her. There, it was all laid out. Pointless for them to get involved but she was compelled to stay and get to know him more. Wanted to get a lot closer to him. No emotional ties. Keeping emotional ties out of the picture wouldn't be that easy with Jake.

Silence hovered over the dining table. "How is Bill?"

Jake's mouth tightened for second. "He'll be okay. Giving the nurses a hard time. He wanted to go home tonight but the doctor wouldn't release him until all the tests were back. He'll be going home tomorrow."

"That's a relief." She sipped her beer, then held the glass tightly between both hands. "Do you mind if I ask what happened?"

He poked at his fajita but didn't eat it. "They're not sure. They thought it was a heart attack but the tests don't confirm that."

Amy placed both hands in her lap and gripped them tightly. "He's going to be okay though?"

Jake put down his fork and rubbed his face. "Sure. Thanks for asking."

"Will you be staying with him when he comes out?"

Jake chuckled. "That's unlikely. He's too damn stubborn for that. I've tried to get him to move in with me but he won't hear of it. He won't even let me buy him a new mobile home. 'Nothin' wrong with this one,' he says."

"Sounds like he likes his independence."

"Just stubborn," Jake said with a smile and a hint of pride. "He's respected as a medicine man. Still participates in the ceremonies. He did that sand painting over the fireplace." Jake pointed to a three-foot-square drawing in black, red, yellow, white and turquoise blue colors above the mantle. A stick figure of a man was embellished with feathers and other designs around him.

"It's beautiful. The detail is amazing. I can't believe it's made out of sand. It looks like it's painted. Does the design represent anything?"

"Sand paintings are created to restore balance for healing or to summon spirits. The Navajo word for sand painting *iikaah* means the place where the Holy People come and go. The objects within this picture are symbolic of the four elements, the four seasons and four directions."

Amy got up from the table, leaving her unfinished dinner aside to examine the painting up close. "Who's the man? An Indian?"

"He's Big Thunder." Jake got up and stood beside her, gazing up at the picture. "People in these painting are called *Yeis*, the Holy People. During a ceremony while the painting is made, everything must be done perfectly or harm could result."

"What kind of ceremonies?"

"Healing ceremonies, religious rituals. There are more advanced ceremonies, secret to only shamans."

"Secret, huh? Intriguing." She took a few steps back, observing the painting from a different perspective. With the early evening light and the flickering candlelight from the dining room, the painting almost appeared to move. "Do you know the secrets?"

A smile twitched at the sides of Jake's mouth. "After the ceremony is over, the painting is destroyed. Permanent paintings like this one are altered in design or color because the original ones are considered sacred and magical."

Amy knew if she asked him how he felt about the supernatural truth of Coyote, she was taking a chance, crossing a line that could change how he felt about her professionally and personally. But she had to ask. That was what she came there for.

"Don't you want to finish your dinner?" he asked. "Were the fajitas okay?"

"Great. They were very good." She lingered staring up at the painting, feeling his presence next to her. Was she making a mistake? Why should she care? She wouldn't be getting serious with Jake anyway. But damn it, she wanted him bad. Her hands trembled as heat rushed through her veins.

"Something wrong, Amy?" Jake put a hand on her shoulder.

She took in a slow breath and turned toward him, not backing away. "This coyote has me worried."

Jake suspected she was upset about something but he had no idea what. Sliding his hand down to the small of her back, he led her to the couch. "Sit. Talk to me. What's going on?"

"Remember Lupi, my neighbor Betty's friend?"

"From the restaurant. I remember, vaguely." The hairs on his arms prickled. He glanced at the mountain lion skin draped over a rocking chair. Last night he had gone into animal form and some of the heightened animal senses still lingered. He could smell her desire for him, even feel the heat rising from her skin. And he wanted her, wanted to stroke her and explore her with his mouth. But beneath her desire was fear—he tasted it—bitter and metallic. What was she afraid of?

Was it his own attraction or was it the animal side of him commanding his desire? Either way the pressure in his groin sent a clear message to his brain on how much he craved to be inside her.

"Lupi was the hiker who died today."

"I hadn't heard the name. I'm so sorry." He took her hand. "Was Betty with him?"

She shook her head, then walked over to the couch and sat down. Her body tensed as she gripped her hands together in her lap, then she glanced around the room as if she was looking for an escape. "Jake, I know this is going to sound crazy but after what your grandfather said about the coyote, I think Lupi's death is connected."

"Connected how?"

"The coyote has been around Betty's house. What if he attacked Lupi?"

Jake stood up and strode toward the fireplace and glanced up at the sand painting. "It wasn't an animal attack. Heart attack, they think." Same thing they said about Bill. For God's sake.

"That coyote keeps coming around my house too. And last night something strange happened." She held his gaze but didn't continue. The hesitancy in her voice was obvious.

"Just say it." He tried to stay calm but he had a feeling he wasn't going to like what he heard.

"I had a lucid dream last night, but it was more than a dream, and it scared me."

"How so?"

She met his gaze, and he saw the hesitancy in her eyes. "Jake." She sighed. "In my dream, you were making love to me."

"That's the scary part?" He couldn't stop himself from grinning.

She smiled. "No. That was kind of nice."

Jake sat beside her and grasped her hand. "Go on."

"Then the dream, or whatever it was, changed. Your eyes changed, and the room became cold as if time passed. Then Dante was standing in the middle of the room and you were gone."

Jake shifted in his seat. "Was that the end of the dream? Dreams can seem real—"

"No. I wasn't dreaming at this point. I was awake, and Dante was in my house." Eyes wide in angry defiance, she yanked her hand away.

Nodding, he waited for her to continue, realizing if he pushed her too much, she'd back off, or worse, leave.

Amy rubbed her arms and glanced around the room as if expecting her old boyfriend to suddenly reappear. "I told him to get out."

"Good."

She opened her mouth to continue, then stopped. Her body tensed, and she turned and looked at him. "Then Dante changed into the coyote and walked straight through the glass door." When she finished speaking she crossed her arms as if waiting for Jake to condemn her words.

He knew better than to say she was imagining it, or dreaming. She seemed logical and not prone to an overactive imagination. He couldn't deny the truth any longer. Coyote was not a myth. This was real. "Where did he go after he left?"

"You're making fun of me."

"No, I'm not. My grandfather believes the man who died today had his life energy stolen by Coyote. He claims Coyote would've done the same to him if it wasn't for his own shaman powers."

"The coyote attacked your grandfather?"

"That's what he said." Jake wasn't sure if he believed his grandfather or not. Didn't he see the coyote change into a man when he was in mountain lion form? But he was under the influence of peyote and in animal form. How could he trust what he thought while in that state? Unlike his brother, Jake rarely shifted into animal form and didn't know the range of his abilities.

She sighed as if relieved. "Now I'm worried about my friend Truly because Dante started dating her. If Lupi died and Bill's in the hospital, maybe Betty and Truly are in danger. Should I do something?"

"I don't think you have to worry. I'll arrange for a humane trap to remove the coyote from the area. I'm sure Betty and Truly will be fine."

"How can you be so sure?"

"I just know." Jake didn't know but once the coyote was gone, he believed the trouble would end. He stood and finished cleaning up the dinner dishes. *Coyote can take many forms. He's a trickster. Maybe he stole the image of Dante from her dreams.* Jake didn't want to overwhelm her with more mystical details.

Amy got up and helped put food away. "So you don't believe the Coyote legend. You think what I said was crazy."

He grimaced and turned to her. "I'm not sure yet. It's not any crazier than most of the stories my grandfather has told me." But with what Amy and Bill had told him, Jake was convinced he would have to use his powers to fight this creature.

Bill was right about one thing. This wasn't the original Coyote legend. He wished it was. Something supernatural was using that myth in a perverted way for some unknown reason.

Amy gazed out across the desert. "So I'm just having nightmares."

Jake didn't answer. Fisting his hands, he searched the plains for the menacing creature. Yes, she was in danger. He had to stop Coyote but he wasn't sure how. "I don't have an explanation, Amy. Just stay away from the coyote."

Obviously Coyote chose her for some ominous purpose. Jake had to stop him.

# Chapter Fourteen

Jake stood at his window, staring out into the desert night for several minutes without saying a word, his hands fisted at his sides. She felt as frustrated and angry as he looked. She moved beside him and peered outside in the direction of his gaze. The twilight cast a muted glow over patches of red earth and sage-colored grass. Purple-gray clouds hovered over the distant mountains and a few silver specks of stars pierced the darkening sky. The air was still, without the slightest breeze to move a branch or a blade of grass, as if the desert was frozen in time. Was he looking for the coyote?

Taking his fist, Amy pulled him away from the window, away from the view of the desert night for the moment. "You don't think I'm crazy then?" she asked.

Jake walked over to the mountain lion fur draped in the rocking chair, picked it up, glanced at Amy with a pained look, then dropped it over the back of the chair again. Stroking the skin, he appeared to be in deep thought.

What was it about that fur that had gotten Bill and Jake in such an argument? She came over and stood beside him, touching the fur too. The coarse hairs were warm to the touch, probably from absorbing the afternoon sun.

"Did you or Bill shoot this animal?" she asked while she stroked the fur, occasionally grazing Jake's hand.

He shook his head, then opened his mouth to speak, closed it again. Finally, he said, "It's been in the family a long time."

She had to tell him. "I think Bill is right about the coyote taking life energy from animals and people. I'd like to talk to him about it when he's well." Amy held her breath, waiting for Jake to dispute her theory.

"When he's up to it, you can ask him."

"I also think Dante's connected. I feel drained after I've...seen him." She didn't want to mention their sexual encounters.

He nodded and fisted his hands in the mountain lion fur, hardly giving her a glance. Did he agree? Disagree? Think she was insane?

She groaned. Typical guy, being evasive. "Why won't you tell me what you think? Just be straight with me."

Jake glanced up at her, then down at the mountain lion skin. "I'm not sure what's real and what's myth yet. I need more proof."

She glided both hands over the fur and his hands touched hers as he stroked the animal skin.

Again, she felt he wasn't telling her everything. How could she get him to trust her? She spread her fingers and pressed her hands deep into the thick fur. The hairs tickled her skin. Jake kneaded the pelt, then intertwined his fingers with hers, pulling her hand toward him. She held her breath as a shiver ran through her body. Despite their baffling conversation, desire coiled inside her belly each time he touched her. She ached to touch his chest, his back, his thighs, everything. Explore, stroke, taste... Her hands gripped his tightly. There was no solution and she didn't want to think about Dante or the coyote anymore.

"You're withholding something," she said, smiling.

He shrugged. "I'm open to all possibilities."

Were they talking about the coyote or each other? Did he want her, or was she pushing?

But she couldn't forget the coyote walking through walls. Tears of frustration burned her eyes. "He seems to have some kind of control over me. I wondered if he can hypnotize people."

"Stay away from him and you'll be fine." His soft laughter was probably meant to lighten the mood but it only made Amy tenser.

"How can I do that when he's my boss?"

"Boss?" Jake looked shocked, then nodded in understanding. "Provided Dante and the coyote are one in the same."

She turned away, pacing in front of the fireplace, glancing up at the sand painting. A little magic could help her out right now.

"Coyote's a shapeshifter. What if they are the same?"

He pressed his lips together but didn't speak.

"Right," she said with a sarcastic tone. "I'm crazy or imagining it all. Except I'm afraid to go to sleep. I think I can resist him while I'm awake but I don't know if I have the power to fight him when I'm asleep." Glancing toward the windows, her stomach lurched.

*God, it's dark.* No, she would not start getting scared of the dark, nor become afraid to go home to her own house. Dreams were just that, dreams. She'd just keep the fireplace poker by her bed.

"Maybe I should go." As she passed Jake, he hooked an arm around her waist. "Don't go." He dropped his arm when she stopped walking and looked up at him, a multitude of emotions battling inside her.

He didn't move and continued to hold her gaze. "Stay here," he whispered.

Again the man of few words had her stumped. "Stay here" for five more minutes, overnight or for eternity? Need to be more specific. "I don't understand."

A glint of mischief sparkled in his eyes and his mouth twitched with the slightest smile. Moving closer, Jake kneaded her shoulders, then pulled her against him. "Don't go home tonight. Stay here with me."

"You think it's too—"

"Don't think," he said and then he kissed her and she forgot what she was going to say.

She melted against him, feeling his arms tighten around her as the kiss deepened and he probed her mouth with his tongue. The chemistry between them was strong since they first met but now the attraction was much deeper.

Her body responded to his touch. Chills slid over her skin and made her nipples hard, her pussy moist.

He tasted faintly of the limes and beer they had. As his kisses slid to her jawline and down her neck, Amy shivered and arched her back and felt his aroused cock pressing on her mound.

"Oh God, Jake." Oh God, she wasn't going home.

He sucked in a breath. "Ah, Amy, you feel good." His fingers roamed around her waist then moved up to her breasts, slowly as if giving her a chance to protest. When she didn't, he cupped her breasts, teased her nipples through the layers of her tank and bra, circling the rigid points protruding beneath the fabric.

"I like that." Her fingers traveled along the waist of his jeans, attempting to reach lower to determine his state of arousal. At the same time she was just as curious to slide her hands under his shirt and smooth her hands over his firm, muscled chest.

Hooking his fingers around the straps of her tank, he soon appeared frustrated with material from her tank and bra. He yanked up her shirt and pulled it over her head, then unhooked her bra and slid that off, tossing it on the floor. "What do you like?" he asked against her neck.

"You touching my breasts. It feels good."

"Good to know. What else do you like?"

She met his gaze and saw the heated passion there. Hesitating, she was unsure how to answer, unsure on how bold she should be. Unable to resist the urge to feel his bare skin, she yanked his shirt out of his jeans and slid her hands underneath.

He sucked in a breath. "That feels nice but you're avoiding my question. What do you like?"

She moistened her lips with her tongue, then swallowed. "Okay. A kiss."

"You've had a few of those already. What else?"

She stiffened. Why all the questions? Not another guy who plays sex games. Her attention focused on the stone fireplace. Maybe it was a mistake coming here. If Dante was a supernatural creature she'd have to fight him herself.

Jake's hand gently lifted her chin. "You okay?"

"I don't like playing games."

He blew out a deep breath and pulled her into his arms. "I'm sorry, I didn't mean it to seem that way." He stroked her hair. "I just want to know what turns you on." He rubbed the back of his neck, looking embarrassed.

Amy closed the distance between them. She fisted her hands at the hem of his shirt and smiled, locking eyes with him. "I'm being way oversensitive. First of all, I want this off." He obliged and the shirt dropped to the floor.

"What else?" He gave her a wicked grin.

She drew him closer by the waistband. Without taking her eyes off his, she undid the button and zipper, slipped her hand inside and grasped his steel-hard shaft.

"Oh God, Amy," he said deep in his throat as his eyelids lowered.

"Yes, you're so hard," she whispered against his lips. "Now take off your jeans."

He groaned. "Okay." When his jeans and underwear were down to his knees, he realized he still had his cowboy boots on.

"Need to take those off first, cowboy," she teased.

He chuckled. "I got that." He kicked off the boots and shoved the jeans to the side. Taking her in his arms again, he kissed her. While his hands reached under her skirt and squeezed her buttocks, his tongue pushed past her lips, darting and teasing inside her mouth. That delicious melty feeling went through her. Her body trembled, dew gathered between her thighs and her nipples tightened. "Oh, damn."

His mouth trailed down to her breasts and sucked hard on a sensitive peak. The sensation made her womb clench.

"Forget anything?" He moved to the next nipple.

She gasped. Dismayed, she asked, "Forget what?"

"Anything else you like."

"Hmmm. Sit down," she ordered.

Her skirt dropped to the floor. She hadn't felt him unzip it. The narrowing glance he gave to her panties was a silent message that said "lose those". Taking them off, she was rewarded by another lustful look.

"Very hot."

Grasping his arms, she pushed him toward the couch. "Sit."

"Would you rather go to the bedroom?"

She shook her head. "Don't want to walk that far. You have protection?"

He nodded. "Yes." When he sat down, she lowered herself between his legs. First stroking him with her hand, she ran her tongue around the ridge of his cock, then up and down the shaft.

Digging her fingers into his thigh, she opened her mouth wide and took him in until he hit the back of her throat.

Jake shuddered and groaned, his fingers threading through her hair. "Jesus."

Pleasuring a man like this gave her so much joy. She loved to listen to his ragged breathing, feel his body writhe and tremble as she brought him to the edge of orgasm.

After stroking his cock with her mouth and hand, she took his balls gently in her mouth which made him raise his hips and groan louder. "Yes, Amy." Hooking his hands under her shoulders, he pulled her up. "Now this is what I want. You sit." He switched places but kissed her long and hard first, then moved to her breasts, trailed his tongue over her abdomen, sending shivers along her skin. His mouth reached her pussy and she lifted her hips.

Her fingers combed through his hair as his tongue circled her swollen bud and instantly set her body on fire. She sucked in a breath, let go of his hair and dug her fingers into the cushions of the couch.

"I only have one request," she said.

"And that is…"

"I don't want to come like this. I want you inside me first." Dante always disappeared right after she reached orgasm. Maybe she was paranoid but she wasn't going to worry about that now.

"Okay." He slipped a finger inside her and held her clit between his lips as he licked her.

"Oh God, Jake. I'm not going to last long."

"Just warn me," he said as the flat of his tongue laved over the most sensitive area and her body was jolted with tiny electric shocks. Bliss, pure gratifying bliss. The pulse deep in her core throbbed and she had to stop. The temptation to let him take her up and over the precipice was maddening. She rocked her hips.

"Jake, come inside now."

He pulled away from her and her pussy continued to throb. After digging into his jeans and sheathing his cock, he settled her lengthwise on the sofa and eased between her legs.

Excitement flared as he nudged the opening of her channel, then thrust deep to the hilt. Arching her back, she cried out in sheer ecstasy.

"Jesus, you're dripping wet," he said between breaths. He pumped harder.

She tried raising her legs to wrap them around his hips but the narrow couch made that movement a struggle. Instead she had to squirm around to obtain the position.

Jake tried balancing his arms on either side of her but again the narrow couch was tricky and he kept slipping off. The length of the couch didn't accommodate his long legs very well either.

His voice chuckled a bit and he quipped, "Want to try something?"

"Sure." Oh, she did like the way he said that. Her stomach gave a little twirl.

Slipping out of her, he took her hand and at first she thought he was going to lead her to the bedroom. Instead he positioned her against the curved, cushioned arm of the couch.

He entered her cunt from behind and plunged deep, so deep her knees wobbled and she groaned. "Oh God, oh God."

Pumping her deep, fast and hard drew out more moisture. She spread her legs for balance and he slid his hand around her hip and found her clit.

Jake rubbed her plump bud with his fingertips, pressing, circling, bringing her to the edge again.

"Come for me now, or let me lick you later," he whispered as he continued to pump and rub her which finally thrust her over the edge.

Suddenly, she gripped his hand and pressed it against her pussy as she exploded in release.

His other hand gripped her hip as he pounded his cock into her. A groan escaped his lips as shudders racked his body. Her channel continued to clench and grip him tightly, squeezing every drop from him.

He slumped against her back and she felt his heart pounding, his breath gasping. The scent of sex only made the rapture that much more enticing.

He turned her around and took her into his arms, holding her close and kissing her.

"I think spending the rest of the night in my bedroom would be more comfortable." He stroked her hair.

"I think I'll have very good dreams tonight," Amy said. She hoped her dreams would be of Jake and not the bizarre ones with Dante.

* * * * *

The glow of the setting sun over the desert slowly became the glow of the digital clock on the nightstand as Amy was drawn out of her dream. What had she been dreaming about? Walking in the desert at sunset? Was anyone with her? She couldn't focus. Two forty-five.

She sighed with pleasure, knowing she had more time to sleep. But it didn't look like her alarm clock. Then something stirred beside her and it took her a second to realize—Jake. She was in Jake's bed. Not accustomed to sleeping with anyone, she wasn't used to waking up next to a man. In his bed.

She liked it. It had been so long since she slept with a man. Certainly never an overnight thing with Dante. He couldn't even commit to making love, never mind waking up next to her.

Ending their bizarre arrangement was a smart thing to do. Dante was a strange man. Thank God, she was with someone normal.

*Damn.* She couldn't stay until morning because Sienna needed to be fed. Amy was about to roll toward Jake and snuggle into him for a few moments before waking him, when she thought she heard the soft pattering of footsteps, like a dog's footpads. But Jake didn't have a dog.

Looking toward the doorway, she sucked in air. The coyote stood just inside Jake's bedroom.

Her mind raced. How did he get in? Then Jake tossed back the blankets, flung himself out of bed and leapt on the coyote.

The animal vanished.

"Shit," he whispered as he stood and ran outside.

"Jake!" Amy grabbed a blanket off the bed and raced after him, switching on the kitchen light as she went out the door. Outside on his deck, Jake stood with hands on his naked hips, his broad back gleaming in the light from the kitchen.

"You saw him?" she asked.

He cocked his head, looking at her, a wildness in his eyes. He nodded.

"Is he out there now?" she asked.

"I don't see him. He's gone."

"He has appeared in my room before like that."

Jake narrowed his eyes. "Before the dream?"

She nodded. "And he walked through the wall when I shouted at him," she added.

He bowed his head, then at her. "Why didn't you tell me the whole story before?"

"Because you said you'd never accepted the Indian culture and rituals your grandfather tried to teach you. I was afraid you'd think I was crazy."

Jake covered his eyes with his hand and groaned. "I've rejected the teachings for a good reason. It has to do with why my father died and why my mother left."

She put a hand on his shoulder. "Do you want to talk about it?"

He sighed and gave her a wry smile. "Later. Not at three in the morning."

"Okay. But I'm sure the coyote and Dante are connected and I think we should talk to Bill."

"Agreed." He took her in his arms. "I'll take care of the coyote."

She didn't know what he planned to do about the coyote and at the moment didn't care. "I need to go home and feed Sienna."

"Okay. I'll go with you." He opened the blanket and slipped it off her shoulders. It dropped onto the deck.

The lust-filled look in Jake's eyes managed to ease any worry from her mind. Cool air whisked over her bare skin, making her nipples sensitive and taut. She shuddered as his hands squeezed her breasts and his fingers pinched her hardened peaks. The soft intake of her breath and the arch of her back seemed to encourage him to touch her harder and more intimately.

Lifting her breast with his palm, he took her nipple in his mouth and sucked gently, rolling his tongue around the tip. The rough stubble on his face rubbed against the soft skin of her breasts, sensitizing them even more. Amy dug her fingers into his shoulders and wondered how this man could make her so turned-on in a matter of minutes. A trickle of moisture slid down her thighs.

Between her legs, his engorged penis was nudging her, teasing her. "Oh, Jake, that's so incredible."

His hand moved down to her pussy and he slipped a finger deep inside, sending her up on her toes. "Ah, yes."

"Ah, Amy, you're so wet."

She gripped his cock and began stroking it. The heel of his hand rubbed vigorously against her swollen clit and the throbbing was about to send her over the edge.

She backed up and he pressed her into the sliding glass window while he massaged her breast and finger-fucked her.

He kissed her hard and she hooked an arm around his neck while she bucked her hips. "I'm going to come, Jake."

"Go for it," he said huskily against her mouth and continued the rhythm on her clit.

Then her climax exploded and she shouted as wave after wave of pleasure surged through her. He pulled her close.

"Jake, take me inside. Make love to me now."

"Quite the little enchantress, isn't she?" a voice said from below the deck. Dante's voice.

Amy let out a yelp. Jake spun around, legs parted, arms slightly raised ready to fight. "Amy, get inside," Jake ordered.

The corner of Dante's mouth quirked. "Well, that's impressive." Tilting his head toward Jake's penis.

"Get out of here," Jake said between clenched teeth.

Amy stood at the open doorway, watching and listening, feeling like a coward. Dante was her ex-boyfriend, shouldn't she just tell him to leave?

"She's mine," Dante said. "I don't need the others if I have her."

Jake approached the edge of the deck, standing above Dante. "Get the hell out of here."

"You can't fight me. Neither can she." The air around Dante seemed to become denser, blurring his image. Then the form of Coyote appeared and Dante vanished. Amy clapped a hand to her mouth and stepped back. Jake didn't move.

Coyote paced in front of the deck, making yipping noises. The sounds made Amy's skin crawl. Then the image changed again and Coyote became Dante again.

"My powers are beyond your understanding," Dante said with an arrogant smirk. "Amy, come here," he ordered.

Jake glared at him. "Stay inside, Amy."

Sniffing the air like a wild animal, Dante glanced wildly from side to side and without a word, dashed into the darkness and disappeared.

"He's gone," Jake said.

"Thank God."

A shadow darted between trees, then appeared in Jake's yard. Dante stood in front of Jake again, this time grasping a six-foot-long rattlesnake by the back of its head. The tail whipped back and forth, trying to coil around Dante's arm. Its rattle sounded like grease sizzling in a hot skillet. "Pay attention," Dante said as he stretched the snake on the ground. After several seconds, a stream of light rose up from the snake's head and entered Dante's mouth. A moment later, the snake lay motionless, apparently dead. Dante tossed it aside. "I can do the same to humans."

"Why?" Jake asked. "And why Amy?"

"Another world depends on it. Amy is one of those rare people who have an excess of white light. I don't need to kill her."

"But you're draining her somehow." Jake backed up toward the door.

"Yes."

Looking over his shoulder, Jake whispered to Amy, "Bring the mountain lion skin to me. And whatever happens, don't be afraid. I'll explain when I get back. Please, please, don't leave."

Animal skin? "Wouldn't you rather I bring you a pair of pants?"

An amused look crossed his face. He touched her cheek. "Not this time."

"Send her out," Dante ordered. "Others will die if I don't have her."

"Like killing small creatures?" Jake shook his head, mocking Dante. "You don't know of my powers."

Amy raced over to the chair and picked up the heavy mountain lion skin then brought it out to Jake. He lifted it from her arms. "What powers?" she asked. He'd told her he wasn't a shaman. But did he know some of their secrets after all?

A worried look crossed his face. "I don't have time to explain. Just trust me. It's okay. Don't be afraid."

"Afraid of what?"

He held the skin over his forearm and approached Dante. Remembering the stories about the sand painting, she glanced over at the painting above the fireplace. Did the sand painting have powers?

Amy wasn't about to cower inside any longer. She strode outside and walked up to Jake. "It's all right, Jake. I can fight him off. I have before."

Dante laughed. "If she doesn't come now, I'll just take her later and maybe I'll stop and visit a few friends on the way."

Jake gave him a warning glare as he slipped the skin onto his back. He glanced back at Amy. "Amy, get inside now and close the door."

Before she had a chance to argue, the mountain lion skin rippled violently then he dropped to the ground and seemed to disappear beneath the fur, like a magician's magic trick. The skin took shape again into the lion form. A low growl startled Amy but she was too stunned to move. Then the animal leapt up onto the railing of the deck. He arched his back, muscles quivering as if getting ready to pounce. Amy clamped her hand over her mouth and stepped back.

"Holy shit," Dante said as he changed into Coyote and tore into the desert with the mountain lion close behind.

At the window, Amy gasped and stood frozen. She wanted to scream but was unable to suck in enough air. The desert was silent, no sign of the two creatures. Only the sound of her racing pulse throbbed in her ears. My God. First Dante, now Jake. What were they? A shiver of dread racked her body at the thought of Jake turning into an animal.

He said, "Stay, don't be afraid." His words played over and over in her mind. How could she stay and how could she not be afraid? Two inhuman creatures had just disappeared into the desert.

# Chapter Fifteen

ꟙ

Dante cursed himself for his overconfidence and stupidity as he waved his hand over the nebula stone and reformed into Coyote. The surroundings were a blur as he bolted, the mountain lion shifter close behind. Coyote bounded around thorn bushes, leapt over cacti and zigzagged around rock formations, trying to gain ground from his enemy.

Obviously the creature was not accustomed to his form or Coyote would've had his throat ripped out by now. And even as an immortal, if Coyote was killed by another shifter, he wasn't sure if he would survive. This was something Gwyllain had never warned him about.

Could Jake be working for Gwyllain too? No, it didn't make sense. Unless Jake wanted Amy's life energy for his offering.

Damn it, but she was his.

Fatigued muscles slowed him down but fortunately he was nearing the saguaro cactus, the center of the portal.

As he got within a few yards of the portal's boundary, he could hear the snarling mountain lion. The moment he was within the circle, he ducked around a large boulder and straightened upright into human form.

Just as the mountain lion bolted around the stone, hackles up, a low growl in his throat, Dante touched the nebula stone and vanished.

After several moments of a sensation of falling, his feet landed hard on the edge of the ocean cliffs of Anartia. This time the nebula stone remained around his neck and he wasn't naked.

Below him, the sea was rough but clear, the sky cloudy but not as stormy. Gwyllain's other Drones must be doing their jobs. Frustration and anxiety radiated through him. He was running out of time and didn't want to meet Gwyllain's wrath if he didn't make his quota. Glancing over his shoulder, he studied the temple. All quiet and he hoped it would stay that way. He didn't want to see Gwyllain or the others. In a few moments, he would return. Moving far from the edge, he walked up the coast for a short distance, giving the mountain lion enough time to get discouraged and leave. This shifter was not of Anartia but he was a threat. Dante would get him away from Amy and knew what to do to destroy him or at least the means of his powers.

After several minutes, Dante reached for the nebula stone, grasping it firmly with eyes closed, then stepped off the edge of the cliff.

Appearing again at the edge of the portal's boundaries, Dante caught a shadow of movement in the distance. The mountain lion's shape disappeared over a ridge, racing back to Jake's home.

Dante knew what he had to do.

* * * * *

Amy paced the window, glancing outside, wondering when Jake would return, when the mountain lion would return. Covering her face with both hands, she closed her eyes for a moment and tried to think. Too much, this was too much.

How could she possibly be with Jake again after this? What was he? What was Dante? And what was she in the middle of?

He'd asked her to stay but she felt she could think better at home. She thought for a moment about their dinner and lovemaking just hours ago, like any new couple starting a relationship. Not like any new couple.

Her boyfriend wasn't human. The crazy thing was, she felt he was trying to protect her. But being alone at Jake's house was surreal and she was beginning to feel like a caged animal.

Home. She had to get home.

After she dressed quickly, she hopped into her car and drove into the pre-dawn toward her house.

When she got home, Sienna was mewing. Amy picked her up, fed her first with some formula then poured some water into a bowl and added a couple of teaspoons of food. Betty had been wonderful the past few days, taking care of her during the day and slowly weaning her off the formula.

Sienna lapped at the water and licked hungrily at the food. Now that the kitten was on solid food the Humane Society would take her. Someone would adopt her. A pang of guilt and regret reverberated through her. Could she give up Sienna now?

Leaving her kitten to finish her meal, Amy quickly showered and changed into jeans and a tee shirt. She returned to find Sienna sitting in the middle of the kitchen as if waiting for her. Amy felt a tug at her heart and sat on the floor, staring at the kitten. *You don't change into a human, do you?* As if Sienna heard her thoughts, she turned and padded across the tile and crawled into her lap.

Amy lost it. Tears came in racking sobs. Clutching the kitten in her arms, she vowed not to give her away even if she moved back to Florida.

After seeing Dante change into the coyote, how would she face him at work? Telling anyone would only make her look crazy. What did he want with her?

The knock at the door made her cry out. She jumped up and started walking to the door, her pulse throbbing in her ears. She had locked the door, hadn't she?

"Amy, it's Jake. Please open up. Let's talk."

She hesitated. "Tomorrow," she said more with a question.

"No, I need to talk to you now. I have to explain this now." The pleading tone stabbed at her heart. She wouldn't get any sleep tonight anyway and she didn't believe he would hurt her.

"Where's Dante?"

"Gone. Disappeared. I'm afraid he may still come for you. Amy, open the door."

She unbolted the door and opened it.

His expression was calm but his eyes were filled with worry, his posture tense.

"Come in," she said barely above a whisper.

He followed her inside and they sat stiffly on her couch, facing the cold fireplace. The only light in the room was from her kitchen.

They sat in silence for a long moment. Jake rubbed his forehead and took a breath several times as if beginning to speak, then stopped. He finally spoke first. "The mountain lion skin is in the Jeep. I can't change without it."

"Good," Amy said, and as soon as she did, she regretted it, fearing her tone was edged with revulsion. She wanted to hold him and run away from him at the same time. How could this work? A huge supernatural wall rose between them. She stared at his liquid, sultry eyes, remembering hot sex, urgent needs and naked, straining bodies pleasuring each other. And also the quiet times and closeness they shared was quickly strengthening the depth of desire between them. "It was quite a surprise. Why didn't you tell me sooner?"

He gave her a pained look. "I didn't want to frighten you by—"

"Showing me something I might not understand."

He nodded. "I'll need to keep the skin close now that I know you're the one he's after. You're the one who's in danger."

She rubbed her forearms, trying to ease the chill that just shot through her. "What did he mean that another world depends on me? I don't understand."

"Don't know but I don't think he'll give up."

"What can I do?"

"Stay away from him."

She stood and walked over by the window. "And how am I supposed to do that when he can walk through walls and enter my dreams?"

Jake stood a few feet away, not approaching too close as if he thought she was afraid of him. She wasn't, damn it. Well, maybe a little. "Then trust me to hunt him down."

Sienna bounded across the room and walked in circles around Jake's legs, nudging him.

"How do I know I'm not in danger from you?"

Anger flashed across his face. He bent down and picked up Sienna and stroked her under her chin. "Do you really believe I could harm you, Amy?" He put the kitten down and she wandered into the next room.

She considered. "No, not you. But what about when you change?"

"I was worried I might hurt you." He dropped back onto the couch. "I demonstrated my skill to a woman I cared about and she freaked. She tried to run out of my house. I was in animal form and animal instincts took over and I tried to stop her." He averted his eyes.

"You injured her?" Amy asked. "How badly?"

"I didn't mean to hurt her. While in animal form I retain human thoughts. I reached out to her and accidentally clawed her leg. She still has the scar. Yes, I'm afraid it could happen again."

She knelt down in front of him and grasped both his hands. "Jake, I'm sorry about what happened with that woman but it was an accident. I don't believe you could hurt me. I'm not worried. Tell me more about your gift."

"Gift? I always thought of it as a curse. Although my brother, Brad, is quite comfortable with the skill. It's called *Eigi Einhamr,* meaning not of one skin. A rare Norwegian trait passed down among males in a family. My father, my brother and I all have the trait."

"You said your father died so you're not immortal?"

Jake smiled, still a sad smile. "No. My father had changed into a wolf, his favored form. Most *Eigi Einhamr*s have a favored form, a skin they are most comfortable in. My father's was a wolf. A hunter shot him. I was nine, my brother eleven."

Amy sat next to him on the couch and placed her head in her hands. "Jake, I'm so sorry about your father."

Taking her hands away from her face, Jake leaned toward her. "You okay?"

She nodded. "This was the time you went to live with Bill. What happened to your mother?"

He looked down at her hands, his mouth tightened. "The change occurs in puberty and my brother had begun to show signs of aggressiveness. My father found him a few skins to practice with and he held the form of a wolf, a leopard and a mountain lion for a few minutes." He hesitated.

She took his face in her hands to make him look at her. "What happened, why did your mother leave?"

"Brad was always the wild one. One night she went into Brad's room as he shifted into the leopard form. Brad leapt from the bed and knocked her off her feet. He snarled at her and she was terrified. A child's prank, showing off his new skills. But after losing my father, she didn't think she could handle two boys with such 'gifts'."

"So Bill was willing to take you in."

"Bill and my dad were friends and Bill learned of the Norwegian trait after my dad was killed."

"Have you ever heard from your mother since?" She stroked his cheek.

"No."

Amy slid her hand behind his neck and kissed him, parting his lips with her tongue. With a deep moan from Jake, he thrust his tongue into her mouth, meeting hers and deepening the kiss. Her body tingled with need.

Then he was brushing her hair back, kissing her cheeks, her neck and palming her breasts. While he continued to kiss her, he yanked up on her tee shirt and leaned back so he could pull it over her head. A quick movement behind her back released her bra and that too went flying across the room.

Hunger claimed Amy as she went directly for his belt, unbuckling it with shaking hands. He let her unfasten his pants while he stripped off his shirt. Squirming to her feet, she pulled him up with her.

She reached into his pants and withdrew his erection. Her eyes widened seeing how hard and thick he was already. As she bent over to take him in her mouth, Jake slipped a hand into her hair to guide her down.

Using one hand to fondle his balls and the other to stroke his length while she licked the head, she then slipped her mouth down to the root.

He groaned, gripping her head tighter. "Amy, that's it."

She matched the rhythm of his thrusts with her hand and mouth.

Everything about this intimate act she enjoyed—the feel of him in her mouth, the taste of him, the hardness within her hand. What got her most excited were his groans of pleasure. As she brought him closer to climax, desire flowed deep in her belly and traveled south. Her panties were soaked, her clit swollen. The confines of her jeans were too much and she wished she had taken them off before she began pleasuring Jake but she wouldn't dare stop.

"Yes, yes," he moaned.

She made soft humming sounds along his cock as he drew faster toward his orgasm. Her head bobbed up and down and now he speared his fingers through her hair.

"Oh God, I'm going to come." He groaned louder as his cum spurted hot and forceful down the back of her throat. She held him in her mouth until every drop of his semen was spent.

Looking up, she met his gaze while she licked at her moist lips. He brushed her hair back and kissed her. "Amazing. Now I need to return the favor." Pulling her up to her feet, he began to unfasten her pants and between the two of them, they worked the jeans over her hips. She kicked them to the side.

Hooking his fingers in the waistband of her panties, he drew them down so she could step out of them. "Much better." He knelt down before her and grasped her hips with his hand. She shuddered at his warm touch on her cool skin and nearly exploded in an orgasm the moment his tongue and lips began to work on her clit.

Hands behind her, she arched her back toward his heavenly mouth. Her buttocks muscles tightened as he slipped a finger inside her channel. "Oh my God."

"You're dripping." He slipped another finger inside, thrust them in and out several times until she was moaning with pleasure. Then he took out his fingers and slipped them into his mouth, licking her juices. "So sweet."

Panting now, she spread her legs for balance but also for him to plunge his fingers into her again. "Jake, I don't think I can stand much longer."

"Hmmm. Then don't. Lie down and let me finish."

As Amy lay back on the couch, she glanced outside. The palest hint of dawn glowed at the horizon. A flickering glow behind a bush startled her. The message of the glow was too clear. She bolted upright.

"What's wrong?" Jake asked.

The glow behind the bush brightened and now she could see flames. Nausea spread through her. She gripped Jake's arm.

"Amy?"

"It's Dante." She pointed outside at the firelight.

Jake muttered a curse as he got up and strode toward the window and peered out. "A locked door won't keep him out." He opened the door wider and stepped onto her deck.

"Don't go out. He's there. He's trying to summon me again." She pressed her hand to her chest, feeling her rapid heartbeat. "Oh God, I can feel him calling. I can feel how strong he is." She shook her head, trying to get control of her breathing. She would not let Dante frighten her like this, take over her life. A deep craving welled up inside, thick and delicious. She wanted to feel his expert hands touching her, teasing her in restrained passion until she reached the point of no return. Her clit swelled and throbbed in response. *No, I'm not giving in to it.* Ignoring the influence Dante had over her body, Amy scrambled into her clothes.

"I'm going out there. He's not expecting me, he's expecting you." Jaw set, Jake slipped into his pants. "Be right back. Stay here." He charged out her door and, moments later, returned, cursing.

"What is it?"

Jake raked his hand through his hair. "I'm going after him anyway."

"What do you mean?"

"He took the mountain lion skin."

Jake exploded out the back door, running toward the fire.

"Then we'll have to fight him together," Amy shouted, as she chased after him. Jake halted and spun around, running back to meet her.

He shook his head and stroked her cheek with his hand. "I'd feel better if you stayed in the house." The heat, the lust and power she saw in his eyes far exceeded the passion she once saw in Dante's eyes.

"Like hell. I don't want anything happening to you either."

He sighed. Cradling her head, he took a step closer. "Nothing will happen to me," he whispered as he took her mouth in a fierce kiss. Slipping his tongue in, he kissed her like he was going away for a long time. She clung to him a moment longer. "I'd still feel better if you stayed in the house."

She gave him a warning look. "Forget it. I can be very stubborn."

"Don't I know it." He sighed with resignation. "All right. Don't get near him. I don't know the extent of his powers."

She agreed, feeling confident that Jake would have no problem defeating Dante if it came down to a fight.

*Oh, this was going to get ugly.*

When they reached the clearing, Dante was standing beside the fire, looking smug and calm. He glanced down at the object burning in the flames and it took a moment before Amy realized what the smoking dark shape was—the mountain lion fur.

Jake hardly gave it a second look. "I expected that from a coward." He kicked the unburned portion of the mountain lion fur into the fire to finish what Dante had started.

Amy clapped a hand over her mouth, crinkling her nose at the smell of burning meat and hair. "Dante, you've burned the fur."

Dante smiled wildly. "Of course. He has no power now. He can't change without a skin. I, however, do not need a skin." Waving his hand over the nebula stone, Dante changed briefly into the coyote, then back again.

Amy gasped and took a step back. But Jake didn't move. "I don't need a skin to stop you. She has fought you before and she will again." Jake took a step closer.

"Where's the Indian blanket, Amy? When I summon you, you're supposed to bring it."

Amy glared at Dante. Did he really think they were going to have sex and in front of Jake? "Why do you need the blanket?"

Dante shrugged. "My gifts are charged with my essence in several dimensional planes to enable me to hypnotize my quarry. But I discovered you are very receptive to my suggestions. Do you remember the office?"

She crossed her arms and didn't say a word. Glancing at Jake, she noticed he had taken a few steps closer to Dante.

Dante smiled. "Oh, she remembers the time in the office. I managed to hypnotize her without the blanket."

"Do the crow feathers work the same way?"

Dante raised his eyebrows and smiled. "Smart lady."

"She's told you to walk away, get out of her life," Jake interjected. "Yet you continue to harass and stalk her."

"I need her power, her aura," Dante said, smiling. "The energy from the animals isn't enough."

"Why her? Why not just kill more animals? Or another human?"

Was Jake baiting him to see if he'd admit to killing Lupi?

Dante glanced at the saguaro as if planning for an escape. Jake must've noticed too because he maneuvered between Dante and the tall cactus, blocking his path. Jake wasn't going to let him leave.

"She has more chi than most. And I need it for the offering. I need a lot of chi. Time is endless unless it's running out for you."

Amy's stomach clenched tight. "What happens if you don't get this chi?"

The two men turned toward her in surprise, not expecting to hear her speak, she suspected.

Jake bowed his head in frustration. He obviously needed to know how this fitted in with his grandfather's theories.

"My portal will close and I'll be trapped in Anartia."

Jake frowned.

"Believe me, it's a place you don't want to visit for an extended time. I could be stuck there for a century, or until the mistress allows me to return to the Earth plane." Dante was inching closer to Amy.

"Amy, get behind me," Jake ordered.

She jogged around the fire, avoiding Dante and stood close to the saguaro. She didn't want to get near either of them if they were going to fight.

"I never planned to hurt her," Dante said unconvincingly. He held his chin defiantly. "I only need one more time with her, that all. And there will be no more animal deaths."

"Not going to happen," Jake said through gritted teeth. "So leave. And leave Amy alone."

"I don't have time for this," Dante said. "I don't have time to find new prey. Only Amy will do now."

"So you did kill Lupi," Amy blurted out without thinking.

Dante looked at her intently. "An accident. His heart failed while I was absorbing chi. Not enough to kill him."

"You had sex with him?"

Dante rolled his eyes. "No. Placed him in a trance and drew the energy from his third eye. Sex just heightens the level of chi." He smiled, obviously pleased with himself.

The fire, which had burned down, left the charred lump of the fur among the glowing coals. While Dante and Amy were talking, she noticed Jake had moved closer to his foe.

The weight of the long night settled on her and she glanced up at the hint of dawn lighting the horizon. All she wanted to do was to have this end so she and Jake could return to the house and they could sleep. Dante raised his hand and her knees nearly buckled.

Out of the corner of her eye, she saw Jake jump Dante. "Stop it," Dante shouted. Before Jake reached him, Dante raised his hand. Jake let out an "oof" as Dante flicked his hand, tumbling him several yards away.

"Jake!" Amy tried to move but couldn't. Jake didn't move for several moments and Amy feared him dead. Then he rolled to his side and struggled to get up. Standing on shaking legs, Jake approached Dante again.

Dante huffed as if he was getting impatient. This time he lowered his head and raised both arms. Jake was lifted off the ground and slammed down again. Jake slowly got to his feet and staggered toward Dante.

"Don't. Dante, I'll go with you," Amy said.

"No!" Jake said as he strode closer.

"Another step, Montag, and I'll crush your chest."

"Fuck!" Jake glared at Dante and didn't take another step. He glanced back at Amy's house, then at Amy.

"That's it, Montag. Go back to the house if you don't want to watch. I won't be long. And I won't hurt her."

She saw something flicker in Jake's eyes, confident and primal, as if he was trying to send her a message. "I'll come back for her then."

"Fine. Whatever," Dante said. "I'll have my quota and be done with this madness for another hundred years."

Jake limped back toward her house as Dante scooped her up in his arms.

"Quota for what?" Amy asked, trying to stall for time.

He lowered her on the sand and brushed her hair back. "My debt for immortality and a means to avenge a wrong."

"Immortality? Avenge what wrong? I don't understand." With great effort she kept her voice steady but she couldn't keep her body from shaking. How would he arouse her when she only feared him now? Isn't that when he took her life energy?

"The man who stole my gold claim during the California Gold Rush in 1855 also stole my wife, then sent men to murder me. The demoness saved me while I was dying and made a deal with me. If I would be one of her Drones, collecting life force energy for her alternative world, she would help me seek revenge on John Reilly."

Amy shook her head, confused and amazed. "But if all this is true, then John Reilly died over a hundred and fifty years ago. How can you get revenge?"

"John Reilly is another Drone but I don't know what he looks like or what his name is. Each cycle we can change our names and appearances. Gwyllain, the demoness, promises someday she will tell me so I can kill him."

Dante moved on top of her and Amy stiffened. "Sorry I don't have a blanket for you."

"I can't." Looking at him, she tried to figure out how to tell him her body wouldn't respond to him when she was terrified.

"Relax, Amy. I'm not going to touch you or hurt you." He raised his hand and she felt the tension ease from her body, comforting warmth reverberated from the roots of her hair down to her toes.

She sighed and wasn't afraid anymore.

A shadowy movement off to her side didn't even startle her, or cause her to turn. Then a low growl sent a shiver through her. Looking up, she saw a bear with thick brownish black fur standing beside the fire. The animal snarled his large teeth at Dante.

Amy blinked, thinking she was hallucinating.

Slowly, Dante stood. With him away from her, her trance began to lift and she realized the bear was real. How in the world could a bear be in her backyard?

The bearskin rug.

When she glanced up at Dante, the bear made his move, lunging for Dante. One swipe of his claw ripped open Dante's shirt. Four bloody slash marks appeared across his chest and the nebula stone necklace dropped to the ground. Amy stared at the necklace for a moment, thinking she had never seen Dante without it.

A flip of Dante's hand sent the bear stumbling away but not nearly as far as it had sent Jake. The bear appeared stunned and took his time getting back on his feet.

The nebula stone has other powers, Amy thought. Didn't Dante touch it or wave his hand over it when he changed into the coyote?

Scrambling to her feet, Amy picked up the necklace. Dante's eyes widened at first with horror then satisfaction and, in two giant steps, he reached her before the bear had a chance to lunge again. He grasped her hand holding the stone and drew it to his chest. She saw the self-satisfied grin he gave the bear as the earth dropped out beneath them. She and Dante disappeared into darkness.

# Chapter Sixteen

ꟻꝺ

Darkness and swirling shadows surrounded Amy as her body drifted, floating on air. Somewhere in the distance, she heard the sound of crashing waves. The ocean? It was a comforting sound, reminding her of Florida and the home she missed. She breathed in the warm, humid air as the sea breeze coated her skin with the salty mist. Then her feet touched down onto solid ground. Squinting, she peered into the darkness and slowly her vision cleared. Far below, waves smashed against jagged rocks. She stood only inches from the precipice.

Her breath was stolen from her lungs as she lunged backward and hit a wall. Turning around, she looked up into the stern brown eyes of the man. He had long blond hair, and a fine unshaved jawline, which gave him a rugged handsome look. Besides towering over her, he was built like a weightlifter. "Step away from the edge," he ordered as he grabbed her upper arm with a tight grip. "The mistress is waiting."

"Where's Dante?"

He angled his head in the direction over his shoulder. "On his way to see Mistress Gwyllain to explain your…ah, unexplained arrival."

She caught a glimpse of Dante then as he ran up the steps of a white building and disappeared inside, leaving her alone with this stranger who didn't seem too pleased that she was there.

Amy swallowed. Images of the man tossing her over the edge raced through her mind. She took steps up the slope and when she slipped he helped her keep her footing.

"Head clear now?" he asked in an even tone.

She nodded. "I need to talk to Dante." Before he was the one person she wanted to be away from, now she wanted to see him since he was the only person who could make sense of this situation. And maybe he would help her get back.

"Come." The man gripped her upper arm and pulled her along the large field toward the white building with columns that looked like a Greek temple.

"What is this place?" Amy thought if she kept asking questions, she wouldn't have a chance to think. "How did I get here?"

The man gave her an annoyed look. He sighed in frustration. "You're here because Dante brought you. Don't you remember?"

"Yes, I remember that." Amy glanced around, trying to figure out how to escape. But where would she go? "Don't you have a name?"

His mouth tightened just a little as if hiding a smile. "Valdon."

"Do you live here, Valdon?"

He cocked his head slightly. "Didn't he explain Anartia to you?"

She shook her head.

As they reached the steps to the white structure Valdon grabbed her arm again to stop her from approaching the stairs. "Anartia is an artificial dimension that exists between worlds—Gwyllain's planet and Earth."

Amy studied him for a moment trying to take this entire situation in. "I'm not sure I understand."

"The engineers who constructed it could explain better. Anartia was created as an exile and a prison for Gwyllain and her lover Tarik, a punishment by Gwyllain's husband. In this world, Gwyllain is the conduit for the power source that maintains the artificial dimension. She controls Anartia and those who have merged with this alternative universe, like Dante, myself and many others. After Gwyllain collects the life force energy, it automatically flows into Anartia."

Her head was beginning to hurt. Most of what he just said made no sense but she wasn't going to ask him to explain it again. "Gwyllain brought you here and Dante here?" she asked.

"Yes, from Earth." As if that made everything clear.

"Why don't you go back? Why don't you send me back?" She just wanted out of there.

Valdon gave her an amused look. "Only the Drones can go back but they must return to Anartia whenever summoned to bestow their offering. The slaves remain to serve her here. After the Drones complete their cycle they remain on Earth." He gripped her arm and led her up the steps and through the entrance of the temple. "Dante serves the mistress now, as will you."

Stopping and taking a step back, she jerked her arm free. Rage boiled to the surface. "I'm no one's servant," she shouted.

Grabbing her arm again, he dragged her up the stairs. Amy winced from the pain of his grip. She tried not to think about what Valdon meant by serving the mistress. If she could just talk to Dante, he would find a way to send her home again, back to Jake. What had Jake done after she and Dante disappeared? She couldn't imagine. There was no possible way Jake could help her. The thought gave her such a hollow feeling, she didn't want to move.

Inside the entrance, she exhaled forcefully at the sight of the giant hall. The great room was about three stories high with rows of white columns on either side. The floors were made of richly veined white marble. About a dozen young women, naked or partially draped in fragments of silky cloth, lay around a large sunken pool in the center of the room. A few sipped from golden goblets, others brushed one another's hair or sat by the edge of the pool, their feet dangling in the water. The women glanced up at Amy and Valdon briefly, then continued with their leisure duties.

Black granite tables, chairs and loungers were scattered around the space and covered with cushions in bright jewel-tone colors. More cushions and rugs were strewn around the floor.

A spicy, woody fragrance rose from a metal incense burner that hung from the ceiling.

"This way. You must be ready before she sees you."

Ready for what?

Amy was dragged along to a side room with no door. A flat rectangular cushion that was large enough to be used for a bed lay on the floor. On top lay a dark blue tunic. Gold sandals were on the floor beside the cushion.

"Change into this. I will return."

"No," she said but recoiled at the sharp look he gave her. "As soon as I explain the mistake, I plan to leave. So there's no need for me to change."

He rolled his eyes and gave her a thin grin. "I will return in a few moments. If you are not wearing that garment, I will change you myself and it will be my pleasure."

She glared at him, getting the message.

He left but he stood right outside her room. Quickly, she stripped out of her clothes and into the tunic. She would be damned if she was going to have that Neanderthal handle her.

Strolling around the room, she went over by the only window. It was long and narrow, too small for even a kitten to slip through.

Kitten. She thought about Sienna and her chest tightened. Who would feed her cat? Tears stung her eyes. How long would she be here? On tiptoes, she peered outside. Blue sky, a couple hundred yards to the edge of the cliff and no other structure for as far as she could see. How could she get out? Between worlds? What the hell did that mean?

She retrieved her pants and felt in the pocket for her cell phone and the turquoise stone. She pulled both out. Bill had given her the stone for protection. *Protection from what? Apparently not from demons.* She flipped open the phone. It was still on.

She stared at the screen which read "No Service". No kidding. What did she expect? She put the phone and stone back into her pants.

"Are you ready?" the man asked without turning around.

"Almost." She blinked back tears and quickly changed into the sandals.

"I'm ready," she said with a shaky voice. "What's next?" Afraid to guess, she followed him out and stood by the row of columns.

"Valdon! Bring her to me," a woman's voice shouted from a lounger by the pool. He cocked a brow and gave her a look that said "you're on".

"She is ready, mistress." Valdon angled his head, directing her toward the great room. "Come meet your mistress. Follow her commands and your life will be worth living."

Amy walked into the center of the room, her sandals slippery on the marble. Alongside the pool, stretched out on one of the loungers was a woman intently watching Amy as she approached. From the arrogant tilt of her chin and the sensuously relaxed position, Amy assumed it was Gwyllain. Another young male and a woman, dressed as she and Valdon were, stood beside one of the columns as if awaiting orders.

The mistress was stunning with long, sleek black hair and she was naked except for a shimmering midnight blue cloth wrapped around her hips. Shafts of sunlight shone down from a dozen huge skylights in the cathedral ceiling, illuminating her bronzed skin and sizable breasts.

When Amy stopped a few feet from Gwyllain's chair, Valdon gripped her arm and pulled her close. The woman wrapped her hand around Amy's wrist, stared into her eyes and said, "Kneel for me."

"Excuse me?"

The woman yanked on her arm. "Kneel. I won't ask again."

Amy did as she was told. The woman looked her up and down, then touched her hair, her cheek, her shoulder. Amy jerked away.

Ignoring Amy's response, Gwyllain stood and held her palms out to her. Without touching her, the woman ran her hands over Amy's body. "Yes, yes, Dante was right. She emits a powerful essence. The vibrations traveled through me without having to touch her. And look." She pointed to the ceiling. "Look how much brighter the sun is now since her arrival."

"I'm here by mistake," Amy said, hopeful she could explain the situation although the woman didn't look like the easiest person to reason with. "I picked up the nebula stone—"

Gwyllain raised her hand to silence her, glaring as if angry that Amy dared to speak aloud. The woman's eyes changed from deep blue to yellow-green, with an eerie inner light and slitlike pupils, giving her a reptilian-like appearance.

Amy resisted the urge to step back. "I can't stay here," she tried again.

"You'll be staying," Gwyllain said simply.

She turned her back on Amy and dropped the blue wrap on the floor, then shot Amy a look as if expecting a comment or compliment on her naked body. Momentarily embarrassed, Amy averted her eyes and looked at Valdon, who looked bored rather than turned-on. When Gwyllain got no response from Amy, she spun around and strode toward the pool.

Amy marched after her, hands on hips. "I cannot stay here."

Stepping into the steamy bath, Gwyllain eased in until the water lapped at her full breasts. Then she sat on an underwater seat. "Valdon will show you what is expected."

"How long do you plan to keep me?" Amy asked, her jaw tight. "Until Dante does something for you?" Her voice was becoming shrill.

Gwyllain frowned, her lips pressed firmly together. Her eyes glowed brighter as she waded through the water toward Amy who was standing at the edge. A predator hunting prey or a snake ready to strike. "You'll call me mistress or Mistress Gwyllain when you address me. Learn some manners."

Amy bit her lip to stop a sharp response. Manners? What about dragging her to Anartia against her will? But she was in this woman's domain and best to play by her rules for the moment.

"How long do you intend to keep me here, mistress?" Amy let the last word out with enough sweet sarcasm that all the other servants turned their heads and dropped their jaws.

Gwyllain turned toward the other male. "Wine please, Chay." He was a few inches shorter than Valdon with wavy brown hair and gray-blue eyes. He too was built like he had been lugging cinder blocks all his life.

"Of course, mistress." Chay strode over to the edge of the pool. Gwyllain raised her golden goblet and Chay poured. She never stopped glaring at Amy.

After a sip or two, she put her glass down. "Oh yes, you were asking about your stay."

"Yes, mistress," Amy said, figuring it was best to go along with the ruse.

"It's permanent."

"What?"

Gwyllain cocked her head. "Manners."

"Excuse me, mistress? What do you mean permanent?" Amy eyed the front door and thought about running out of the temple but even if she managed to escape, where would she go?

"Yes, as in for eternity. Your life force will help maintain Anartia and your appearance suits me. Dante wouldn't kill you, so I've agreed to allow you to live here as my slave."

"I can't agree to that," Amy argued, trying not to show fear.

Gwyllain laughed. "There is no choice. Once Tarik has you merged with Anartia, you will be bound to serve my needs and in exchange you'll have eternal life."

Amy swallowed several times, forcing herself not to cry but feeling tears well up in her eyes. Eternal life without Jake, any life without Jake, would be hell. She couldn't stand the thought of never seeing him again. The ache bore deep. Not only Jake but what would happen when she didn't return? Her family, Sienna, her house, her job? Wasn't there some way out? Her hands in fists, she frantically looked around the room, looking for an alternative plan. But what would she do if she could escape? How would she get home?

Gwyllain probably took Amy's lack of response as resignation. "I'd like to finish bathing in privacy. Chay, have Sakari show her what is expected of her."

"Yes, mistress."

"And, Amy." Gwyllain smiled as she sipped her wine. "There is no escape."

# Chapter Seventeen

ꙮ

The moment Amy and Dante vanished, Jake slipped out of the bearskin and kicked it aside. He strode forward and stared at the exact point where they had disappeared. Swearing, he roamed the area for an hour in a circular formation, trying to find signs of where they had vanished—an opening between rocks leading to a hidden cavern or crevice. There was no sign that they had ever been here. He thought he caught the whiff of an ocean breeze but it quickly faded. Although his animal senses were still acute, they were of little use. He was fighting otherworldly beings who had supernatural powers far beyond his.

Stunned and disoriented from returning to his human form, his mind raced for the next logical step. He gave a humorless laugh. How could he find logic in this insanity? How could he possibly help Amy? When he'd thought he could finally use his shapeshifting skills for good, see his heritage as something other than a curse, he ended up causing someone a lot of pain. And he'd put Amy in danger. The curse would forever haunt his life. He'd lost his father because of a hunter, lost his mother because she couldn't handle the stress, lost Alison because she couldn't accept who he was and now he'd lost Amy.

He doubted his grandfather or his people had the power or skills needed to help in this situation but Jake couldn't think of another option. He kicked sand to smother the fire and smoldering mountain lion fur. His fur was destroyed but he would find a way into the Otherworld and find a way to bring Amy back. Picking up the bearskin, he marched toward Amy's house.

*****

They'd been hiking for three hours and Bill was barely winded.

Jake traversed the steep trail, following behind his grandfather toward the rocky bluff. If he hadn't been close to Bill, he might have strayed off the overgrown path in the hazy twilight. Stunted pine trees, dried grasses and sage brush obscured most of the trail. Tied to his backpack was the bearskin and a knife—the only objects his grandfather told him he would need. Inside the pack Jake also brought provisions for a few days—clothes, food and water—although he had a feeling he wouldn't be using any of it during the ceremony.

"Just up ahead." Bill pointed to a shadowed overhang in the rocks. Jake realized it wasn't a shadow but the cave entrance. A few cairns or stacked stones, spaced every few feet, marked the last several yards of the treacherous trail.

"What is this place?"

"An ancient cliff dwelling. Dates back to the third century. Not very impressive looking. Nothing like Montezuma's Castle. And tough to find without a map."

"Where's our map?" Jake asked as the last stretch became steeper and he had to do hand over hand to climb.

"Back at the house, on the front porch. I decided I didn't need it. Wanted to test my memory."

Jake gritted his teeth. "Amy's life is in danger and you wanted to test—"

"Wait 'til you see the petroglyphs."

"Petroglyphs?" Jake shook his head. "I don't care right now about any freaking petroglyphs. All I care about is Amy. Shouldn't we be going over the details of this ritual now?"

Bill ignored him and continued talking. "The prehistoric cave paintings are in good shape. Do you want to know what kind of animals they are?"

Jake huffed, losing his patience. "Petroglyphs are carved paintings. Pictographs are painted. Are they carved or just painted?"

"These are the carved ones. There's a bear, a hawk and a deer, or maybe it's a mountain goat." Bill glanced back at him with a mischievous glint in his eyes.

"Oh, for—" Jake rubbed a hand over his face to stop from swearing, because he understood what his grandfather was doing, trying to distract him from worrying. "Sounds great, Bill."

As they reached the top of the bluff and stood outside the entrance to the cave, Jake's stomach tightened. "Have you done ceremonies here before?"

"Sure, but never one like this." Bill turned and glanced back at Jake. "Keep focused on your quest. It may save your life."

A puff of gray smoke coiled out along the cave opening and streamed up like a gray serpent toward the purple sky. The scent of a campfire and copal incense drifted out from the dark hole. Jake heard the faint thumping from a couple of hand drums, men sang a monotone Navajo chant.

"Who's in there?" Jake removed his pack and gripped it in his hand.

"This ritual is a dandy and needs the power of many shamans."

"Are you sure this will work?"

Bill's blank expression gave Jake no reassurance. "Nope." Bill turned and entered the cave. Jake shrugged and followed him inside.

The flickering light from the fire projected eerie shadows along the stone walls. His anticipation mounted in his gut. "What if I get there and I can't find her? What if I do find her, how do I find my way back?"

"Come inside," Bill ordered. "It's time."

The warmth and pungent wood fire stung his eyes and burned his throat as Jake entered the main room of the cave. The circular space was about twelve feet in diameter with a fire pit in the center. Seven other men, bare-chested and wearing long pants, sat around the fire cross-legged. One continued to beat a drum with a padded stick.

Another man poured sand from his hand in a fine stream, creating a design on the ground. As Jake moved closer, he saw the sand painting on the cavern floor. The pattern was of a spiral with concentric circles of alternating colors in black, orange, tan and white sands. Resisting the urge to ask all the questions running through his mind, he sat when his grandfather signaled him to do so. Bill was to Jake's right and the man doing the sand painting was on his left.

"Thank you for coming," Jake said.

The men laughed. Jake wasn't sure what was so funny. Apparently, they weren't too serious about this ritual, which convinced him even more, that it would never work.

Bill shook his head. "I told you he never took to our ways. Still, he is a brave man and you know of his powers."

"He'll need more than bravery to survive this journey," the one making the sand painting said.

The words sent a chill up Jake's spine. Did he even have a chance in hell?

"If he returns, he must demonstrate this shapeshifting skill as payment for the ritual."

"If I return? You don't sound too hopeful."

The men exchanged glances but made no comments. The man sitting to Bill's right who was called an elder said, "We have not done a ritual of this type of quest before but it should work."

Should work? Perfect. Staring at the opposite wall, Jake noticed the animal petroglyphs in the flickering light. The rough sketches in black did depict a deerlike creature, a bear and a hawk or large bird.

"A person's destiny is a sacred thing. Always keep your mind and your heart open and search for truth," the elder said. "While on your journey, it doesn't hurt to keep your eyes open too. The doorway back may arrive unexpectedly." He passed an earthen mug to Bill. His grandfather took a sip then passed it to Jake.

Jake sipped the bitter liquid and grimaced.

"Take another drink," the elder ordered.

Jake did, then handed it to the sand painter. The man took a drink and passed it around.

The shamans began a soft chant, a song Jake didn't understand but his body quickly felt the effects of the drink. He was relaxed and lightheaded. The room seemed to brighten and expand.

"Watch the animals on the wall," the elder shaman said. "Soon they will come alive and be your guides to the Otherworld."

What? Jake tried to speak but the word didn't make it from his brain to his mouth. With his gaze focused first on the elder shaman, then on the wall paintings, Jake blinked as his vision kept blurring.

Bill got up and slipped Jake's backpack onto Jake's shoulders with the bearskin still attached. Would he be able to take all these objects with him to this Otherworld, assuming the ritual would work?

"The animals come alive? You mean they're hallucinations?" Jake finally spoke with slurred words. He rubbed his face with his hand. "How can hallucinations carry me to this Otherworld? I don't understand."

With a firm grip, Bill held Jake's arm, giving him a warning look that said "shut up". The elder cocked his head toward the sand painting that appeared to be moving like a whirlpool.

*Yep, I'm starting to hallucinate.*

"This sand painting holds ominous power and magic," the elder said. "The Great Spirit permits the outward and inward integration in these sacred ceremonies. Through this test you will be initiated into the mysteries and ways of the shaman."

Out of the corner of his eye, Jake thought he saw movement. When he turned and looked at the animals on the wall, the petroglyphs appeared normal. The flickering light from the fire was playing tricks on his eyes. "Why are we wasting time?" he asked, his head spinning.

Bill squeezed his arm to silence him but he had to think of Amy's life. "I honor and respect your beliefs and my grandfather's. But Amy's life is at stake here. The longer we wait…"

"You love her?" one shaman across the fire pit asked.

Jake sighed impatiently. "Yes, I can't lose her."

"Good. Your desire will give you more power."

The chanting got louder and Jake shook his head. The room spun.

"It's almost time," the elder announced. "Jake, follow your totem animal into the vortex, into the sand painting. If you see a dark swirling cloud, step into it. That should take you to the Otherworld. Find Amy."

Jake turned slowly toward the sand painting. It was spinning like a two-foot whirlpool. He looked back to the elder. "And how do we get back?"

The elder smiled and shrugged his shoulders. "Don't know. Haven't done this ritual before."

"Great." Jake rubbed his face. *If I find her, we may not have a way back. But what choice do I have?*

"I'll do what I can on my end," Bill tried to reassure him.

A shadow across the room caught Jake's attention. When he raised his head, the stick figures of the cave drawing expanded away from the stone and moved to the next stone on the wall.

Jake held his breath. He could hear the shamans chuckling. Did they see them too? The black stick-figured animals followed each other around the walls like a moving picture. When they reached the opening of the cavern room they paused.

Jake laughed. "Run out of wall?"

The chants of the shamans grew louder. Then the three animals swelled, became three-dimensional and jumped out of the stone wall.

Jake sucked in the smoking air and choked, then turned to Bill "Can you see—"

Bill silenced him again with a hand on his arm. "It's time to go. Stand."

Panic rose inside with his racing heartbeat. He stood on shaky legs. All along he'd hoped he would find a way to rescue Amy but he'd never thought this ceremony would work. Now he feared it would work but still he would fail her. Unable to decide what he should do, he glanced to each shaman for guidance. They stared back with blank expressions.

What was he thinking? He wasn't a shaman. He didn't know their ways, their signs. How was he supposed to use their magic to save Amy and himself? He would die today and he would fail her, fail his grandfather.

Glancing at Bill, Jake raised his arms, begging for help, while the deer, the bear and hawk moved around the fire circle.

His grandfather smiled. "I am proud of you, son. Keep your mind and eyes open like the elder said. Look for the vortex and follow the hawk spirit. He will guide you." He pointed to the deer as it dived into the swirling sand painting and was sucked into the whirlpool.

"Oh God," Jake whispered.

"Get ready," Bill ordered.

Then the bear dived headfirst into the sand painting and vanished. Jake's throat tightened. He moved to the edge of the sand painting, peering down but not seeing anything in the two-foot area but moving sand.

The hawk flew around the room in its black shadowed form, dipping down toward the shamans and passing close to Jake.

"Go with the blessing of the Great Spirit," Bill said as the hawk flew down the whirlpool.

"Now!" the elder shouted.

Gripping the straps of his backpack, Jack stepped into the swirling sand. His stomach dropped as he was engulfed in darkness.

# Chapter Eighteen

ꟃ

Amy spent her first day on Anartia training with Sakari, learning her slave duties. The alternative was punishment. When Valdon pointed to the chains and shackles attached to the column at the far end of the main room, the meaning of the type of punishment was quite clear. He didn't need to explain further. Until she could find a way out or talk to Dante, she would obey.

"The red wine should be opened in the early evening before the mistress has finished the offering with one of the Drones or her favored time with Tarik," Sakari said as she placed a bottle on a tray along with two goblets.

"Offering?" Amy asked.

Sakari gave her a sly smile. "Don't worry about it. You'll understand all that later. Learn this now to save yourself grief from Gwyllain." Sakari helped Amy cut and arrange cheeses, tropical fruits, fine meats, seafood and pastries.

"Where does all this food come from?" Amy followed Sakari into the main room with a tray of cheeses and canapés and placed them as directed on a side table near the pool. On another table, Sakari poured wine into two goblets.

"Tarik manifests all the food through the portal. He scans swanky parties and events and acquires what he needs."

"Acquires? You mean he steals."

Sakari shrugged.

"Gwyllain said she was immortal and would make me immortal too. If they're immortal, why do they need to eat?"

"They wish to duplicate the routines and indulgences of their home world. They can never return, even if Tarik manages to break Anartia free."

"Why can't they just leave?"

Sakari glanced over her shoulder toward Gwyllain's quarters, then quickly picked up two of the miniature pastries, handed one to Amy and popped one in her mouth. "Anartia's existence depends on Gwyllain and she cannot survive without Anartia. Neither can exist without the other. If she were to leave for any length of time, Anartia would be destroyed and its destruction could have catastrophic effects on Earth.

"Tarik continues to search for a way to free her with his experiments."

The idea of experiments brought to mind old movies of Frankenstein and she didn't want to think about that. Those movies, as silly as they were, always frightened her as a child. "What does Gwyllain mean by merging me? Is that part of the experiments?"

"Tarik explained it to me once, although I don't understand it. He said merging is altering the magnetic resonance of your body to align you with Anartia."

Amy frowned. "Doesn't make sense to me either."

Sakari retrieved a pair of snips from her pocket and began cutting bougainvillea from the numerous ceramic pots surrounding the pool. Brilliant blooms in red, pink and lavender clusters grew on gnarled branches with thorns.

"Ouch." Sakari sucked on her finger and carefully handed the cut flowers to Amy. "Mind the thorns. We may be immortal but we can die if seriously injured on Anartia. Gwyllain reminds us of that flaw in her world and holds the threat of our destruction over our heads," Sakari said. They walked back into the food preparation area and she handed Amy a crystal vase for the flowers.

"Is Dante with Gwyllain now?"

"Tarik is with the mistress this afternoon in her private quarters. They should be coming out for their evening bath soon. I haven't seen Dante. Maybe he went back. If his cycle is complete, he won't return for many years."

Years? Oh no. Panic rose inside Amy's chest. There had to be some way out. "When do you think Tarik will perform this merging on me?" Maybe Dante hadn't left yet and she could convince him to help her get back before that happened.

"Probably tonight after their bath."

Amy tried not to look alarmed at she continued to add bougainvillea stems to the vase. "Then what?"

"He'll make you immortal and unless they continue to the next step and make you a Drone, you can never leave Anartia."

A thorn pierced Amy's thumb, she jerked her hand, knocking over the crystal vase. The loud crash made Sakari cry out. Shards of glass and broken blooms spewed across the floor.

* * * * *

A fierce storm howled around Jake as if he was in the middle of a hurricane. An invisible force yanked on his limbs and he feared he would be ripped apart. Then his feet touched down onto solid ground and the storm calmed. The wind died to a gentle breeze filled with the scent of the ocean and grass.

Twilight replaced darkness. He stood in the middle of a grassy field in front of a large white building with columns. To his left, the field sloped down to the edge of a cliff and beyond was the rolling green waves of an ocean. Looking up and down the shoreline, he didn't see any other buildings. The coastline appeared steep and treacherous. If Amy was anywhere, she had to be inside that building. He searched for the hawk, the totem creature that Bill said would be his guide. There was no sign of any of the three animals who'd led him there. Had the peyote worn off? Weren't they hallucinations anyway? How could a hallucination help him? He still didn't know how he would return.

*Find Amy first, then worry about getting back.* He ran up the steps, skipping two at a time and entered the structure.

Inside, he saw a man and women reclining in chairs around a pool. Two women in blue toga-like outfits stood off to the side, like Grecian waitresses. Around the pool, several women, mostly naked and young, lounged in chairs or on the floor. It took him a moment to realize one of the women in the blue robes was Amy.

"Amy!" he cried out before thinking. He took one step then was slammed sideways into a column. The wind was knocked out of him and he crumpled to the floor. When his head cleared, metal shackles were clamped around his wrists, ankles and neck.

His backpack and its contents were dumped next to the couple's lounger. The bearskin lay beside them on the floor. *Shit.*

Wincing at the throbbing pain in his head, he managed to stand but found he was chained to one of the columns and couldn't move more than a couple of feet. The man and woman glanced at him, then went back sipping drinks and snacking on plates of food. Finally, the woman sat up a little straighter and raised her chin toward Jake.

"Welcome to Anartia. I am Gwyllain. Why have you entered my world?"

Jake was surprised she didn't ask how he'd gotten there. He glanced around and saw Amy was leaning against the other woman and weeping. If he could only get the skin on he could get himself free of the chains and get Amy out.

Dante came out of a side room, walked up to Amy and handed her something. She looked at him with a strange expression. Was he trying to hypnotize her again? "The man came to take Amy back with him," Dante answered.

"Stay away from her," Jake said, struggling against his chains.

Dante laughed and put his arm around Amy. "If I want her now, I can have her in any way I wish," he taunted.

This seemed to please Gwyllain who gave a shrill laugh. "I will miss you, Dante, until your next cycle. I do enjoy your offerings."

The man next to her shot Gwyllain a disapproving look. A jealous lover? Jake wondered. "We don't need another Drone at this time. Send him back."

Gwyllain considered her lover's request, not taking her eyes off Jake. "But your experiments. Couldn't we use another Drone? I think this one pleases me."

Tarik shot Jake a look of hatred. "The woman slave is all we need at the moment," Tarik insisted as he drew circles around her naked nipples.

Gwyllain inched closer to him. "I suppose."

Dante stood behind Amy, wrapped his arms around her and began kissing and whispering in her ear. Amy frowned and shook her head, then glanced at Jake.

"Damn you. Leave her alone." Jake jerked on the chains until the skin around his wrists and ankles was raw.

"Jake, stop. You're hurting yourself," Amy said. She tried to pull away from Dante and failed.

"Tarik, my love. This is so entertaining," Gwyllain said as she eased onto her lover's lounger and began stroking his chest. "I'm getting excited again. Maybe Dante will make love to our new slave for our pleasure." Seeming to forget Jake for the moment, she paid full attention to Tarik. The man was obviously aroused beneath a silky cloth covering his hips. Gwyllain pushed the cloth aside, exposing him and gripped his erect shaft.

*What is it with these people?* Jake turned his attentions back to Amy, trying to figure a way to get out of the damn shackles. If he did, he would wrap the chains around Dante's neck.

Dante rubbed Amy's arms and ran his tongue from her shoulder, up her neck and to her ear. She twisted away from him. "Hmmm. That would be a pleasurable send-off. I would like to take her to my room and prepare her first," Dante said.

"No," Jake roared. "Let her go and I'll stay in her place."

Tarik raised his head from sucking Gwyllain's breasts. "Very noble but the mistress has decided to keep you both. We'll use you as a Drone." Tarik didn't seem pleased but the man didn't look like he would argue with Gwyllain either.

Jake didn't bother to ask what Drone meant because he was watching Dante lead Amy around the pool. The cruel bastard let Amy stop as she passed Jake.

"Say goodbye," Dante said to Jake.

Amy rushed into Jake's arms and kissed him, ignoring the laughter from Tarik and Gwyllain. "Jake, I'm sorry. I promise I won't leave you."

"Amy, I'm sorry I couldn't get you out of here. We'll figure out something, I promise." How could he admit that he had absolutely no idea how to rescue her?

Dante pulled her away and Jake spat out a string of curses.

* * * * *

In the hallway outside the pool room, Dante placed the nebula stone necklace around Amy's neck. "You'll need this. When you get back home, keep it in a safe place. Do not destroy it."

"You're helping us escape?" Amy touched the stone, felt its coolness where it rested between her breasts.

"You're a Sha Warrior, Amy. You are a guardian of the Earth. You have more life force energy than most mortals. Tarik believes that you and other Sha Warriors may be the key to safely break Anartia free from its inter-dimensional ties to Earth and end our prison exile. He has begun his experiments.

But he has not told Gwyllain because he doubts she would agree to the destruction of her kingdom."

"Rather rule in Hell than not to rule at all?" Amy asked.

Dante nodded. "Exactly. Gwyllain thinks he's trying to discover a way to collect and store power more efficiently."

"I still don't understand why you're letting me go."

"To keep you safe until Tarik figures out how to utilize the Sha Warriors' power. We need to find others like you. You're my bargaining chip."

"Then what? Will you kill me then?" She raised her chin, glaring at him.

"No. It won't come to that." He looked her in the eyes when he said that but she wasn't sure if she believed him. "Hurry," Dante said, "before the mistress becomes impatient with your absence." Amy was led out another entrance at the end of a corridor.

"What about Jake?" Amy asked as he took her hand, nearly dragging her down the steps, toward the ocean cliffs.

Dante glanced at her but didn't answer. He continued to run down the grassy slope, pulling her along beside him.

"Dante, I'm not going anywhere without Jake."

"I know. You'll have to wait down here. I'll go back for him."

"Not without Jake." Amy jerked her arm free.

"I'm already risking more than you know by sending you back. You'll have to do it my way." Dante took her arm again and urged her on. They reached the edge of the cliff and he stopped and faced her. "When Jake comes, hold the stone in your right hand, like this." He made her grip the pendant in her right hand and pressed it to her chest. "Do not let go and do not let go of Jake. Understand."

She nodded. "I'll wait here. Thank you, Dante."

"Remember to keep the stone safe. I'll return someday and retrieve it. Destroying it will upset the balance between Anartia and Earth, causing great upheavals on both worlds."

"I understand."

"Hold the stone now and keep it close to your chest."

"Why?" Holding the stone to her chest, she took a step back and eyed him suspiciously.

"So you don't forget. I may not return to show you how to go through the portal."

"All right. Tell me." She spread her legs, bracing herself against the gusts of winds rising from the ocean.

"When Jake comes, hold him close as the two of you move toward the edge of the cliff. You must be holding the stone like I showed you." Dante moved behind her and wrapped his arms around her. "Then you both must step off the cliff together to enter the portal."

"What if I let go of the stone?"

"You'll fall to your death onto those rocks." He pointed downward. She had seen someone jump off when she and Dante first arrived. He was telling her the truth.

Amy shuddered. "Oh my God. I don't know if I can do this." She leaned toward the edge and peered over, staring down at the waves crashing against the rocks far below. "This is the only way?"

"Yes, this is the only way." Dante kissed her hard and fast, then picked her up and tossed her over the cliff.

Amy tried to scream but the air rushed out of her lungs as the sensation of falling hit her and she held tight to the nebula stone.

The moment Amy hit the ground she ripped the nebula stone from her neck and ran toward her house. She wasn't taking any chances that the pendant or the powers of the portal would transport her back to that place.

Jake. She stopped and turned around, staring at the saguaro, expecting it to move or come alive. That was the center of the portal or the landmark Dante had used to locate the portal. Would he send Jake back too? There had to be other nebula stones. The image of Jake chained to the column tore at her heart. She couldn't count on Dante.

Dante had a reason to keep her safe—she was supposed to be a Sha Warrior. Why would he help Jake? He wouldn't.

She glanced at her cozy house, then at the tall saguaro. The cactus appeared malevolent now—the doorway into hell.

Searching on the ground, she found the nebula stone and picked it up. *God, I'm not a warrior but I can't stay here.*

She closed her fingers around the stone and slowly brought it to her chest. The air rushed out of her lungs as the desert floor dropped from beneath her feet.

* * * * *

After several minutes, Jake watched Dante enter the main room without Amy. "She's getting ready," he said to Gwyllain. He walked over to Jake's backpack and turned to Jake. "I see you brought an interesting souvenir." Dante lifted the bearskin. "I think this would be the perfect place to make love to Amy, right in front of Jake. It would create the most drama, don't you think, Gwyllain? The amount of chi produced between Amy and Jake should be quite intense."

Bastard. Jake yanked on his bindings until the shackles dug into his skin again. Afterward, Dante would probably burn the bearskin like he had the mountain lion skin, or cut it up. Instead he took a few steps toward Jake.

"Excellent idea but move the fur closer to me." Gwyllain focused her attention on Tarik's cock, stroking him. "I can't see with it so far away."

Dante gave Jake an odd look, dropped the skin on the tile out of reach, then continued to stroll past Jake with a look of contempt. *What was the guy up to?* He leaned toward Jake and whispered, "Amy is safe back on Earth. Gwyllain won't bother with her now that she has her life energy quota for this cycle. It's another Drone's turn. You're on your own, man. I can't do anything more for you without risking my neck."

Torn between wanting to punch him out and wanting to thank him for saving Amy, Jake stared at Dante without a word. Jake would be trapped on Anartia and Dante would go back to Earth to be with Amy. Some rescue. At least she was safe.

Dante shook his head as if he didn't know what else to say and left the hall.

What burned Jake the most was that Dante had helped Amy escape, not him. With Jake out of the picture, did Dante have the power to sway her love as well as seduce her?

Dropping to the floor, he stared at the bearskin. It lay just out of reach. The ankle and wrist chains rattled as he attempted to find a comfortable seated position. What was the use of the fur now? Even if he could change and manage to overpower the mistress and her lord, how would he return home?

The two were busy fucking on the lounge chair at the moment, oblivious to Jake, probably enjoying the audience or not giving a damn. *Damn, how the hell can I get out of here?*

Gwyllain straddled Tarik and was rocking her hips fiercely, her breasts bouncing with every thrust. Tarik gripped her buttocks, his fingers digging into her ass cheeks.

Shit. He wasn't going to watch this for an eternity. He had to get back and fight for Amy somehow. Reaching out with his foot, he tried to drag the bearskin to him. It was out of reach. Then he took a length of chain and tossed it toward the fur. The chain landed on the skin. The noise alerted Gwyllain.

Without missing her stride, she glanced over her shoulder at him. Jake smiled, trying to send her the message that he was enjoying the show. Gwyllain seemed pleased by that and cocked her head back, twisted her body to give him a better view of her breasts. She lifted them with her hands, pinching the nipples.

Jake smiled wider and responded by stroking himself through his pants. Gwyllain laughed and was surprised when her lover switched positions, flipping her on her back and continuing his thrusts. The attentions of her audience seemed to be quickly forgotten and Jake again tried to pull the chain and the bearskin.

The chain slid over the fur without moving it any closer. Damn it.

Outside the wind howled around the columns and the light filtering down through the skylights grew darker. Sun going down?

Then the entrance door swung open and Sakari ran inside, eyes wide, chest heaving as if she had been running. She ran toward Gwyllain, then seeing her mistress was in the middle of sex with her lover, she hesitated, glancing around, unsure of what to do.

"Mistress, I'm sorry to disturb you."

Gwyllain looked up and shot Sakari a look that said "you're an inch from death".

"Not now."

"But, Mistress, there is a tornado outside. It approaches the temple."

"Impossible," Gwyllain said. "Anartia does not have the power to produce a tornado. Do not disturb us again."

Sakari nodded. Keeping her head bowed, she backed away.

"Sakari!" Jake called as he stood up. Gwyllain glared at him for a moment. "Could I trouble you for some water?"

Sakari looked at Gwyllain for approval. Gwyllain rolled her eyes and flicked her hand, giving Sakari permission then wrapped her slim legs around Tarik's hips which brought a groan from him.

Sakari returned with a pitcher and a goblet.

"Thank you." Jake poured some water into the glass and took a drink. "Would you mind bringing the fur closer so I have something to sit on?"

"Sure." She looked at the fur for a moment, at first repelled by the head and the claws. "It's an odd piece. I've not seen anything like it." Picking it up by a side far from the head, she dragged it across the floor to him.

"Thank you, Sakari. Where did you see the tornado?" He remembered the shaman elder's words who said to look for a dark, swirling cloud, a vortex and to step into it. Grandfather and the shamans did well. He set the goblet down and stood. The wind rose to a roar, rattling the windows and skylights.

She pointed toward the front of the building.

"Leave this room now and don't return until the tornado is gone," Jake said as he picked up the fur.

"You're leaving?"

"It's dangerous for you to stay," Jake said as he placed the fur on his shoulders but did not give himself the will to change his form.

She nodded. A puzzled and pained look crossed her face, then she turned and padded across the room, disappearing into the room where she retrieved the water.

Jake slipped the bearskin over his head. The tornado was his summons to return to Earth. Willing himself to become one with the bearskin, Jake felt his muscles thicken, his body grow heavy. The shackles around his wrists, ankles and neck snapped. At the sound of the chains dropping to the floor, Gwyllain lifted her head and screamed. Her lover took them to be screams of passion and held her down, pumping her harder and, by the sound of his groans and the scent of sex that Jake could now detect, Tarik was climaxing.

The bear growled, a deep guttural sound that sent the women slaves shrieking and running out of the room in all directions. Jake ransacked the room, swiping at the wall sconces, shredding pillows and wall hangings, tossing loungers and chairs into the pool. Small fires broke out around the hall. At first Tarik was apparently oblivious to the commotion, or ignored it, too focused on his own gratification with his mistress. Jake stalked toward Tarik and Gwyllain. Standing at his full height, he roared, showing sharp teeth. He pawed the air with his long claws and shoved the lounger closer to the pool. Both demons stared in horror, unable to react.

Before Tarik or Gwyllain had a chance to scramble off, Jake picked up the lounger and dumped them into the pool. Then Jake bounded out the front entrance, knocking over three marble columns on his way out.

Outside, Jake slid out of the fur but draped it over his shoulders in case he was pursued. The wind had died and the sun was setting over the ocean. Where was the tornado, his ride home? Spinning around, he searched the horizon in all directions, looked into the sky and saw no sign. Damn, he'd missed it. He'd wasted too much time tearing apart the temple.

Above him a hawk shrieked, then flew about a hundred yards away. With outstretched wings it circled downward in a large spiral. He watched it for a moment as the bird spun faster and faster toward the ground. The damn thing was going to crash.

A commotion behind him signaled pursuit.

As he turned around, the door to the temple flung wide and he saw Gwyllain, Tarik, Dante and another male running toward them. Even if he was in his bear form, they had more power and strength and could easily overpower him. He caught them off guard before, now they were ready for him.

Now what? He glanced up at the hawk, searching for some kind of guidance. The swirling flight of the hawk had again created the tornado. The wind howled as the twister darkened and grew in size and strength and the ground rumbled with the power.

The wind stirred up clouds of grass and dirt, obscuring the view of his pursuers. The energy of the tornado pulled at him, vibrating through every muscle. As Jake ran toward the center of the tornado, the yells of his pursuers were cut off.

The hawk flew into the tornado. Last chance, the creator of the tornado was leaving. He had to leave now. Before he entered the black, swirling cloud, he glanced one last time over his shoulder at his pursuers. He caught a movement along the ocean cliff.

Amy!

Quickly, he stepped away from the tornado, out of its path and ran toward her. "Amy!" The tornado vanished. *Damn it.* "We need to go now, hurry."

"Jake. I know. Hold on to me. The portal is this way. We have to jump."

"Off the cliff?"

"Yes. I have the nebula stone. Dante showed me how." With one arm around Jake's waist and the other hand holding her pendant, she tried to pull him toward the edge.

"And you trust him?" Jake grabbed her upper arms.

She nodded.

"No, Amy, the way back is through the tornado. That's how I got here." But the wind had died, the tornado had disappeared and so had the hawk. "Damn it." Gwyllain and her minions were racing toward them. Dante was following behind and signaling urgently to Amy and him. It seemed like he was trying to tell them to go.

"Trust me," Amy said with a smile.

He stared down at the crashing waves far below and his stomach flipped at the thought of jumping. Then he glanced back at Gwyllain and her crew—no time. "Over the cliff?"

"Yes, hold on to me. Don't let go."

He groaned. "Shit. Okay, let's do it!" They ran to the edge.

He wrapped both arms around her and jumped.

# Chapter Nineteen

ഗ

Dante stood at the edge of the cliff, not daring to look directly at Gwyllain.

"Go after them," Gwyllain ordered.

"No, we don't have the energy to spare right now," Tarik argued.

Gwyllain huffed, narrowing her eyes at Dante. "How did they escape?"

"She must have taken my nebula stone from my room." He hoped Gwyllain bought that, then turned to Tarik. "I'll need another so I can return to Earth. My cycle is completed."

Tarik looked to Gwyllain for approval.

She approached Dante, her expression tight. Gliding her hands over his chest, she leaned up and kissed him. A goodbye kiss? Or a kiss of death? When she stepped back, her eyes glowed yellow-green.

He was in deep shit.

A few trickles of sweat dripped down his chest beneath his white buttoned shirt. "You're responsible for the destruction of my temple."

"It will be repaired to your satisfaction," Dante reassured her.

"Yes, it will and you'll be staying on as my slave." Her hand slid down to his groin and she palmed his cock. "Sakari will join the other Drones."

Dante resisted the urge to pull away from her touch. He hardened slightly. The demoness was a beautiful seductress even though she was a controlling…minx. Not death but a disagreeable alternative. He knew to protest would anger her even more, maybe send him over the cliff without the nebula stone. An unpleasant death and an end to eternal life, with no chance to destroy the man who had stolen his wife, his gold claim, his life. Slave he would be, bound in exile until Gwyllain agreed to make him a Drone again.

At least Amy was safe, the Sha Warrior was safe.

* * * * *

Jake plummeted through the swirling mist, darkness engulfing him. Amy was in his arms and he could hear her rapid breathing. After several moments he rolled hard onto solid ground again. The desert greeted him. Amy's backyard.

They stood and brushed sand off themselves. "You okay?" he asked her.

"Fine." She grabbed his shoulders and kissed him hard.

"Why did you come back?"

"I didn't want to leave without you but Dante tricked me."

"Like the Trickster."

She laughed. "He threw me over the cliff."

"Let's move away from this area while you have the nebula stone. I don't want to be making that trip again any time soon."

"Never again, I hope."

He took her hand and they walked back to her house. "Get your hiking boots on, we have someplace to go."

"Where?"

"A sacred place but we need to stop at my grandfather's and get a trail map. Now I know why Bill left it behind."

"Okay, but I have to feed Sienna first. Poor thing must be starving by now."

* * * * *

A couple of hours later, they approached the cave, the scent of smoke and burning sage greeting them, then the sound of drums. It took Jake a moment for his eyes to adjust to the darkness. Amy followed behind him. His grandfather stood when they walked in, came up to Jake, smiling and gave him a hug, then hugged Amy. "Welcome back, son."

The colored sands of the sand painting were still in motion, spinning like an eddy in a river. With the palms of his hands, the sand painter swept over the swirling sands of the design, destroying the pattern forever. On the cavern wall, the deer, the bear and hawk carvings were back in place. The drumming ceased and the other men stretched.

"How long?" Jake asked.

"A day," Bill answered.

"Bill, why did you have my name written on the map?" Amy asked. Then she turned to Jake. "Is he psychic too?"

Bill grinned. "I had a vision. I saw the two of you walking into this cave together. Amy is truly a Sha Warrior, one who has much white light surrounding her. A strong spirit."

Jake hugged her to his side. "I have to agree. She's very special."

"So are you. You have a special gift," Amy said.

"One you'll demonstrate for the men here. But another time," Bill said.

"It's okay," Amy said, hugging him. "Show them."

She tightened her arms around him for a moment and he didn't want to let her go. Even knowing what he was, *Eigi Einhamr,* she wasn't afraid. No, he wasn't cursed, he was blessed. She stood back to give him room as Jake untied the bearskin from his backpack, then slipped it over his head. He willed himself to become one with the animal and had no fear of frightening Amy. He even saw admiration glow in her eyes. God, he loved her for that.

The change into bear form was easier this time. No pain. The power and strength surged through his muscles, creating his new shape.

Delighted by the startled expressions and shouts from the shamans, Jake stalked around the fire pit on his rear paws and gave a deep growl. Bill laughed with pride.

Jake slipped out of the skin. Now back in his human form, he approached Amy. She was laughing too. He took her into his arms while the men's voices rose in loud in discussions. "I love you, Amy," he whispered into her ear. "God, I love you."

"I love you too," she whispered.

He picked up the nebula stone hanging around her neck. "Will he come back for this?"

She frowned. "Someday."

"Then destroy the damn thing."

"I can't. Dante said it would be dangerous if I did."

* * * * *

Three weeks later at Jake's house, Amy sat curled on the couch, gazing into the fireplace. The flames dancing around the log almost hypnotized her to sleep. With her head on Jake's shoulder, she fought to keep her eyes open. They had spent the last few days moving her belongings into his house. Her parents had been disappointed when she told them that she wasn't moving back to Florida but they were happy to hear she'd found someone special. They'd already asked if she and Jake would be coming for a visit over the Thanksgiving holiday. Besides Bill and the other shamans, Truly was the only person who knew what had happened to her and Jake. The story of her journey to Anartia would always remain a secret as well as Jake's shapeshifting gift.

"Since Dante has not returned to the lab for weeks, Human Resources has posted the management position to replace him. I've applied for it. Phil said he's fairly sure I'll get it."

"Great news," Jake said.

"The bosses were surprised Dante'd just disappeared. Police came to the office and wrote up a report but didn't seem too hopeful that he would turn up. As long as he didn't steal from the company and he didn't leave a forwarding address, there wasn't much the police could do."

Jake hooked his arm under her knees and pulled her legs over his thighs, then wrapped his arms around her. "I think I could sleep right here tonight," Jake said.

"Me too but I prefer your bed. So much better." Never had she imagined to feel so relaxed, safe and at home than with Jake in his house.

"We can finish unpacking your stuff tomorrow."

She closed her eyes and snuggled closer. "Thank God, I can't look at another box."

"We do have something to discuss though," he said in a serious tone.

Opening her eyes, she leaned back and studied him, trying to figure out if something was wrong. "No, I'm not moving back to Florida." Sienna paced over Jake's lap, then over hers, finally settling in a curled lump on her thighs and began to purr.

"I kind of figured that. No, that's not it."

"I don't have to worry about my lease because Truly is going to buy my house. She said you can keep the bearskin. The owner doesn't want it and neither does she." The bearskin was in front of the fireplace.

He shook his head.

"You don't like cats? But I can't part with Sienna now." She frowned.

He turned her around so she would look at him. "No, I like Sienna. That's not it." He petted Sienna. The cat lifted her head and licked his hand. He paused a moment for Amy as if she knew what he was getting at.

*Men. I don't read minds.* "What then?"

"It's been weeks and you haven't mentioned the nebula stone. Where did you put it? You never explained why you can't destroy it. How come?"

She sighed. "I can't destroy it. Dante told me the balance between the worlds could be harmed. Anartia is a prison to those tied to it, an exile that is connected to Earth in an altered dimension. The nebula stone is a link. If it's destroyed, there's no telling what could happen. I didn't want you to worry."

"I'm not worried. Where is it?"

"In a safe place."

He studied her, trying to understand her reluctance. "Why won't you tell me where it is? Don't you trust me?"

"I know how much you hated Dante and I was afraid you would try to destroy it. I know Dante was motivated by selfish reasons but I believe him about the stone. I think it is dangerous, especially if we destroy it."

"I don't like the guy but he did help you. I won't destroy it."

It occurred to her that someone had to know about the stone besides herself. "Okay. I wrapped it in a protective cloth and hung it on the hook behind the sand painting of Big Thunder." She pointed to the picture above the fireplace.

Jake glanced up at the Holy One, Big Thunder, who was guarding a very dangerous pendant. He hoped the painting had enough magic to protect it and to protect the two worlds. "I wonder if Dante or another from Anartia will return to claim the necklace." Jake picked up Sienna and placed her on the bearskin, then sat beside Amy. He trailed his fingers through her hair, down her neck, the side of her breast, then slipped a hand under her tee shirt and cupped her breast.

Amy caught her breath and moaned. Arching into his hand. His rough hand brushed her nipples and instantly made them hard and sensitive. "Was Sienna bothering you?" she teased.

"Nope. I wanted her mother's full attention."

"Ah. Good." She yanked at Jake's shirt, pulling it out of his jeans. The rush of passion and desire surged through her as she touched his heated skin beneath his shirt.

On second thought, making love in his living room wouldn't be a bad idea. She didn't think they would make it into the bedroom. Amy glanced up at the sand painting of Big Thunder and could swear the figure moved. The stick figure's arms and legs seemed to do a dance while the lightning bolts flashed along the sides and changed color. But it must be the flickering light from the fire, a trick of the eyes. "Something about that painting…"

"What about it?"

"There's magic in it."

"Think so?" He kissed her forehead and hugged her close.

"Yeah, I think so."

"I think you're right." Jake slipped his hand under her tee shirt and quickly pulled it over her head. "Maybe the magic is in you. Maybe it's us."

## *Also by Kathy Kulig*

ഗ

Seducing the Stones

# About the Author

ꟃ

Kathy Kulig spins stories with passion and adventure. Her characters enter both paranormal and contemporary worlds with steamy or erotic romances woven in. Gutsy heroines and hunky heroes face the unexpected and overcome formidable odds, because with courage, true love can find a way. These are the stories she loves to read and the stories she loves to write.

Besides her career in writing, Kathy is a cytotechnologist and has worked as a research scientist, medical technologist, dive master and stringer for a newspaper. Propelled by her love of travel and adventure, Kathy has visited a few places not usually considered vacation hot spots-and lived to tell about it. When not writing or dreaming up her next story, Kathy enjoys traveling, relaxing by the beach with a book, mountain biking, movies and dinners out. She lives with her husband in a 100-year-old Victorian house in Pennsylvania.

Kathy welcomes comments from readers. You can find her website and email address on her author bio page at www.ellorascave.com.

*Tell Us What You Think*

We appreciate hearing reader opinions about our books. You can email us at Comments@EllorasCave.com.

## Why an electronic book?

We live in the Information Age—an exciting time in the history of human civilization, in which technology rules supreme and continues to progress in leaps and bounds every minute of every day. For a multitude of reasons, more and more avid literary fans are opting to purchase e-books instead of paper books. The question from those not yet initiated into the world of electronic reading is simply: *Why?*

1. ***Price.*** An electronic title at Ellora's Cave Publishing and Cerridwen Press runs anywhere from 40% to 75% less than the cover price of the exact same title in paperback format. Why? Basic mathematics and cost. It is less expensive to publish an e-book (no paper and printing, no warehousing and shipping) than it is to publish a paperback, so the savings are passed along to the consumer.
2. ***Space.*** Running out of room in your house for your books? That is one worry you will never have with electronic books. For a low one-time cost, you can purchase a handheld device specifically designed for e-reading. Many e-readers have large, convenient screens for viewing. Better yet, hundreds of titles can be stored within your new library—on a single microchip. There are a variety of e-readers from different manufacturers. You can also read e-books on your PC or laptop computer. (Please note that Ellora's Cave does not endorse any specific brands.

You can check our websites at www.ellorascave.com or www.cerridwenpress.com for information we make available to new consumers.)

3. ***Mobility.*** Because your new e-library consists of only a microchip within a small, easily transportable e-reader, your entire cache of books can be taken with you wherever you go.
4. ***Personal Viewing Preferences.*** Are the words you are currently reading too small? Too large? Too... ANNOYING? Paperback books cannot be modified according to personal preferences, but e-books can.
5. ***Instant Gratification.*** Is it the middle of the night and all the bookstores near you are closed? Are you tired of waiting days, sometimes weeks, for bookstores to ship the novels you bought? Ellora's Cave Publishing sells instantaneous downloads twenty-four hours a day, seven days a week, every day of the year. Our webstore is never closed. Our e-book delivery system is 100% automated, meaning your order is filled as soon as you pay for it.

Those are a few of the top reasons why electronic books are replacing paperbacks for many avid readers.

As always, Ellora's Cave and Cerridwen Press welcome your questions and comments. We invite you to email us at Comments@ellorascave.com or write to us directly at Ellora's Cave Publishing Inc., 1056 Home Avenue, Akron, OH 44310-3502.

Cerridwen, the Celtic Goddess of wisdom, was the muse who brought inspiration to storytellers and those in the creative arts. Cerridwen Press encompasses the best and most innovative stories in all genres of today's fiction. Visit our site and discover the newest titles by talented authors who still get inspired - much like the ancient storytellers did, once upon a time.